Caballito

Robin Baker

Copyright © 2013 Robin Baker
www.robin-baker.com

ISBN 978-1-62646-467-4

All rights reserved. No part of this publication may be reproduced, stored in a retrieval system, or transmitted in any form or by any means, electronic, mechanical, recording or otherwise, without the prior written permission of the author.

Robin Baker is represented by:
The Susijn Agency
3rd Floor, 64 Gt. Titchfield Street, London, W1W 7QH, UK
www.thesusijnagency.com

Except for the historical figures and events listed in the Acknowledgements, the characters and events in this book are fictitious. Any similarity to real persons, living or dead, is coincidental and not intended by the author.

Published by HARD NUT books, 2013
Email: hardnutbooks@gmail.com

Printed in the United States of America on acid-free paper.

Dedication

To all the staff, students, villagers, poachers, beer-drinkers, dart-players, cricketers, 'ghosts', free-spirits and lovers who together created the magic that was Woodchester Park, Gloucestershire
1972-1992

ALSO BY ROBIN BAKER:

FICTION

Primal
The Hitchhiker's Child

NON-FICTION

Sperm Wars
Baby Wars
Sex in the Future
Fragile science

For more information:
http://www.robin-baker.com/books/

Chapter 1

'There's a madwoman in the Ladies.'

'Wino? Bag-lady?'

'No, she's young. Nearly as young as us. Really pretty, too. Brownish skin. Long black hair. But she's just standing there, stark naked, staring into the mirror with this sad look on her face.'

'Her clothes are in the toilet. There's water all over the floor.'

'Oh my God! Don't look. She's coming out.'

'What are you four staring at?'

'Nothing,' we said in unison, looking away, Leo and I wide-eyed, Gemma and Aisha trying to stifle giggles. But as soon as the woman turned her shapely back on us and struggled onto one of the tall stools near the bar, we stared again.

The flushed and overweight landlord appeared, brushing himself off as from a visit to the cellar. On seeing the woman, he froze, his face slowly turning crimson. Then he started shouting and swearing at her, but when all she did was laugh and demand a coffee he picked up the bar phone.

The police arrived – a man and a woman. The man seemed angry, speaking to the naked woman as if he knew her, as if she had done this before. But she refused to be covered or to leave quietly, so he dragged her kicking and shouting from the room.

'Imagine doing that,' said Aisha.

Gemma blushed. 'Well, actually. After last summer's exams…'

'Right across the Downs and back,' chuckled Leo. 'How's that for a streak?'

Gemma looked at me and Aisha. 'Not ever?'

'Those two? Of course "not ever." All that "naked-in-the-jungle" rubbish. It's just not in them.'

I bristled. 'Yes it is. And one day I'll prove it to you. But it's time and place, Leo. Doing what the locals do. And in case you haven't noticed, around here the locals wear clothes.'

'And a great shame it is too. Don't you think, Max? Eh? A few more like madwoman, that's what we need. I wonder what the police are doing with her?'

Chapter 2

An earth-trembling thunderstorm drove me to shelter in a second-hand bookshop just a few hundred metres from my home. Browsing to fill the time, I was tempted by a copy of *Coming of Age in Samoa* by Margaret Mead, the once-famous American Anthropologist. 'Why the cellophane wrapping?' I asked the shop owner.

He winked at me. 'Because of the photographs.'

'So which edition is it?'

'First, I think.' His eyes were wide, his face sincere.

I laughed. '1928! It can't be.'

He took the book from me, then made a show of examining it through the cellophane. 'Sorry. My mistake. 1961, this one.'

'Can I take off the wrapping?'

'Best not.'

'How much?'

'A pound.'

'How about fifty pence?'

Back in my apartment, the contents of the 'book' spilled onto the floor. But when I tried to put the pages back in order, I found that many were missing. There were no photographs either. As a book it was worthless, but it soon didn't matter. The bookmark was value enough.

It wasn't a real bookmark, more two sheets of writing paper folded together to serve as such. When unfolded, one side of each sheet bore handwritten prose scribed in the most beautiful italic lettering. Yet somebody obviously hadn't approved because on each sheet two lines had been drawn from corner to diagonal corner to form a single large censorious 'X':

My uncle was prone to allude to my people as "animals". 'They are too bestial even to wear clothes,' he would tell me, 'I know it for a fact.' The addition of 'fact' was typical. 'They know only wood and stone for weapons,' he would say. 'They are too ignorant and lazy to build houses or to grow food.' He would gaze indignantly at me. I met him with equal indignation. Even then I thought it intolerable that he should speak so knowingly about matters of which in truth he was ignorant. It was futile to contradict him, but nobody knew my people then, and I wonder ... Would it be too presumptuous of me to claim that I am the only outsider – if indeed I can describe myself as such – who has ever truly understood them?

I struggle to know where to begin. At Newnham perhaps, such an agreeable shock; those few merry weeks of study and tea parties. Or with the strength bestowed upon me by that single brief but memorable meeting with the beautiful Cicily. At first, she bewildered me because instead of seeking to escape in a distant world, she wished to change the world right here in England. But she was so deliciously determined that she dazzled me into believing that anything was possible. So it was not a great surprise, on my return over fifty years later, to discover that she and her many friends had succeeded in their quest. How much Cicily achieved, how many books and articles she wrote, and such famous 'lovers.' Que gran honor, that after we parted she should change her name to mine.

For my part, I craved to be the adventurous Marianne, and marvelled at the coincidence: that she had died exactly six Full Moons before I was born, and at a place so near. But now with the wisdom that comes with age, I know my spirit to be hers.

> A chaperone in the jungle seemed such silliness, and the more Aunt Matilda demanded that we turn back to her brother's Mission, the more determined I became to travel ever onwards. Until, seized with an emotional impulse to which I could not attribute a cause, I sank the canoe, forcing us to leave the river for jungle tracks. I ached to be alone, to be lost and vulnerable, to mimic my romantic Isabel. I yearned to savour animal fear, then to taste the sweet joy of rescue.
>
> It was Matilda who took the first arrow, a yard-long shaft piercing her chest, her bright red blood soaking her BB and blouse, oozing between her teeth to spill from her open mouth. The poor Indian bearers took the next three. Suddenly, I was alone with a savage and utterly nude murderer, and it would be a whole long year before I could ask my Capuchin why he chose to spare me.

I let the book fall apart again, this time deliberately, all over the floor. Then I shuffled the printed pages with my bare feet, looking for further sheets of handwriting, but there weren't any.

***

While finishing a coffee at my apartment window, I looked out across the Bristol Downs to the Suspension Bridge. The morning rush-hour was in full flow, and it was raining. I sat in front of my word processor. *Chapter 15: Future Work* the screen said; nothing more.

'Last chapter? Always the most difficult,' my PhD supervisor had once told me, trying to console me, to spur me on.

Rain began lashing the window pane, enticing me back across the room to stare out at the people scurrying on the pavements beneath, struggling with their umbrellas; at the cars and buses too, with their headlights on full and their windscreen wipers working at top speed. I smiled to myself. According to the weatherwoman, it was raining even harder in Liverpool.

'But there aren't any undiscovered stone-age tribes,' Leo had once scoffed. 'And even if there were, you'd never find them. And even if you did, they'd kill you as soon as look at you. Why the hell would they let somebody like you live with them?'

'No, you're wrong,' I growled back at him. 'There are still uncontacted tribes. About a hundred, it's reckoned. Mainly in the rainforests of Brazil, Peru and Indonesia. Governments even know roughly where they are but they're protecting them. It's just a question of slipping through the defences, that's all.'

'And you think you're the person to do it?'

'Sure! Why not?'

'What I don't understand,' said Gemma, 'is why you think it's such a big deal. Surely loads of people have lived with rainforest tribes and written about them. That's what Anthropologists do, isn't it?'

'But that's the point. They always go to study, not to live. They wear modern clothes, take medicines, introduce technology, bring tools and provisions to barter for information, ooze approval and disapproval. It all has an influence. You have to become one of the people. Embrace everything: their technology; their nakedness if need be; and their morals.'

'Morals! Now I get it,' laughed Leo. 'You want to screw native girls. Why didn't you just say so? I'll come with you.'

Only Aisha had taken me seriously, lying in my arms, cocooned beneath my duvet, reluctant to crawl out into the dank chill of my bedroom to start another day. We would discover a tribe together, we told each other. Live a stone-age life together; write about it together. But now three years on she is a headmaster's wife somewhere, and I have a thesis to finish.

Suddenly inspired, I strode from my window back to the word processor and typed a whole paragraph. Then I read it through, deleted every word, and wandered round my flat again. The rain outside was easing. A large lorry drove by beneath my window, a badly-loaded lorry, probably from the M4 Motorway. I picked up the phone and dialled a familiar number in Liverpool. 'Hi Gemma. Did I get you up? How are your ankles?'

'Oh, Hi Max. No, it's OK. My ankles? Panic's over. Swelling's nearly gone. Just one more week of taking it easy, the doctor says – unless I can persuade him to make it two.'

I chuckled. 'How's Leo coping?'

'Leo cope? Don't be silly, Max. Anyway, how about you? Found anybody to share that massive bed of yours yet? That new tenant of yours on the ground floor you got so excited about?'

'Total disaster. Turns out she hates hairy chests. She wanted to take a razor to me.'

'Unlucky! But maybe it's for the best, eh? How's "Future Work" coming along?'

'It's not. I daren't write anything in case I'm actually expected to do it. But that's not what I want, Gem. It really isn't.'

'Then tell him.'

'Oh, sure. And have him give the fellowship to somebody else.'

In my final undergraduate year, an eminent Professor had urged me not to "waste" my upcoming postgraduate years living in some remote jungle, but to write computer models about tribal evolution instead. 'All life, all history, all explanations can be digitised,' he enthused. 'You'll be a pioneer in the anthropological world, my boy. This work will make your name. Our names.' He had been waiting, he said, for a first-rate student to appear who also had a talent for mathematics and computing. And now, with my PhD nearly complete, he was so "enthralled" by my work that he desperately wanted me to continue. The fellowship was mine, if I wanted it.

'Look, Gem... The reason I'm phoning... You know that course-module on Suffragette Literature you did at uni. You didn't come across a woman called Cicily who changed her name, wrote loads of stuff and had famous lovers, did you?'

Chapter 3

'Hi, stranger,' said Gemma from the open door as I walked up the path, her appearance a shock though not a surprise.

'Hi, Gem.' I threw my holdall into the hallway and gave her a long hug. 'You look great.'

'Liar!' She closed the door behind me.

I had to tell her. 'Do you know how many badly-loaded lorries I saw on that journey? Ten! Bristol to Liverpool, just a hundred and fifty miles – ten!'

She gave a gentle smile and placed her hand on my arm. 'It's been two years, Max. Let them go. Move on.'

We went into the kitchen. 'So what's so important about this accountants' conference that Leo has to leave you on your own this week of all weeks?'

'It's in the Caribbean, it's free, there'll be lots of women, and everything here is totally freaking him out. And I wanted him to go. Until it's over, I really am better without him. Besides, I'm not alone, am I? You're here. He trusts you. We both do.'

***

Gemma sat on her lounge floor peering down at my bookmark, her long fair hair tumbling around her pale angular face. I was so used to seeing her slim and sexy that her globular mother-earth body seemed an anomaly, as if borrowed from a different person.

'So somebody starts to write a story, doesn't like it and gives up.' She looked up at me on the settee. 'Why are you so interested?'

'So you think it's a story?'

'Don't you?'

'I'm not sure. If – as you say – there really was a Cicily who changed her name and bedded both Charlie Chaplin and H.G. Wells...'

'Oh, yes. Let me show you.' She made to struggle to her feet.

'No, stay there. Just tell me where.'

She slumped back down again. 'There. Third shelf down. The thick red one. Pass it here.' She found the page. 'Here it is. "Rebecca West. 1892-1983. Born Cicily Fairfield in London. Father left the family in 1901 and her mother moved with the children to Edinburgh. Cicily returned to London in 1910."'

'Does it say when she changed her name?'

'Not exactly. It says that in 1911 Cicily joined the staff of the feminist paper *Freewoman* and started to use the name Rebecca West.'

'So our bookmark woman could be a Rebecca. And we're talking about a meeting with Cicily in 1910, 1911-ish. Yes? Before Cicily changed her name. Sounds promising. Fits with chaperones and tea parties, anyway. Maybe the article mentions our woman as the inspiration for the change of name. Does it?'

Gemma scanned the encyclopaedia entry. 'It says here that Rebecca West named herself after the "passionate, self-willed heroine in Henrik Ibsen's play *Rosmersholm*." Nothing about a Rebecca from Newnham.' She handed me the book so that I could see for myself. 'So you think your bookmark woman might be a real person?'

'Doesn't she feel real to you?'

'Not really. More like a character dreamed up for a novel, I would say.'

'What about these other women? "Adventurous Marianne"? "Romantic Isabel"? Can you place either of them? Or do you think they're fictional too?'

She shook her head. 'No idea. But even if they were real, all it means is that the author did some research to get the setting right for his or her main character.' Gemma struggled onto her knees, then shuffled to kneel in front of where I was sitting. 'Come on. What's on your mind, Max?'

'Oh... Nothing, not really. Just crazy thoughts, not worth talking about. Besides, right now...' I smiled at her. '... I don't know about you, but I'm hungry, and in great need of alcohol.'

She smiled back. 'OK. I get the message. To the kitchen woman, and stop asking questions. So what do you feel like?'

'No! I'm chef and shopper this week. You're going to take it easy. Just keep my wine-glass full and I'll do the rest.'

'Really?' Gemma laughed; a delightful musical laugh that I had missed since she and Leo moved north. 'Then that's definitely a deal. Do you know – in all our six years together, the nearest Leo has ever come to cooking me a meal is heating up a takeaway.'

***

The following morning, Gemma thrust a scribbled note into my hand. 'I don't really want to distract you from your thesis – but Leo phoned last night. I told him about your bookmark and he has this idea who your "romantic Isabel" might be.'

I glanced at the name on the paper. '"Isabel Godin"! How the hell does Leo come up with a name like that?'

'Oh, you know Leo. Ask him what colour my eyes are and he won't have a clue. But show him some obscure crossword...'

I smiled. 'Look, can I borrow Leo's library card?' It was an old deceit that Leo and I had used often when students. Although his face is thinner than mine, his long hair curlier, and his beard slightly longer, any difference in appearance was always too subtle for stressed librarians to notice. And so it proved again, allowing me to take out on loan just the book I needed: *Perils and Captivity* was in three parts, the last entitled, *Voyage of Madame Godin Along the River of the Amazons in the year 1770.*

'I've found her Gem,' I said as I returned. 'Deep in the library archives. 1827! They don't write books like this anymore. I'll start reading about her after dinner.'

But I never had chance. Gemma started reading first, then couldn't stop. 'This is so romantic. Shall I read it for you? Make some notes?'

I knew her offer was to allow me to work on my thesis, but the next morning with a shout of 'Just going to the library again. Back for lunch,' I instead went to re-immerse myself in a previously unknown world that I had discovered the day before. And after phoning Gemma to check that she wasn't about to give birth on the kitchen floor, my morning in the library turned into a whole day.

If I had possessed any preconception of middle- to upper-class Victorian women it was along the lines that they stayed at home, dedicating their life to their family and domestic responsibilities. They were socially responsible, wore stiff corsets and long dresses, went to church frequently, and spent their time worrying about servants and children. And I daresay many were just like that, but as my second day in the library unfolded I learned just how many exceptions there were. Stories of crossing the Atlas Mountains to the Sahara, of cycling fourteen thousand miles through the towns and jungles of the Indian Plain, or of being in sole charge of a caravan of two hundred slaves and porters in nineteenth century Africa, astounded me. So did the tale of an "adventurous Marianne" that I found. She was Marianne North who, it seemed, travelled the world, often alone, painting the flowers and plants of far-flung countries. Her paintings were still hanging in a gallery named after her at Kew Gardens in London – and she died at Alderley in Gloucestershire on 30 August 1890.

I checked in the library's almanac. There was a Full Moon that night.

***

After dinner, Gemma told me the story of Isabel Godin. 'She was born high up in the Andes, in Peru – except it's Ecuador now. A place called Riobamba, a Spanish colony. When she was fourteen, she married a Frenchman called Jean Godin…'

'Fourteen! How the hell does a 14-year old Spanish Peruvian girl meet a Frenchman to marry? And when was this exactly?'

Gemma checked her notes. 'The marriage was 1741. And he was on an expedition. The world's first "geodesy" expedition to the equator. What's "geodesy"?'

'No idea! But go on.'

'Eventually, Jean Godin decides he wants to take Isabel and their children to France. One child's already been born, the other's on its way. But what does the idiot do? A test run without his family right across South America to the Atlantic coast, the whole length of the Amazon, west to east, just to make sure it's safe. Can you believe it? It took months.'

'He was being cautious.'

'Crazy, more like – and it totally backfired. Because when he arrived, the Portuguese and Spanish authorities wouldn't let him go back up the Amazon to collect his wife and family. So for years and years they were on opposite sides of South America, totally unable to communicate with each other. She couldn't even tell him their two children had died of smallpox. All he could do was keep writing to Europe asking for help.'

'You mean he could write to Europe but not to her? Or her to him?'

'Seems that way. Anyway, eventually the King of Portugal sent a "galiot", whatever that is.'

'Does it matter?'

'Not really, except it came with thirty oarsmen to do whatever was necessary. Which in the end meant that it went as far up the Amazon as it could and just sat and waited for Isabel to make her way down from the Andes to meet it. By then, it was twenty years... Twenty years!... since Jean had left her, yet they'd stayed faithful to each other all that time...'

I chuckled.

'They had,' she insisted. 'It was really romantic. And when the news about the boat reached her, she didn't hesitate. She just set off across the mountains and down the tributaries to find the boat.'

'Alone? She can't have gone alone.'

'Not at first, and this is where it gets really awful. To begin with there were... wait a minute...' She looked through her notes. '... forty-two people, though thirty-one of them were Indian bearers. They all crossed the Andes by foot and on mule. But when they arrived down in the Amazon Basin, the mission station they'd been relying on to give them more provisions had been abandoned. Everybody had died from a smallpox outbreak. It scared the bearers shitless. They all deserted.'

'Can't say I blame them. So that left… How many? Eleven?'

She nodded. 'Isabel and six others set up an emergency camp, and four went on ahead in a small canoe they found. Those four were supposed to send back transport big enough for them all, but it never came – and one-by one those in the camp died from disease and infection.'

'So now Isabel's alone?'

'And nearly dead, too. For days, she just lies on the forest floor, delirious, surrounded by stinking corpses. But she recovers, then wanders totally lost through the jungle for nine days, living on fruit, nuts, partridge eggs, and what she calls "palm-cabbage." Then, virtually naked because her clothes had been shredded and torn from her body by branches, she stumbles across four Indians.'

'Did they attack her?'

'No! They were nice to her. Took her to the nearest mission.'

'And did she and Jean ever make it to France?'

'They did! Three years later. And nineteen years on, that's where they both died. Within six months of each other. And I don't care what you say, I think it's a really romantic story.' Gemma's blue eyes were glistening, holding back tears.

'I was only kidding. I think it's romantic too. And that's brilliant. Thanks. That's got to be her, don't you think? So that's the lot. All the women in the bookmark seem to be real, and Isabel's story plus the Capuchin reference pins the story to South America. We're talking Amazonians, Gem. It couldn't be better.'

'So now are you going to tell me where all this is going?'

I hesitated. 'OK. Look... Something a bit like this bookmark story happened once before. Back in 1935, a young white Christian girl called Helena Valero, about 12 years old, was captured by Amazonian Indians and forced to live with them for twenty odd years. Everything you can think of happened to her, including having four children. When she eventually escaped, she was interviewed by an Italian Anthropologist who then wrote her biography. It was a fantastic book. Everybody raved about it. Completely unique.'

'So...'

'The point is, the tribe in that book were Yanomamö. They were horticulturalists. Shamanists. Male-dominated. Warmongers. Quite advanced on the Amazonian scale and fairly specialised. But this tribe in the bookmark: stone tools, naked hunters and foragers, nomads... That's just about as simple as human society gets, yet even in the early 1900s there really were tribes still living like that. So suppose Rebecca really existed. Suppose she really did spend over fifty years with such people. Her story would be amazing.'

Gemma was shaking her head. 'But you can't interview her, can you? Even if she lived, she's got to be dead by now.'

'I know. But... Suppose the bookmark was the start of an autobiography. Obviously it was never published otherwise the whole anthropological world would know about it, including me. But suppose it's just lying around in a draw or an attic somewhere. That's anthropological gold dust, Gem. Nobody really knows what the lives of the forest nomads were like in the early 1900s. But the manuscript could tell us. I could write papers on it, a book even. I'd be given money to re-visit the tribe, see if it still exists, how it's changed. It's totally mind-blowing. The chance of a lifetime.'

Gemma was chuckling. 'Max, calm down. I can see why you're excited, but – come on – this is pure fantasy. The bookmark is no more than scribbles for a novel. It's fiction. Forget it.'

'I can't forget it. It's there in my head, all the time. I tell you Gem. If I didn't need the money, just a sniff that Rebecca was real... I think I'd chuck the fellowship and throw everything into researching her life and tracking down her tribe.'

She peered at me. 'Do you need the money?'

I laughed. 'Sadly, yes. My inheritance was good, but it won't run to gallivanting off to South America for years on end.'

'Well that's a relief. You won't be tempted into doing anything silly then. Because, whether you like it or not, you're brilliant at what you do. Look at all those papers you've written. Not to mention the lectures you've given – and you're even at Cambridge next month, aren't you? You've got a fantastic career ahead of you, Max. You'd be crazy to jack it all in just because of some stupid bookmark. Which is a work of fiction, I promise you. Cicily, Marianne and Isabel might all be real, but Rebecca isn't. She can't be.'

'Of course she can. Give me one good reason why not.'

'OK. Just ask yourself this. Would any real person in her right mind deliberately try to repeat an adventure as appalling as Isabel Godin's?'

Chapter 4

'Remember me?'

'Can't say that I do.'

'Nearly two months ago you sold me a 1961 copy of *Coming of Age in Samoa*.'

'Did you enjoy it?'

'It was unreadable, but I'll make you a deal. I won't tell anybody what state it was in, and I'll let you keep my pound…'

'Fifty pence.'

'…if you'll tell me where the book came from. You do keep records, don't you?' Then I told him about the bookmark.

With a disinterested air he disappeared into the back of the shop. 'It was part of a job-lot,' he said when he returned. 'A favour for a friend of mine, about five years ago. He used to do house clearances. But he was giving up. Closing down. The big C. Six months, they told him – but he only managed three.'

I voiced my condolences but all he did was shrug.

'So where was his shop? Somewhere in Bristol?'

'No, Nailsworth. Tiny place. Over in Gloucestershire.'

Back at home, I checked on a map. As the spirit flies, Nailsworth was just a few miles to the north-east of Alderley, where Marianne North had died.

***

I phoned Liverpool. 'Hey, you're home. Congratulations. How's the baby?'

'You mean the little pink one, or the big hairy one?'

'I mean the little pink one. But did Leo really faint in the delivery room? Or was he just stringing me along?'

'No, he fainted. Did you think he wouldn't? And the pink one is gorgeous, but very noisy, very hungry, and doesn't understand sleep. Leo's just taken her out to buy some breast pads. For me, not her. I'm leaking all over the place. We've decided to call her 'Solymar' by the way, and before you say anything, it's my idea and I like it.'

'Then so do I. No, I mean it. 'Sun and Sea'. That's great. Very you – and Leo.'

'Mmm. So how's life in the academic rut? Finished your thesis yet?'

'Just about.' Then I told her about my visit to the bookshop.

'Still doesn't prove anything. You'll have to do a lot better than geography to convince me Rebecca is real.'

***

Budding academics don't often get invited to lecture at Cambridge University before they can put 'Dr' before their name. Admittedly, my hosts were only a student society, interested more in computer modelling than in anthropology itself, but there were a lot of famous people at the university who might just be tempted to come and listen to me.

'Where did you put the posters advertising my talk?' I asked the gushing undergraduate who met me late-afternoon and introduced himself as chairperson of the society. 'Which departments?'

'Loads.'

'Anthropology?'

'Of course.' He looked unusually nervous. 'The only problem…' But before he could finish, other committee members appeared and as they led me to the lecture theatre for my five o'clock start we became enmeshed in a round of introductions and polite small-talk. At the lecture hall, the projectionist asked for my slides, and I took up position at the lectern to wait for the auditorium to fill.

Five o'clock arrived, but not my audience. 'They're always late,' said the chairperson with a weak smile as he drummed his fingers on the bench before him. 'Five more minutes? Give them chance to get here?' I shrugged and poured myself some water from the bottle provided. Then to make it look as though I cared I began fingering my lecture notes – but something very different was on my mind.

Days before, by phone, I had negotiated with the Newnham archivist to be allowed access to some of the College records, and for this I had arrived in Cambridge before lunch. The woman had listened to my bookmark story with fascination, then suggested that to err on the safe side I should examine the details of all students who registered between 1905 and 1915. While trying not to become despondent as the possibilities shrank, I scanned through seemingly endless Marys, Margarets and Winifreds, telling myself that there had to be at least one Rebecca, even if she wasn't my Rebecca – but there wasn't.

'OK, shall we start?' the chairperson said at last. 'I'm sure that what we lack in numbers, we make up for in enthusiasm.' He forced a smile then in a ludicrous sop to protocol stood to introduce me, his delivery only lightened by three further people sidling into the back row. My audience had reached double-figures.

'First slide please,' I shouted, and a fumble or two by the projectionist later, the title of my talk was on the screen and the theatre lights were dimming. But once I started speaking... Once the theatre was dark, apart from the projector light and screen… The three latecomers on the back row sidled out again.

'Next slide please.'

'Sorry, the projector's jammed. Just give me a moment.'

I took a sip of water.

At the back of the theatre, through a door that doesn't open, a young woman appears and fills my mind. Beautiful, of course, and tall and elegant, she has an hour-glass figure with hand-span waist all doubtlessly tortured into shape by corsetry. Dark though the room I see her clearly, her outfit Gainsborough blue from head to toe. Her bell-shaped skirt drags on the floor as she glides down the steps towards me, and her taffeta petticoats rustle with every hidden stride.

'Sorry, I'll have to turn the lights up for a moment.'

There is no sun, but Rebecca's parasol with its frilly frothy rim of muslin is raised above her head. Her high-necked blouse drips with lace, and her wide hat has a windmill bow and a lavish brim sweeping around her face. The hat seems suspended on her head by magic, but in reality must be resting on her long dark hair, pulled together into a flat coil and drawn up onto her crown.

'There, that's done it.' The theatre lights dimmed again and my next slide appeared on the screen.

Smiling at me, Rebecca comes to rest in front of the lectern, enveloping me with the scent of her lavender perfume. I am privileged: the only person to know that beneath her fashionable innocent subservient exterior there beats a fierce heart aching for adventure, yearning to "savour animal fear", to emulate her "romantic Isabel." I look straight through her at the people sitting on the front row – and shout at them.

'No! For pity's sake turn the lights back up again. This is a total farce. A complete and utter waste of time. Mine – and yours. I really appreciate the invitation,' I said to the chairperson. 'And I thank you others for coming, but I know perfectly well that, like everybody else in Cambridge, you'd much prefer to be at Richard Dawkins' defence of *The Blind Watchmaker*. And so would I if I didn't feel so pissed off and stupid for actually starting to lecture to the seven of you. Look, if we stop now, you can still get to Dawkins' lecture in time. I won't even hold you to taking me out for a drink and a meal afterwards. Just pay me my expenses and I'll entertain myself.'

The students at the front exchanged sheepish glances. 'How did you know?' said the chairman.

'Big posters everywhere? How could I not know?'

He stood and moved out towards me. 'I'm really sorry. It's my fault. But I honestly didn't know when I invited you.'

'It's OK. Don't feel bad about it. These things happen. Go! Go! All of you.'

And nearly all did, and quickly too, though the chairperson did pause long enough to shake my hand and thank me, and the projectionist did collect and return my slides. But one person stayed, her pretty face, dark hair and shapely body unnervingly reminiscent of my imagined Rebecca. 'I'm the treasurer,' she said with a smile. 'And in case you missed it the first time, my name's Anya.'

'No, I didn't miss it. And thanks for hanging back, but it's OK. There's really no need to pay me now. I'll send you an invoice. Just go. You'll be late.'

She shrugged. 'I've heard Richard before. Several times.' Her smile grew coy. 'Look, I was wondering... I mean, if you prefer to be on your own, fine. After this cock-up, I wouldn't blame you. But, if you'd like company for a while, I'm all yours. And I do have the society's cheque book.'

    I smiled at her. 'Do you drink?'
    'I'm famous for it.'
    'And do you like Indian food?'

***

With a couple of hours in a pub behind us, and poppadams and a first shared bottle of wine finished, Anya and I began a second bottle and waited for the main dishes. 'Obviously she'd have been stripped,' she said, her blue eyes wide. 'The women would have been desperate for those gorgeous clothes.'

    'Mmm. Maybe.'
    'And raped. Who was to stop them?'
    I had told Anya everything, including how I nearly missed finding Rebecca in the Newnham archives that afternoon. "Mary R. Downing" the record card said, so I passed it over during my first search while looking only at students' names. But during my second much slower and more-painstaking search, I checked birth places and dates as well. "Nailsworth," the card said; and "23 February 1891" – exactly six Full Moons after Marianne North's death. If that wasn't link enough, Mary R. Downing had attended Newnham to study Botany in 1910, and had stayed for only three weeks.

    'It has to be her,' I said to the archivist, hardly able to contain myself. 'Is there any way you can check whether that "R" stands for Rebecca?' And after a full half-hour in the far-reaches of her domain, the wonderful meticulous woman returned with a piece of paper and a beaming smile to confirm that it did.

Meal over, the waiter cleared our table and Anya asked for the bill. 'As Rebecca survived,' she mused, bubbling with interest, 'somebody must have protected her, mustn't they? The chief's son? He fell in love with her at first sight and stopped the other men from hurting her? Married her? She had his babies. Probably lots of them. She became a baby machine. Oh, I'd love to know.'

'And so would I. I can hardly think of anything else. But, what you've just said... So much depends on what sort of tribe it was. Some – the hunter-gatherers – didn't really have chiefs as far as we know. Everybody was equal. As for marriage... Now that's something I'd really like to know. There certainly won't have been any ceremony. Even the Yanomamö didn't have weddings. For them, marriage was... Oh, sorry.'

'Sorry? Why?'

'I'm lecturing again. Bad habit. Just tell me to stop.'

Anya reached across and gave my hand a timid and very brief squeeze. 'No. It's OK. I want to know. Go on, please. What was marriage to the Yanomamö?'

'Well, it was political. Possessive. Polygamous. Girls were traded. Promised to somebody when really young. Even before the girl was born sometimes. And all the men beat their 'wives'. Even killed them sometimes if they were unfaithful.'

'So the women were too afraid to cheat?'

'You'd think so, wouldn't you? But it seems not. If a woman really fancied a man, she always found some way of having sex with him.'

'Really?' Anya laughed as the waiter collected the cheque. 'So nothing's changed very much then?'

'I guess not.' Then, standing, I asked if she knew where my hotel was.

'Sure. I walk past it every night on the way to my flat. It's about ten minutes from here.' She checked her watch. 'Shit! We've missed last orders.' Briefly, she looked disappointed. 'Off-licence?' Then her face lit up. 'What about your mini-bar? In your room? How about it? Let's get really pissed at the society's expense – and you can tell me everything you know about sex in the Amazon.' Then, on seeing my expression, she said, 'Oh, don't worry. My first lecture tomorrow isn't until two.'

***

On a real high when I returned home the next day, I phoned Gemma and told her my news.

'That's brilliant, Max. Especially about Rebecca. You were right and I was wrong. Congratulations. And what about the girl? Did she make her two o'clock lecture?'

'Just about. We shared a taxi. I dropped her off on the way to the station.'

'And are you going to see her again?'

'Probably not. It was fun, but we both knew it was only a one-off.'

'Oh! OK. So what's next with Rebecca?'

***

At the end of a two-day visit to Nailsworth, I sat alone in an ostentatiously quaint café. Between pouring tiny and ever-stronger cups of tea from an elegant if slightly stained silver pot, I ate scones topped with cream and strawberry jam.

I had arrived in the picturesque Cotswold town full of hope that I would discover something about Rebecca and the Downing family. I visited graveyards, churches, pubs, and the offices of the nearest local newspaper in Stroud. I found the site of the old bookshop, now a sweetshop, where my copy of

Coming of Age had first surfaced. I even stopped old people in the street and asked questions. But over the whole two days I learned nothing. '"Nailsworth" could mean any of the villages around here,' and 'Maybe the family left before World War I,' were the nearest things to helpful answers I received. I may have proved Rebecca to be real, but I still had no idea how to find her.

Chapter 5

Artist's model wins the right to sunbathe naked

An artist's model has been given the right to continue sunbathing naked in her back garden after a court cleared her of indecent exposure. Alice Doberfield, 39, a widow, was prosecuted after her next door neighbour filmed her on a camcorder and complained to police that her behaviour was offensive.

The court heard that Mrs Doberfield was unaware she was being filmed as she strolled naked in the garden of her cottage in Llan-y-Bont, Gwynedd, north-west Wales, last June. Her neighbour, Owen Jones, 45, a father of four, took the video to police who arrested Mrs Doberfield and charged her with indecent exposure.

Acquitting Mrs Doberfield, the chairman of the bench, Simon Belfry, told her: "Public nudity is not in itself an offence; it is your motive that matters and that alone which must be judged. You have admitted sunbathing naked from time to time and we accept that this has become a normal pattern just as nakedness is a normal part of your profession. We do not accept the prosecution's case that your motives were sexual or that you intended to cause harm or distress."

Mrs Doberfield, who has a 9-year-old daughter, said after the case: "I intend moving away from the area and getting on with my life and occupation. Since this blew up, my daughter has been ostracised at school and we have both been treated as lepers in the village. It has been horrible."

This is not the first time that Mrs Doberfield's pursuit of nakedness has led to her moving home. In October 1983, the naked body of her husband, John Doberfield, was found hanging from a tree on the Mary R. Downing estate in Gloucestershire. An inquest returned a verdict of 'suicide.' Reports at the time spoke of local hostility to the pagan naturist sect of which Mrs Doberfield and her husband had been members, a sect rumoured to consist of Animists and Wiccans.

***

I had rehearsed my introduction, designed to put Alice Doberfield at ease and at least get me inside the house, but the preparation proved unnecessary. A young girl opened the door.

'You're not Red,' she said. 'You're a different Red. And you're late. Mummy doesn't like it when men are late.' Her dark eyes studied me. 'Well… Come in.'

The hallway into which I stepped on my way to the lounge was tiny. Cigarette smoke hung in the air. So did the rancid smell of old chips. 'Mummy's upstairs in the bathroom. She won't be long.' The furnishing in the lounge was minimal: a rug, portable television, gas fire, threadbare settee and a stained mattress that although standing on its edge against the wall looked as though it could fall to the floor at any moment. Perched precariously on top of the mattress was a battered Polaroid camera.

'What's your name?' I asked.

'Yito.'

'That's an unusual name. What is it? Japanese?'

'Don't be silly. Do I look Japanese?'

To which the answer could have been yes. Not full-blooded, but with her long black hair, olive complexion, and the hint of oriental eyes one of her parents could easily have been Japanese.

'Besides, Yito is Spanish,' the girl continued. 'It's short for Caballito.'

'Little horse, eh? Foal?'

'Not telling you. Is that a real camera? With film you have to take to the chemist?'

I had brought my camera in case Alice Doberfield possessed photographs of the Downing estate, or even of Rebecca herself. If so, I intended to ask to copy them.

Yito scampered barefooted across to the mattress and fetched the Polaroid. 'This is my camera,' she said. 'Red bought it for me. And every time he comes to see Mummy he brings a new film for me to use. But he keeps all the pictures.'

I told her it looked a very good camera, which seemed to please her. She gave an engaging smile, displaying several gaps where milk teeth had been lost.

'Now can I look at yours?' she said.

She twisted it this way and that, as if in awe, then began playing with the lens while looking through the viewfinder. 'Wow! You can get closer. And further away. All without moving. What are these other things for?'

I told her.

'You mean... You can actually make things darker or lighter? And you can stop things being all blurry if they're moving?'

'Up to a point, sure.'

'Wow!'

Zooming in and out, she framed a picture of me, then began chuckling.

'What's the matter?' I asked.

'That lamp-post outside the window looks silly – like it's growing out of your head. And there's too much pattern on the curtain. It makes the picture look messy.' She looked around for a better angle and eventually found one that pleased her. 'Can I take a picture of you? Close up? Please? Your beard looks really furry with all the light behind. And your nose makes a nice shape. Is this the button I press? Can I? Please?'

And I hadn't the heart to say no, either to the first picture or to the next five.

'How many pictures can it take?'

'Only 20, then you have to change the film.'

'Have you got another film? Can I finish this one? Out in the garden? Please? While you're with Mummy. Will it photograph flowers?'

***

'You're late. I don't like people being late.' I spun round, then tried to hide my surprise; expecting either oriental or Spanish, all I saw was Anglo-Saxon – and I saw a great deal. Technically, Alice wasn't naked, but her knee-length dressing gown was so transparent she may as well have been. She hadn't even bothered to tie the belt. 'On the phone, you said you wanted the afternoon. That ends at five and I charge per hour – from when you were supposed to arrive, not from when you did. So what exactly do you want? Tell me, and I'll tell you what it costs. Money up-front.' Her body was on the fat side of voluptuous but her feet – she was bare-footed – looked dainty apart from the hint of a bunion on the left. Her shoulder-length hair was mousy-coloured and tied in a pony-tail.

'Actually, all I want is to talk.' My throat was dry; not from embarrassment but in case the tardy man I was impersonating suddenly arrived and blew my cover.

Alice grunted. 'One of those, eh?' and walked over to the mantelpiece to light up from a packet of cigarettes. She didn't offer me one. Through her robe her buttocks showed, pocked with cellulite. 'Well, even talking costs. Ten pounds an hour. Fifteen pounds if you want either of us to be naked, twenty if you want us both to be, and thirty if…'

'No, naked isn't necessary. Please… Go and get dressed. And an hour will be plenty.' I fumbled in my back pocket, found a ten pound note, and handed it to her. Ten minutes later, we were sitting on opposite sides of a small wooden kitchen table. She was still smoking and I was sipping a steaming cup of tea that she had generously provided at no extra cost.

'So what do you want to talk about?'

'I read about you in the paper.'

'Which one?'

I told her.

She had thrown on a loose-fitting red sweater and an old pair of jeans but was still barefooted. 'Must be someone else. I can't afford adverts in posh rags like that.'

'It wasn't an advert…' and I told her about the article.

'Are you a journalist? Digging for dirt? If you are my price has just gone up.'

'No,' and I explained who I was. 'And to be honest, no offence, but it's not really you I'm interested in. Nor your court case. The newspaper article mentioned a Mary R. Downing. Did you ever meet her? Or do you know anything about her? Any photographs? Where exactly was the estate by the way?'

'The estate? Hidden away, middle of nowhere. Even most of the locals didn't know it was there. Perfect for...' Then she hesitated and took an extra long draw on her cigarette. 'The crone was a Downing,' she said eventually. 'But her family – and the rest of us – called her Ipomoea.' She hesitated again. 'I don't think she called herself Mary though. I could have sworn John said she was Rebecca.'

'When you say "family"...'

'Her grandchildren. Though they didn't look a bit like her. They were South American.'

'South American? Could they have been Amazonian?'

She eyed me suspiciously. 'How did you know that? But yes, they were. And there was some sort of Spanish link as well. The children's real names were crazy, unpronounceable, but the crone had given them all Spanish nicknames. Not José or Maria or Antonio or anything like that but Sol, Nubes, Mariposa... There were six of them: four boys, two girls.'

'Sun, Clouds, Butterfly,' I translated aloud. 'All from the natural world.'

'I guess so. Actually, I liked the names. That's why Yito...' Her voice petered away, as if she couldn't think how to finish the sentence.

'So how did you become involved with Rebecca Downing? The newspaper said there was some sort of sect on the estate. Animists and Wiccans? Was your involvement through that? Was your husband a Wiccan?'

Again she looked at me suspiciously. 'We both were. And, I may as well tell you, John wasn't really my husband. Not legally. We went through a Handfasting ceremony. Have you heard of it?'

I shook my head.

'No? I don't suppose many people have.' She gave a wry smile. 'All the women wanted to marry John, and eventually most of them did. But I was the first. And he made me his High Priestess. Anyway... He was the connection. He'd met the crone in South America and agreed to come back with her to teach the children, but they were unteachable.'

'Language problems?'

'Not really. Sure, most of the time they jabbered to each other in their own language, whatever it was, but they understood English well enough.' She laughed as if at a memory. 'It was really weird; they spoke English with exactly the same posh accent as the crone. No, the real problem was that apart from Noo they couldn't see the point in learning about things they couldn't use.'

'Noo?'

'Oh, short for Nubes. That's what we called her.'

There was silence as I sipped my tea. Then I cleared my throat. 'Alice... Did the crone – Rebecca... I mean Ipomoea... Did you ever see her writing anything? Something big? An autobiography perhaps?'

Alice didn't look at me, just stared at her hands as she slowly shook her head. 'An autobiography? Ipomoea?'

'Why not? Her life sounds incredible.'

Alice shook her head again, then drew on her cigarette.

'No? Are you sure?'

'Sure!' she said emphatically.

Out of the corner of my eye, through the kitchen window, I could see Yito wandering round the long but narrow back garden, her short flared red summer dress flapping in the swirls of wind. She wasn't, as I'd expected, snapping away aimlessly with my camera but she was walking studiously from place to place. I never saw her take a photograph.

'Nice kid,' I said. 'Really pretty.'

'She's my life. All I've got left.'

'Of John?'

'Of everything. All my past. All my future.'

Alice was staring at her hands. I studied her for a moment. 'She seems really bright. Quick on the uptake.'

'Only with cameras. I take it that's yours. She won't want to give it back, you know. You got any kids?'

I shook my head.

Almost for the first time, Alice made eye-contact with me. Her eyes were greenish-blue and impassive, like a cat's. 'I never thought I would have one, you see. And I was getting so desperate. Then suddenly, out of the blue, there was Yito. If it hadn't been for her, I think I would have…' Again a sentence faded away, unfinished.

I held her gaze and smiled. 'Why did Yito call me Red?'

Alice also smiled, and for a moment – despite her nicotine-stained and slightly uneven teeth – I glimpsed how pretty she might once have been. She stubbed out her cigarette in an overfull ash-tray. 'A couple of years ago, I gave her a kiddie's picture book for Christmas. It was about Rob Roy MacGregor. Do you know him? Eighteenth century? Scottish folk hero? Outlaw?'

'Yes, of course. And his nickname was Red. But he really was a redhead. I'm not.'

Now she even chuckled. 'I know. But he also had this wonderful beard. Yito was fascinated, and ever since, every man she's known with a full beard she's called Red, no matter what colour his hair.'

I smiled at the story. 'Sounds as though you – and Yito – know a lot of men with beards.'

'I'm a model. Artists and photographers come here. Of course we do.'

Despite the way Alice's hands trembled as she lit another cigarette, she seemed to be relaxing, so I asked my question again. 'Are you absolutely sure that Rebecca – Ipomoea – didn't write an autobiography?'

Immediately, Alice began stubbing out her newly-lit cigarette. 'I'm sure! OK?' Then she told me that my hour was up – the hour since I should have arrived. Even if I wanted longer, she said, I couldn't have it. She'd just remembered something she had to do. It was time for me to go.

'This camera's wicked,' said a breathless Yito, coming straight in when she was called. 'I love the feel when you wind on the film. And does the picture really look the same as through the hole?'

She glanced at her mother, then at me. Suddenly her eyes were pleading, open wide, bright. 'Can I have it? Please? Please can I have it? I'll do anything you want, won't I Mummy? Just say.'

'Yito! No! Give it back.'

Yito didn't argue, just pulled the strap over her head and handed the camera back to me, looking as though she was going to cry. 'I didn't finish the film,' she said, dark eyes shining. 'I only took the good things. Will I be able to see them?'

'Of course! I'll get them developed and post them to you. And…' I looked at Alice, then back at Yito. '…I'm going to be buying a new camera before long. And when I do, you can have this one. I'll post it.'

'Really? Do you mean it? Promise?'

'I promise.'

'Not that we can afford the film,' said Alice. 'Besides… We're moving on. Very soon.'

I wrote down my telephone number and offered it to Alice. 'Let me know your new address,' I said. 'And if you ever want to tell me more about Rebecca Downing or your time with the sect – particularly if you remember anything about a manuscript – just let me know and I'll come running.'

***

I had Yito's film developed quickly and sent her the prints. The exposure was wrong on most of the outdoor shots, but other than that… How many untrained 9-year olds would have photographed mud squeezing between her bare toes? Or the shape of a footprint on a squashed flower? So, with the prints, I enclosed a note not only praising her eye for a picture but also explaining what had gone wrong with the exposure. I also told her that the six photographs she had taken of me, although each was more a silhouette than a portrait, were among the most interesting anybody had ever managed. And not wanting to miss the opportunity, I enclosed a sheet of the many questions I still wanted to ask Yito's mother.

There was no reply from either of them.

Shortly afterwards, I bought the new camera I wanted and tried to honour my promise that Yito should have my old one. But I was already too late. My phone calls received only a recorded message that the number no longer existed, and a provisional letter came back, 'Not known at this address.' I waited for Alice – or maybe even Yito – to phone me, but neither did.

In the months that followed, I visited the offices of Stroud's local newspaper several times. There I pored through paper after paper looking for an obituary for Rebecca Downing and coverage of John Doberfield's suicide. I thought that either could provide a clue to the whereabouts of the manuscript that Alice had insisted so unconvincingly was never written. But I found no obituary, the suicide reports told me nothing new, and nobody at the newspapers' offices could or would remember John Doberfield's death for me. 'Over ten years ago, mate. Everybody's moved on.' Apart from an incongruous picture of the tree from which John Doberfield hung himself, the articles were scarcely more than mentions of the event or the result of the inquest. There wasn't even a by-line saying who had written them.

'It's weird,' I said to Gemma during a phone conversation. 'John Doberfield's body was found by a search party out looking for a young girl from the local orphanage. But there's a lot more coverage of her and her disappearance than there is of this juicy suicide in a pagan sect. It doesn't make sense.'

Chapter 6

Wind howled through tiny gaps in the window-frames, rain cascaded from blocked guttering, and the branches of trees insistently tapped the panes of the upstairs windows; my first night in my new house and I did briefly wonder if I would prefer to be back in the city.

Manningford Bruce is a tiny village in rural Wiltshire; a picturesque collection of houses nestling near the River Avon in the Vale of Pewsey. Set almost a mile from the main village, my cottage had a thatched roof and a rambling overgrown front garden separated from cow fields by nothing more than an electric fence. At the back it had trees, trees and more trees. Six hectares of trees to be precise. It seemed perfect for an established Lecturer in Theoretical Anthropology and well worth the extra commuting.

Southern England was in the middle of a minor heat wave when Leo and Gemma, with six-year-old Solymar and their year-old son, first visited my new home. 'For Christ's sake,' I said as I emerged from the house carrying a tray of iced fruit juice. It was the Sunday of their long weekend visit, and another swelteringly hot August day. 'Will you lot please stop chasing each other around and put some clothes on. That's the third time that helicopter has flown over us in the past fifteen minutes.'

'Don't be such a spoilsport,' said Gemma, her lightly tanned body glistening with sweat as she walked elegantly over to collect her and Solymar's drink. 'Just give in and join in?'

I shook my head. All weekend my visitors had been playfully trying to get me to take off my shorts, though little

Solymar was the only one to try the direct approach: from behind with a yank. But nobody had succeeded yet.

'I'm going into the woods,' said Leo. 'Take a long stroll. Anybody coming?'

Gemma and Solymar declined – and I laid down a condition. 'Only if you get dressed first.'

'Why?'

'Because people do sometimes wander in from the road. They don't realise it's private property. You could be seen.'

'Doesn't bother me. It would serve them right. Give them a double shock if you were too.'

'No thanks. I have to live here.'

He eyed me. 'Have you still never walked naked and barefoot through a wood?'

In the end we compromised: barefooted, but wearing shorts – and I made Leo go in front so that if there were thorns lurking out of sight, he would step on them first. On finding a clearing created by a fallen victim of Dutch-elm disease, we sat on the trunk, made ourselves comfortable and soaked up the sun and atmosphere. But suddenly, the sylvan peace was shattered. Through the background noise of singing birds and rustling leaves, voices emerged; angry voices, a man's and a woman's. The voices' owners were still out of sight when a moment's silence was followed by the woman shouting 'No!' before screaming. Then we saw them, running towards us through the trees on the far side of the clearing. Neither was laughing.

The woman was youngish, perhaps in her mid-twenties. Her long fair hair was flapping round her face, her blouse open as if ripped; as we watched, the material caught on a bush, slowing the woman down and ripping further as she struggled free. She was still wearing underwear, but no skirt or trousers, and seemed also to have lost her shoes. Just a few yards behind and closing, the man, probably also in his mid-twenties, looked maniacal. After catching her by the shoulders, he wrestled her to the ground and they disappeared from our view. We could still hear her shouting at him to stop, screaming for help, until her voice was muffled.

I jumped off the trunk, but Leo restrained me. 'Just wait a moment,' he said. 'Maybe it's not what it seems.'

'Bugger that.' And when I ran to help, Leo ran with me.

I daresay we were an intimidating sight, two semi-naked bearded wild-haired men running across the clearing, bellowing loudly. Certainly our apparition was too much for the would-be rapist who scrambled to his feet and stumbled, hopped and ran from us as he tried to hitch up his trousers. It was also too much for the girl who sat and shuffled backwards until she was against a tree, staring up at us with wide frightened eyes. 'Don't touch me,' she screamed. 'Stay away! Please! Don't hurt me.'

'It's all right,' said Leo. 'You're safe with us. Come back to the cottage. My girlfriend's there. She can give you some clothes.'

'No!' exclaimed the girl.

Leo and I exchanged glances. 'OK,' he said. 'I'll go and fetch her.'

'I'll stay. Make sure matey doesn't return.'

Staying on the ground, the girl stared up at me with fearful suspicion, pulled her tattered blouse around her top half as if cold, folded her knees up to her stomach and half-turned away.

'Look... I'll move. Out of sight. I'll be over there. OK? Shout if you need me.' But she didn't shout, or even move until Gemma arrived with a dressing-gown and took her back to the cottage and straight upstairs.

Leo and I heard the bath running and occasional voices chattering. Eventually, we heard laughter. When the pair of them came downstairs to join us, the girl, now dressed in Gemma's clothes, began by thanking us and apologising for doubting our intentions. We made light of it, saying we wouldn't have trusted us either. Her name was Jenny and she lived about thirty miles away at Stroud in Gloucestershire. 'I'm going to drive her home,' said Gemma. 'I'll probably be gone a couple of hours.'

'Are you sure you're OK?' I asked Jenny while we waited for Gemma at the gate.

'Just about. Though if it hadn't been for you three…' She gave a slight shiver. 'I seem to be such a bad judge of men.'

I smiled. 'So... What do you do?'

She gave a quiet laugh, almost as if embarrassed. 'I'm a sort of curator – for the Museum of Local History. Probably sounds really boring, but it has its moments.'

'I didn't know Stroud had a museum.'

'It hasn't. It did have, and hopefully it will have again – if we ever get a lottery grant that is. Until then, somebody's got to look after all the documents and collections. And that lucky person is me. Only part-time, of course, but it's better than no job at all.'

'Local History… Does "local" go as far as Nailsworth?'

'Further.'

'Really! Have you ever heard of the Downing family?' and I gave her a brief summary of what I knew and wanted, how it all started, and how my investigation had stalled.

'The Downings,' she shook her head. 'No, sorry.' Then she looked at me and smiled, as if she hadn't properly noticed me before. 'You are really excited about this, aren't you? The thought of this Rebecca and all those other women adventurers? And I can see why. They sound like amazing women.'

Gemma arrived at the gate with the car. Jenny opened the passenger door, but before getting in she turned to me. 'Look… If the Downings owned an Estate near Nailsworth as recently as '83, we're bound to have something about them. We have copies of all the Registers from way back. And maps, magazines, newspaper cuttings, the lot. Would you like me to have a look for you? See what I can dig up? Until we get that grant, I'm not exactly overworked. I'd like to help. We need more stories of strong women out there.'

***

The phone rang. 'I have something for you.' It was Jenny, just a couple of weeks after her offer.

'Great! What is it?'

'Oh, I need to show you really.'

'OK. So where shall we meet?'

'Why not at yours? This Sunday?'

'Fine, if you're sure. I'll cook you something. A sort-of thank you.' But when Sunday came, my bottle of wine and a three-course meal seemed excessive. All Jenny had found was an early twentieth century reference to an estate owned by somebody called William Downing, plus a land-registry map of the general area from the seventeenth century.

'The estate is called Inchfield Park,' Jenny said as side-by-side and occasionally shoulder-to-shoulder, we examined the map on the kitchen table. 'Its origins go back to the mid-sixteenth Century. An entire valley was turned into a deer park, complete with a ten mile long boundary wall.' The long red-varnished nail of her slender index finger traced the course of the wall for me on the map. 'And there, at the western end, that's a hunting lodge.' Her green eyes shone brightly as she looked up at me. 'Exciting, eh?'

'Well... Yes... Inchfield Park. Sixteenth century. It's a start, at least.' I waited for more, but nothing came. She just sipped her wine and continued looking at me. 'So, nothing about Rebecca?' I asked. 'Or the break-up of the sect?'

She shook her head.

'John Doberfield's suicide?'

Now she laughed. 'Give me chance, Max. I do have a job to do as well, you know.' Then she looked around. 'I love your cottage. You're so lucky, living in a place like this.'

***

The following Friday, Jenny phoned again. 'I've got the next instalment for you. Is Sunday OK again?'

'Sure. Shall I come to you this time?'

'Absolutely not. My place is tiny. And a tip. And I share. And I so love your house.' She paused. 'This time I'll do the cooking. How's that?'

She still didn't bring answers to any of my main questions, just another map, this time from the nineteenth century. 'Can you see what they've done? They've landscaped the valley. Converted the river and fish ponds along the valley bottom into a series of lakes – really deep according to this note here. And they've turned the hunting lodge into a Manor House. And look at this...' She unfolded a sheet of paper. 'It's some sort of Parish commentary. The owners never actually lived in the Mansion. It was just some kind of retreat, but it must have been impressive. George III visited there in 1801.'

'Were these owners the Downings?'

She shook her head. 'No. But... Wait for it. Just a couple of days ago I found a record that the Downings bought the estate in 1850 – for one hundred thousand pounds. Can you imagine? That was Charles Downing, "a recent convert to Catholicism."' She pointed at the phrase on the paper; this week her nail-varnish was clear.

'Catholicism, eh? That sounds promising. Fits with "Mary," anyway. And with her uncle having something to do with a Mission. Maybe not with "Rebecca" though. Is Rebecca a catholic name?'

'It can be. Let's wait and see. Now that I've found Charles, I might be able to check the family through. If so – maybe next weekend?' She turned to face me, smiling with satisfaction, her mouth wider than average, lips shiny with gloss.

'Ah. I can't. Sorry, I'm busy next weekend. Do you want to tell me by phone?'

'Well... No, not really. I'd rather meet, wouldn't you?'

I smiled. 'Actually... Yes... I think I would. So how about the weekend after?'

'Brilliant! So, what now? Shall we open that wine I brought? Then I'll start cooking. The meal takes a while. You can talk to me. Tell me what it's like being a lecturer. Ooh, and an Anthropologist. That must be so exciting. I've never met one before.'

***

A fortnight later, Jenny was hardly through my cottage door before she was searching for the corkscrew. 'Desperate?' I smiled.

'Excited! Wait 'til you hear what I've got for you. You'll want to celebrate too.' And within moments she was handing me a very large glass of a very strong red wine and attacking hers with gusto. 'OK? Ready? Charles Downing had two sons and a daughter. The daughter, Matilda, never married…'

'Matilda? Brilliant.'

'I know – and there's more.' Standing in front of me, wearing a long V-necked cardigan over jeans, Jenny was more made-up than on previous occasions: mascara, blue eye-shadow, a hint of pink lipstick. Her perfume was more noticeable than usual too, and her fair wavy hair extra glossy. 'The elder son trained to become a Jesuit and went off to do missionary work in Spanish South America. The younger son – that's the William we've already talked about – took over the Estate when Charles died in 1895.'

'And did William have any children?'

'He did! Just the one. Are you ready?' She took another large swig from her glass, her eyes never wavering from mine as she waited for my reaction.

'A daughter? Rebecca?'

'Absolutely! Your girl from Newnham College. And, rumour has it in a village magazine I have from 1911, that she and her father fell out and he sent her to South America to do missionary work with his brother. How's that?'

I smiled at her excited face. 'So that is the family, and Inchfield Park is their Estate. The place Rebecca grew up in – and came back to.' Jenny was smiling back at me, her eyes soft, almost maternal, as if taking pleasure from my excitement. I shook my head, and gave a quiet chuckle. 'That really is fantastic, Jenny. I could kiss you for that.'

Jenny drained her glass and placed it on the kitchen table, then turned back to face me, her green eyes open wide. 'I was hoping you'd say that,' she murmured.

***

First out of bed the next morning, Jenny opened the curtains and then disappeared onto the landing on her way to the bathroom. A few minutes later, she returned.

'You could have used my dressing-gown,' I said. 'You must be frozen.'

She slithered back into bed then shuffled under the covers to embrace me with arms and legs, her body very cold against my skin. After a while, she began fingering my beard, then playing with my chest hair. 'My last boyfriend… He hated body hair. He used to shave his chest, and his pubes. Even under his arms. I didn't really like it.'

'Yet you…?' I said, placing my palm on her groin.

'He insisted. Said he liked women to look like little girls down there. And actually… He turned out not to be a very nice man in the end.' She gave a weak smile. 'I didn't cope with it too well I'm afraid. But… I'm OK now. Water under the bridge I suppose. So… Would you like me to let it grow again? Can you put up with bristles for a while?'

'It'll be worth it.' I kissed her on the nose which felt cold between my lips, then I glimpsed the bedside alarm clock. 'Oh God! Sorry Jenny. It's gone eight. I've got to go.' I wriggled free from her, then sat up. 'I'm lecturing this morning.'

'Can't you phone in? Make an excuse? Just this once? I don't work Mondays. We could go for a drive. Spend the day together. Stonehenge! How about it? It's years since I've been there.'

I laughed. 'Tempting… but I can't. Sorry.'

She also sat up, pulling the duvet to her shoulders for warmth. 'Do I really have to wait until next weekend to see you again?'

'Actually longer. I'm lecturing at a conference in Newcastle next weekend.'

'Oh,' she groaned. 'What about?'

'"Factors in the transition from hunter-gatherer to agriculturist economy." Riveting, eh? Why?'

'Can I come with you? Please? I'd love to hear you lecture, even though I probably won't understand a word you're saying. Maybe we could stay in a hotel together?'

I grinned at her, then instead of getting out of bed, I slipped back under the duvet and began delivering a rain of below-the-waist kisses, making her giggle. 'What are you doing? I thought you had a lecture?'

After poking my head out into the open, I looked up at her. 'I have, but it's not until twelve. I've just remembered.'

Chapter 7

Mother forced daughter, 8, to act as prostitute

A mother has been found guilty at Leeds Crown Court of forcing her 8-year old daughter to engage in acts of prostitution. In order to protect the identity of the daughter, now aged 14, the mother cannot be named.

The Court heard that the mother, 43, a widow, between 1991 and 1996 forced her daughter to take Polaroid photographs of her in sexual acts with men. She also forced her daughter to take part in such acts which the mother then photographed.

Presenting what it called an 'irrefutable case' the Prosecution showed the court a collection of diaries and photographs taken from the family home.

The mother, who described herself as an 'Artist's Model,' pleaded not guilty to abuse and said 'I have never forced my daughter to do anything. It is my belief that girls even as young as eight have the right to make their own decisions. My daughter wanted to raise money to buy film for her camera and this was the way she chose to do it.'

Sentencing the mother, Mr Justice Andrew Priest said ' In all my experience I have never before come across a case in which a mother has so callously and blatantly allowed a daughter so young to be debased, defiled, hurt and degraded in such an obscene way. You are clearly not fit to be her mother and I recommend that the child remains in care until she reaches the age of at least sixteen.'

***

Graphic images flashed into my mind of what Alice had been expecting of me the afternoon I visited her home in Wales, followed by others of young Yito being stripped and abused by bearded men on the filthy mattress in that squalid house while her mother took photographs. There was another image too: of Alice behind bars. She couldn't escape me in jail.

I called friends who worked in social services and asked them to help me track down both Alice's jail and Yito's whereabouts. Within a fortnight I had the address of both: Alice was in Styal Prison in Cheshire; Yito in a children's home in Yorkshire. I wrote to Alice, asking to visit and talk to her again. Then I tried to keep my promise to Yito over my camera by writing to her Principal. I explained who I was, the significance of the camera, and requested permission to send it to Yito. Alice replied by return to say that she had nothing further to say to me. Yito's Principal took a little longer to respond.

***

'I so look forward to these weekends,' said Jenny. 'Being here, with you, out in the countryside.'

She had just taken off her hat, scarf and coat when there was an insistent knocking on my cottage door. Outside were two hefty and unsmiling policemen.

'What is it? What's wrong?' asked Jenny as she saw them, but they weren't interested in her. After being asked to confirm who I was, I was shown two fairly poor faxes: one of a photograph of myself from the series that Yito had taken, and the other of my unaddressed note, praising her photographs, that I had signed as 'Red.' As soon as I acknowledged both, I was arrested on suspicion of the sexual abuse of a minor and driven to a police station near Swindon for questioning. My final image of Jenny was of her standing in my hallway, looking stunned.

The next twenty-four hours were the longest and in many ways the most frightening of my life. The sense of injustice and fear for the future were bad enough but the way I was treated made matters much worse. Feelings were running high in the station, a number of the police behaving as if I had abused their own daughters. Nothing was explained to me, and even a request to visit the toilet was treated as salacious. I was 'the scum of the earth,' 'a turd,' 'vomit.'

I was allowed a lawyer, a diffident bespectacled man in his fifties who could not prevent me being taken before the police doctor to have my genitals man-handled this way and that while a photographer zoomed in from every angle. These images were to be compared with photographs that had been found in the house of the 'poor girl,' pictures of men's genitals that at times had been in the act of penetrating her.

'How many times did you visit?'

'How old was she when you first fucked her?'

'How much did you pay her?'

'What perverted kick did you get from being photographed?'

'Why did she call you "Red"?'

The questions went on and on, the same ones repeated time after time, detectives working in shifts. Every truthful answer was countered by, 'You're lying.'

The most aggressive interrogator was a Detective Inspector with shaven head, cold piercing blue eyes and a goitre neck that bulged over his too-tight collar. 'We know you're lying. The child kept diaries and she talks about you all the way through. 1991 – Red came. 1992, 1993, Red came, Red came. She's written Red under your photo. You've signed yourself Red on your letter. 1994 – Red came, Red came. 1995. 1996. You're in all of them. She describes what you did to her. What she did to you. She has photos of your dick, you perverted bastard. Come on. Make it easy for yourself. Admit it!'

'I visited once, to talk with her mother. I never touched either of them. Yito called every man with a beard Red.'

The next afternoon, twenty hours after I'd been arrested, more evidence arrived: a book that the police claimed was Yito's 1992 diary plus the originals of my picture and letter.

'Yes… Of course that was me,' I said. 'Haven't I said so? A thousand times I've admitted that's me. But I only visited once, and I never, ever touched her. I've no idea who these other Reds are. Give me some dates. I'll have alibis.'

'We have no dates. The girl just scribbled anywhere in her diaries.'

'Then ask the mother what I did. Ask the daughter.'

'We have. Can't believe them, though, can we? They're protecting you. Probably terrified of you.'

Then a whole day after I'd been arrested, the latest interrogation was interrupted. A stooping detective came into the room, carrying a sheath of papers and photographs and took my skin-headed DI to one side; when they started arguing, they left the room. They were gone for a long, long half-hour.

'OK. You can go,' my interrogator said when he eventually returned. 'Pick your things up at the desk. And think yourself lucky you've got those two moles on your balls.'

My solicitor half-heartedly asked for an apology but 'Just doing my job,' was all I received.

'The DI...' I said to my solicitor as we parted. 'What was his name again?'

'Blakely. CJ Blakely. Child Protection Unit. He's based in Gloucester. Just promoted. Why?'

The atmosphere in the police car that took me home was still hostile. There was no apology, no polite words of farewell. They just dropped me at the track to my cottage and accelerated away. As I opened the front door, I heard a faint metallic sound: Jenny's keys were on the floor.

***

Not until my fourth call was the phone answered. 'Hi Jenny. I'm back. What a nightmare. You won't believe what they put me through.'

'So... Did they charge you?'

'Charge me! No, of course not. So where have you been? I thought you might still be at the cottage. I was getting worried. And what's with the keys?'

'Oh, I did wait. For a while. You know, just thinking about... Trying to make sense of... An hour – maybe. Or two. But then... After the shock. After I'd thought about... Well, I realised. I couldn't stay anyway. So I came home.'

I gave a quiet laugh of confusion. 'I don't understand. Couldn't stay?'

'You know... Charged, not charged. Guilty, not guilty. It was the end whatever.'

'End! Of what? Why? And of course I'm not guilty. I couldn't have sex with an eight-year-old if you tortured me. Surely you know me...'

'Know you? How does that help?' She gave a strained laugh. 'I knew that guy in the woods. He seemed really nice. And my ex... Especially my ex. Yet look what he... But you. I was so... I even told my Mum: "He's lovely," I said. Then in walk the police. It's hilarious really: "Jenny's done it again." So I thought... Well, better to finish it now than...'

'Finish! Jenny...'

'Best for me. I mean... How could I ever be sure? Every time a young girl... Every time we have sex, I'll be thinking... And that's just me. What if one of my friends...? Or my parents...? You don't know them. "No smoke without fire, our Jen. He'll not be welcome in this house."'

'Jenny... Look, let me drive over. Are you alone? Maybe you need somebody with you.'

'No, I'm fine. Absolutely fine. "A lesson learned" my Mum would say. If I told her. Which I won't. She despairs, you know. And she's still not that well. And... The thing is... In some ways Max, you really are the worst yet. No, you are. You got my hopes so... so... Because you were so nice to me. And it was such fun. When you gave that lecture... All that applause. And now... I'd actually thought about it, you know? Worked it out. How not to end up with a...' She paused. 'You do understand, don't you?'

I took a deep breath, then spoke as gently as I could. 'Are you sure you don't need me over there Jenny? Are you sure you're going to be OK?'

'Of course I'm going to be OK. This is nothing. After my ex... No Max. I'm fine.'

'Well, if you're sure...'

***

'Ah, Max. There you are. Come in. Come in.'

'Duncan. What's all this about?' I closed the door behind me.

'Yes… Well… Look Max. I'll come straight to the point. Probably best, eh?' He stood there for a moment, mouth open, looking at me. Then he turned round, walked over to his floor-to-ceiling bookcase and peered as if looking for a particular volume. All I could see was his back. I waited. When he turned round, he took off his spectacles and began cleaning them on his unbuttoned cardigan. 'Enjoyed your last paper by the way,' he said. 'Insightful. Excellent.'

'Thanks. But did you see the mauling it received in *Nature*?'

'Ah, yes. Was that the one? Really? Most unfortunate. You should have let me give it the once-over before sending it off.'

'I did, and you did.'

'Did I? Oh. Well… You know your fellow academics. Axes to grind, and all that. Anyway… Look, Max, the point is. We've known each other a long time, yes? How long is it now?'

'Ten years.'

'Really? Goodness. Tempus fugit, eh?'

'Duncan. What is this about? My promotion to Senior Lecturer? Is there something wrong with my application? I mean, surely that mauling in *Nature*…'

He took a deep breath. 'Not married, are you Max. No children.'

I laughed. 'Well… No. But…'

'Girlfriend?'

'Not any more. Why?'

With stilted movements, he half-turned to look out of the window for a few moments, then turned back, but lowered his eyes and looked at the floor. 'The thing is... You're a good lecturer, Max. No doubt of that. Brilliant, even. You get rave reviews. Every year your course comes top. The students love you. And your work... Well... But the thing is... The thing is...' He cleared his throat. 'The Vice Chancellor has had a phone call.'

'Phone call?'

'Yes. Some policeman. DI Blackman, Buckley, something like that.'

'Blakely?'

'Probably. Do you know what it's about?'

I nodded, very slowly. 'But why would he phone here? It was all a mistake.'

'Checking alibis he said.'

'They let me go.'

'I know. "Insufficient evidence" he said.'

'Insufficient! Absolutely no bloody evidence at all. I'm totally innocent. It was all one big mistake.'

With his hands, he gestured for me to calm down. 'And I believe you, Max. Of course I do. So does the Vice Chancellor. And we'd like to just ignore it, of course. But...'

'But nothing. They didn't charge me. I didn't do anything.'

'I'm sure. But the thing is...'

'For Christ's sake, Duncan. Will you stop saying "the thing is" and get to the fucking point.'

'Oh. OK. Language, Max. The point is, at the moment this unfortunate business... Well, at the moment it's totally under-wraps. Just the Vice-Chancellor and me, so far. And you, of course. No harm done. So, if you leave immediately...'

'Leave!'

'Of course "leave". You don't think you can stay here, do you? We can't have students being taught by a suspected paedophile.'

'Paedophile!'

'You know what I mean. The papers would have a field-day. So would the parents' lawyers. We'd have mobs. Demonstrations. Look at the animal rights business. And Cuthbertson in Sociology. That harassment thing. He denies that too. But it makes no difference. No, you've got to go – now – then if anything does blow up…'

'Nothing will blow up. It can't. Because I didn't do anything.'

'Come on, Max. If only life were that simple, eh? We'll give you a glowing reference. Love to. You've earned it. Well… As long as… So you shouldn't have any trouble getting another job. Maybe abroad, eh? And if all goes smoothly, the Vice Chancellor says he might see his way to putting together a small lump sum for you. Ease the burden, so to speak.'

'What are you saying? You're sacking me?'

'Sacking? No! No, of course not. Far too risky for us, though we could, of course. If we had to. No, no. Resign. That's the way to do it. We'll waive the three-months notice. Let you quietly slip away. Best for you. Best for us. Say it's for personal reasons. You need to nurse your sick mother, something like that.'

I hung my head, and spoke quietly. 'My mother's dead, Duncan. So's my father. Crushed by a lorry. You sent me a "Condolences" card. Remember?'

'Sorry, didn't catch any of that.'

Staring at him, I gazed into his eyes for so long he began to fidget. 'How old are you Duncan?'

'Eh? Sorry?'

'How old? Sixty? More? Just a couple of years to retirement?'

'Actually, sixty-three. But I don't see…'

'And you've been here thirty, forty years?'

'Stick to the point Max. You'll go, yes? No fuss? I can tell the…'

'But this is the point, Duncan. Very much the point. You've lost all pride in what you do. Because there's no joy in Universities any more, is there? They're just businesses, scared shitless of scandal and litigation in case they lose their precious reputation and all the money that goes with it. And there's no joy in the subject any more, if there ever was. A subject you begged me to take on. Theoretical Anthropology! My God. I wanted to work in the field. Do you remember? Get my hands dirty. I know you did too. So what were you doing? Making sure I didn't get what you didn't dare go for?' I gave a quiet laugh. 'You're doing me a favour. No really, you are. Ironic, eh? So… Yes! I'll go. Glad to. Go and get your pat-on-the-back from the Vice Chancellor. And tell him I will take that "little lump sum." Only it isn't going to be so little. You make sure of that.' I opened the door, then paused in the doorway, looking back at him, his mouth open. 'Send me the paperwork, will you? Save me from coming back here again. I've got a new life to begin. Enjoy your retirement Duncan.'

***

'You did what?' said Leo when, over a week later, I finally told him the news over the phone. 'Are you crazy?'

'No. I'd had enough. It's been building for years. Ask Gemma.'

'But what sparked it off.'

'Not much. Just a disagreement over my last paper.'

'How the hell can you give up a bloody good job just because somebody doesn't like what you've written. What does Jenny say about this?'

'Oh, we've decided to call it a day. It wasn't going anywhere. We could both see that.'

'Idiots. So what are you going to do now? How are you going to fill your time? What the hell are you going to live on?'

'I'll manage. I've got just about enough money to survive – if I'm careful. And I've got plans. For starters, I've applied for a grant to research the life of Rebecca Downing. I've found this Trust set up by some Gloucestershire philanthropist to encourage research into local history. That will help, if I get it.'

'I thought you came to a dead-end on that story years ago.'

'I did, but then Jenny came up with a few more leads, and that Wiccan woman who knew Rebecca has just surfaced again – in jail.'

'In jail! Christ! So she's going to be really useful then. Anyway, it's your life, Max. I just hate seeing you make such a mess of it.'

***

For a fortnight after my arrest, a parcel lay unsent on my hall table. Every day I looked at it in passing, and sometimes I even picked it up then put it down again. It was addressed to Yito, and inside was my old camera plus a letter reminding her who I was, wishing her many brilliant photographs, and giving her my address. Also in the letter, I offered not only to send her a film once a month but also to have it developed if she sent it back to me. Eventually, I made my decision, took the parcel to Pewsey Post Office, and mailed it Recorded Delivery. A week later, I received a postcard with Van Gogh's *A Starry Night* on the front and "Thank you. I do remember you. Yito" written neatly on the back.

Yito's mother, on the other hand, never once replied to anything I sent her.

Chapter 8

On a cold and showery April morning, I drove through Nailsworth on my way to find and explore Inchfield Park. According to my map, I first had to locate the single-track B-road 'with passing places' which meandered the few miles between Nailsworth and Pegbury. And halfway along that, at a T-junction, would be the only access road into the Park. In the event, this 'road' proved to be no more than a very narrow dirt track with unkempt hedges either side and weeds growing along the middle. After winding between cow fields for about half a mile, the track finally ended at a gate, with signs:

'Private Property.'
'Trespassers will be Prosecuted.'
'No Admittance.'
'Danger – Electrified.'

The gate was iron, padlocked, stretched right across the track, and to judge from the vegetation hadn't been opened for some time. The temptation to blunder on was tempered by the need to know more about the seriousness of what I would be doing. I looked at my watch.

The Crown was empty apart from the landlord from whom I ordered a half of bitter and a packet of crisps before asking what I would need to be allowed into Inchfield Park.

'A permit, I reckon.'
'Who from?'
'No idea.'
'Who might?'
'Nobody round here.'
He looked at me. 'How long are you staying?'
'Why?'

'Well… My Missus'll be opening the kitchen in a minute. Here's the menu. The first three are off. Eat here, buy a proper drink, and maybe I'll introduce you to Hood. If he comes in. Often has a quick one, Saturday lunchtime, does Hood. Then he goes to the Park fishing for the afternoon. He's the only one who dares, see. Buy him a drink and he might even take you with him.'

'So… He's got a permit, this Hood?'

'Shouldn't think so. Doesn't need one. His cousin used to be a policeman.'

While I waited for my plate of egg-and-chips – the only meal 'on' on the menu – and slowly sipped a pint of Best Bitter, assorted people drifted in, each greeted by a shout of 'Shut that bloody door.' Then suddenly the door flew open, letting in both the rain and a bearded man who was virtually blown into the room. I would have guessed who he was even without the give-away shouts of 'Alright Hood?' that rippled round the room. On his head was perched a grubby green Robin Hood hat, complete with Pheasant's feather. Wearing Wellington boots, faded brown corduroy trousers, and an old leather waistcoat he looked from a different age.

'Bloody weather,' was all he said as he took off his hat and dislodged the raindrops by knocking it against his trousers.

The landlord had started pouring a pint of beer the moment Hood appeared. The pair of them talked, occasionally looking in my direction, but it was several minutes before Hood walked over to my table. Without word or invitation, he pulled up a chair. 'Thanks for this,' he said, holding up his pint glass. 'I hear you want to go to the Park.' He looked under the table. 'Reckon you'll need better shoes than those, though. Wet grass and cow pats.'

'I'll cope.'

'Reckon we'll need something warm inside us as well.'

'Like...?'

'Bottle of whiskey would do it, I'd say. Two if you want some as well.'

***

'Aren't you worried they'll get stolen?' I asked Hood as he collected a net and fishing rod from a tumbledown ivy-covered building alongside an Inchfield lake.

'Witchery, ghosts, and deaths, that's all this place is known for.'

Behind the wheel of a battered dark-blue Ford Prefect, Hood had driven past the access road I had explored and parked instead in a passing space further towards Nailsworth. And from there – over stiles, across cow fields, through fences and over a broken part of the high boundary wall – we had arrived half-an-hour later in the valley bottom.

'Deaths?'

Large drops of rain began to measle the otherwise smooth lake surface.

'Over forty so far, so they say. And hardly-a-one natural... so they say.'

'Hence the ghosts?'

'Maybe. Eight in the valley at the last count: an angel that hangs about over one of the lakes; a Roman centurion on the east path; a ragged dwarf; a headless horseman; a naked temptress; a floating coffin; a black dog; and a man in his night-shirt who was savaged by his own dogs. Mind you, he could be the angel. Oh... And there's a large black cat, a sort of panther – but that one's probably not a ghost.' I was watching his face closely, looking for a twinkle in his clear blue eyes, but I didn't see one. 'Don't see a living soul here from one month's end to the next,' he continued, 'which suits me fine. And I daresay it'll stay that way until the old place gets flattened.'

'Flattened?'

Hood took the bottle of whiskey from his pocket, unscrewed the cap, took a long swig, then wiped his mouth and moustache with the back of his hand. 'You wanted to come here and I've brought you. Now I'm going fishing and you're going to leave me in peace. Meet me back here in three hours and I'll show you how to get out, but that's it. If you want to ask questions, you can do it in the pub this evening over a few drinks. OK? Now, make sure you don't get lost. And don't go in the old house, either. That's haunted, too.'

***

Winding along the valley bottom, the main track occasionally allowed a wonderful view of the lakes, but mostly it was bordered by bushes and trees. Everywhere, thick woodland clung to steep slopes, and being April the new spring leaves formed an intricate mosaic of shades of green. The recent shower had muddied the track and filled the air with the smell of damp vegetation, punctuated occasionally by the rancid scent of foxes – or was it the odour of rotting corpses? I kept glancing over my shoulder, straining my ears to identify strange sounds masked by those normal for an English forest. All around me, unseen songbirds were chorusing. Overhead, circling crows and rooks were cawing. Was that a twig cracking? Did something slip and fall? Then suddenly…

Round a bend, in a clearing, I was confronted by a monstrous house. An enormous stone edifice adorned with a tower, gables and buttresses. A kestrel swooped from the air to disappear somewhere into the clearly crumbling roof. A flock of jackdaws was circling overhead and a pigeon flew out through one of the huge vaulted and evidently unglazed windows. As I drew near I saw a series of animal-shaped gargoyles high up on the mansion's walls: a grotesque bat, an owl, a boar, several ravens and various hideous griffins. The old house looked just like a medieval monastery, and despite Hood's warning I had to go inside. This was, after all, Rebecca Downing's family home. George III once stayed here.

There was no conventional way in; no grand entrance to welcome or impress the visitor. Just a huge heavy sombre wooden door that was either jammed or locked. So I climbed in through one of the vast windows, noting fragments of glass all around. Once inside, I found the floor littered with lumps of stone, some small others huge, all once part of a ceiling; there was more to fear in the house than just ghosts.

The wind whistled through the building, and I shivered. The whole place was eerily magnificent – but also dark, cold and wet. You could smell the dampness, almost taste it. But not all of the scattered wooden furniture had yet rotted. Some had been protected by the fallen stone and debris. I tugged at the protruding arm of a chair but nearly started a landslide, so I left it.

I moved over to a window to gaze outside, up the wooded slope – and immediately felt all colour drain from my cheeks. Something or somebody was among the trees. Narrowing my eyes to focus, I could make out a solid shape within the dappled mosaic of light and shade. Were those legs? Were they bare? A gust of cold wind blew my hair over my eyes. I brushed it back and looked again. Now I glimpsed buttocks, side-on, half-hidden by the branches of a tree. Was I looking at a deer? A Roe or Muntjac, perhaps. Wind blew the branches and the creature turned. Was that a triangle of black hair? A naked woman? Or just a shadow? I was being stupid. What woman would go naked in such weather? Unless... I fumbled in my pocket and took out the whiskey bottle.

***

'Ah, that's her, that's the temptress,' Hood said as I described what I'd seen. 'It's always her bottom half you see. Mind you, I'm not complaining.' He gave a dirty laugh.

The pair of us were walking in single file, the rain by then relentless. Hood was in front carrying his afternoon's catch of a Roach and two Tench – 'not bad considering the weather' – with myself bringing up the rear, slipping and sliding while struggling uphill on a narrow muddy badger track through the forest.

'Who is she supposed to be?' I shouted forward.

'Reckon she's the ghost of one of those jungle witches that lived here for a while. They all died. Of the cold, most like. Either that or they ate each other.' He laughed again.

'Do you know anything about them?'

'Bits and pieces. Get me really drunk later on and I might tell you. Has been known. But right now, I'm going home to the warm to enjoy my fish.'

Hood didn't invite me to share either his fish or the warmth of his home, just informed me that *The Crown* could be bribed into renting out rooms for Bed-and-Breakfast if I wanted to stay the night.

***

'You the guy waiting for Hood?' asked a large apple-shaped man as he joined a trio playing dominoes on the table next to me. Red-faced from the sheer effort of standing, he hooked his walking stick over the nearby coat-stand and slumped onto the wooden bench. The spaniel with him squeezed behind the man's legs and curled up as if expecting a long evening.

I nodded.

The man took a gulp from the pint of beer that had been waiting for him. 'Now what would a bloke like you be wanting with a country bumpkin like Hood, I wonder?' The men on the tables near me stopped playing their cards or dominoes to listen to my answer.

I told them as briefly as I could.

'So you're a university feller then.'

'Used to be. I'm freelance now.'

With raised eyebrows and sombre glances, everybody went back to their games. A few minutes later, Hood arrived and eventually made his way to my table.

'Alright Hood?' said the apple-shaped man as Hood sat opposite me.

'Alright Cuz?' echoed Hood.

'Cuz?' I asked quietly.

'Cousin!' replied Hood loudly. 'And a right fat pain in the backside he is too, aren't you Cuz?'

The landlord brought over a pint of beer and a whiskey chaser for Hood, and another pint of beer for me. 'Thanks,' I said to Hood.

'No need. You're paying,' and without any further pleasantry, Hood downed the pint without stopping, drank the chaser in one as well, and finished off with a belch of appreciation. 'First is always best, don't you reckon?' He signalled to the bar and the landlord immediately began preparing a further round. 'Now, what can I tell you?'

According to Hood, the villagers around the Estate had known William Downing as a devout, doddery and reclusive old man living in the crumbling house with just two or three servants almost as old as himself for company. And

Hood was still a young man when he heard that a woman had turned up at the mansion claiming to be William Downing's long-lost daughter. Nobody but a doctor, a solicitor and a priest had seen William after that, and eventually the old man was carried out in a coffin. 'Day before his hundredth birthday, so they say. Refused to go to hospital, didn't he. Wanted to die in the house. Silly old sod!'

'You sure you're alright Hood?' came from the next table.

'Never better.'

'Hood!' shouted dart players from across the room. 'Make a four?' And without apology, he went to join them. When eventually he came back, he didn't even sit down. Just drank more of his beer.

'So what happened to the house and Estate when William died?' I asked as he stood there. 'And who owns it now?'

'What happened? Don't rightly know. Wheeling and dealing, I shouldn't wonder. Rumour has it that old man Downing didn't exactly own the place. Some Trust did – Park something or other – and still does. But now some big-shot company is interested. Except it's all on hold. Some daft story about rare plants and animals.' He drained his glass, and the landlord delivered the next.

'Best slow down Hood,' said Cuz.

'Slow down yourself. Alright? When have I ever lost the plot?' And taking his new drink with him, Hood went to the dart board again.

'What was the old woman like?' I asked when he returned. 'Did you ever see her?'

'Once or twice. Only in the valley, mind. She had grey hair. Tits flat as pancakes down to her waist. Slim, though – and she could scamper up and down those slopes like a young one.'

'So you visited the valley while she was there?'

'Did I? Christ! Not to see her, though. Them others.' Hood gave the dirtiest laugh yet. 'Me and the lads used to go for a gander sometimes in the summer. Took binoculars. Saw some really tasty sights. Know what I mean? Used to sit around a bonfire near one of the lakes, didn't they? All starkers.'

I gave a polite smile. 'Look, Hood. This is all great stuff, but what I really want to know is what happened to the old lady. Did she die in the valley? Move away? Was that why the sect broke up?'

'Hood! A word,' demanded Cuz. Then he glowered at me. 'A private word.'

I went to the 'Gents', but when I came back into the room, Hood, Cuz and others seemed to be arguing, so I stayed around the bar for a while, waiting for them to calm down. When I finally returned to the table, Hood greeted me with a frown. 'I'm needed for a game of dominoes. Probably nowt else I can tell you anyway.'

'Yes there is. The old lady. I really need to know what happened to her.'

Hood grunted and wiped beer off his moustache and beard. 'Search me. One summer they were all there and the next they were all gone. They could have buggered off back to the jungle for all I know, old lady and all.'

I groaned. 'OK. So when was that last summer you saw them? 1983? The same year as the suicide? Was that part of the break-up?'

Hood's mouth fell open but he said nothing, and the people around us seemed finally to lose patience. 'Hood! Dominoes! Now!' Hood immediately began to stand.

'So the suicide was part of the break-up,' I said quickly.

He dithered for a moment, then leaned towards me. 'Look, you wanted to hear what I know, and you just have. Now I'm going to enjoy myself, and you're going to leave me in peace. Fair enough?'

Chapter 9

Every month a film from Yito appeared through my letterbox – and on my next shopping visit to Marlborough or Devizes, I handed the roll into a chemist's for a 60-minute development service. Knowing that Yito was always impatient to see the results, I mailed back the developed negatives, one set of prints, and a new roll of film as soon as possible, along with any comments I might have on her pictures. I also kept a full set of prints for myself.

'She is pretty,' Gemma remarked when I showed her the latest photographs containing self-portraits of the now nearly sixteen-year-old Yito. 'You can't see any sign of suffering in her, can you?'

Only three of the photographs were of Yito's face. The rest were of parts of her body – hands, feet, fingers and toes – all in some way juxtaposing with nature. There was a foot in a goldfish pond, the toes being nibbled by fish; a bleeding knee poking through a gap in a pile of rough hewn logs...

'Pretty? Mmm, I suppose she is. Look... I've already got her next roll of film. Don't suppose you could have it developed for me while you're in London, could you? I'm really short of time to finish this report. At the rate my money is running out...'

Leo laughed. 'You mean the fools are still paying you? Haven't they worked out it's all a waste of time and money yet?'

'No, but they will when they read this "progress" report I'm writing. I don't even know where in the Amazon Rebecca went. I've written to all the old Jesuit colleges in the UK, trying to track down where her uncle was trained and which mission he went to, but so far: nothing. If I could just get my hands on that damn autobiography…'

Leo threw up his hands. 'Which might not even exist.'

'You didn't see Alice's face when she was denying it. That manuscript is out there somewhere, and the place to start looking is wherever Rebecca died, but I can't find that out either. Even the Family Records Centre in London doesn't have a record of her death. Not that I can find, anyway.'

'Maybe she's not dead yet,' said Gemma.

I laughed. 'Do you know – and this is how desperate I've become – I'm actually phoning all the Old People's Homes I can find listed. But she'd be 109. Come on!'

'Didn't her father live to be a hundred?'

'A hundred is one thing, but 109… No she's dead. She's got to be. And what the hell is this link with John Doberfield's suicide that keeps cropping up? Basically, I'm stuck – again. I can't think what to do next.'

'I'll tell you what to do next,' said Leo. 'Give up, get your old job back, and find yourself a woman. Have you fucked anybody since you gave Jenny the elbow?'

I shrugged. 'A couple of half-hearted affairs, that's all.'

'You see. Now that's not healthy. And on top of that, your house is falling to pieces and your garden's a jungle. How much longer can you carry on like this?'

'Leo, stop it,' said Gemma, mother-earth again: eight months pregnant with her third child. 'And don't listen to him Max. I think it's brilliant the way you've persevered with this.'

'Thanks.'

'The word is obsessive.'

'Leo! Come on, be nice, be helpful. Tell Max what you told me on the way here.'

'Why? It'll only delay the inevitable.'

'Leo!'

'Oh, OK. Look Max. Maybe you should check out that Trust your poacher-friend mentioned. What was it called? Park something?'

'Why? What good would that do?'

'Because my guess is you'll find it's a Discretionary.'

'A what?'

'A family trust, if you prefer. Huge tax benefits for people like the Downings. And if I'm right, a list of the trustees and beneficiaries over the years could make interesting reading.'

'Leo… I haven't the faintest idea what you're talking about.'

'And the rest,' Gemma urged Leo with a scowl.

He groaned. 'OK, if you want, Max, I'll volunteer to look into it for you. Unlike you, I know what I'm doing – and I've got the contacts.' He looked at Gemma, as if for approval, then back at me. 'But I still think you'd be better just giving up.'

***

Two days later, I heard the pair of them stalking up my garden path after their weekend break in London. Moments on, the cottage door flew open and Gemma stormed into my kitchen. 'Don't ever ask me to do anything like that again,' she shouted. 'I have never been so embarrassed in my whole life.' The yellow envelope she threw on to my kitchen table flew off and slithered under the dishwasher. Laughing, Leo dropped to his knees to retrieve it.

Gemma blustered on. 'I was sent to the manageress, like some naughty school-girl. I had to put up with this sour-faced bitch in her fifties looking down her nose at me through her glasses. Did you know what was on that film? Because if you did…'

Leo placed the package back on the table. 'Calm down, Gem. Come on. Sit down.' Then grinning broadly at me he added: 'It's funny really. Get her a drink and listen to this.'

So I made Gemma a gin and tonic which despite her condition she accepted, taking rapid angry sips before speaking. 'She was so snotty to me. "The negatives I have to return to you," she said, "but I can only let you have five of the prints because it is company policy – in fact our obligation – to destroy all prints that might be construed as pornographic. And in this particular case we decided that all of your close-ups of a young woman's groin fall into that category."'

My mouth dropped open. 'Oh God! I'm sorry Gem.'

Leo, chortling away in the background about the word 'groin', made further gin-and-tonics for him and me.

'Did you know?' Gemma asked me, narrowing her eyes.

'No! Of course I didn't. What did you say? I hope you told them the film wasn't yours. That you were developing it for a friend.'

'Of course I did. And she said she would let it pass – this time. The bitch. I felt that small.'

I reached for the package. 'Have you looked at the negatives?'

'Of course we've looked at the negatives,' sniggered Leo. 'But don't get too excited. They're more biology than *Playboy*.'

'A couple of snails mating on her pubic hair, like it was a lawn. And a couple of earthworms half-in, half-out of her. Totally disgusting.'

'And lots of mucus stuff everywhere. Not a turn-on, I promise you.'

'It's as if she's portraying being dead.'

In the package I mailed to Yito, I included a letter explaining what had happened. I also said that if she wished to take such photographs then she must either go back to using an instant camera or learn how to develop the film herself. I suggested she switch to using positive film – slides – which she could develop privately in a simple container in her bedroom. She wrote back by return and said she'd love to – and would I pay for all the chemicals and equipment.

***

'How's the new baby?' I asked Leo when he phoned.

'Handsome, hungry, and already hung like a horse.'

'Not yours then. Decided on a name yet?'

'Jealous sod! No, not yet – and I didn't phone to talk babies. I've got the low-down on Park Trust for you, and it took some doing, so be grateful.'

'OK. I'm grateful. Anything interesting?'

'All sorts. First, Park Trust is an old one. Nineteenth Century. The guy who created it was William Downing's father, Charles, and its assets are listed as the entire Park, all buildings, and quite a few fairly clever investments. The terms of the trust were, and still are: any bloodline descendant has automatic right to become both a trustee and a beneficiary on reaching the age of 25; co-opted non-bloodline trustees must never outnumber bloodline; and a quorum is two. Then there's all sorts of other stuff about voting rights, adding and removing trustees, proxy representation, and so on. Are you with me so far?'

'Just about. So what's interesting?'

'Several things. First, your poacher-friend was right. The Trust is up for sale and some big leisure park chain has an option on it. But there's a hitch. The local naturalists are trying to get the valley declared a site of special scientific interest – bats, moths, orchids, that sort of thing – but nobody's being allowed in to do any proper research. So until all that gets sorted out, the sale is on hold. There's probably a lot of money at stake.'

'So who will benefit if the sale does go ahead? Who are the current trustees? Not Rebecca, surely.'

'No! She was – but only until 1983.'

'There's 1983 again. Does that mean Rebecca died in that year too?'

'Or opted-out. And soon after, one of the grandchildren became a trustee…'

'Male or female?'

'Can't tell. The name was about 20 consecutive consonants. Meant nothing to me. Anyway, in 1984 the grandchild came off the list and the family interests were taken over by a proxy company – *NB Holdings* – which probably means that all the bloodline descendants had left the country. Your poacher guy could be right. And it's this company that is receiving Trust money at the moment in the form of fairly hefty "administration costs," and part of their current remit is to sell the Trust.'

'Can they do that?'

'Probably. I daresay there's a fifteen year or whatever abeyance clause: if all bloodline descendants die or fail to call a meeting in that time, the proxy and non-bloodline trustees have the right to liquidate the trust, and that's what's happening now.'

'Do we know anything about this *NB Holdings*?'

'Not much. Two directors. Same name, so two brothers, sisters, maybe husband and wife. I'll look into them if you like, but I don't think you'll learn anything about Ipomoea or the family from them, especially if they really did return to the jungle. The Downing legacy is as good as over.'

'So… Another dead-end then?'

'Afraid so. But, there is one thing that might interest you. Guess who Ipomoea co-opted to help run the thing for her while she was a trustee – and who stayed on briefly to help the grandchild?'

'Who? John Doberfield?'

'Spot on! Somehow, he got a foot inside the family fortune door before he topped himself. Interesting, eh?'

Chapter 10

It was a July evening and just warm enough for me to be drinking outside. Surprise visitors should have been impossible because the gravelled path amplified footsteps as they crunched ever nearer. But this night the early-warning system failed, the rooks overhead making too much noise. Suddenly, somebody was watching me. Turning too quickly to face the shadowy figure, I slopped my wine.

The intruder wasn't threatening. Just a pretty young woman in her late teens. She had long dark hair and was wearing a bohemian-looking outfit of a short denim jacket and floral skirt with old trainers poking out under the hem. Over her shoulder she was carrying a heavy-looking green rucksack. She looked as panicked as I was shocked. 'I'm sorry,' she almost blurted, 'but I haven't enough money.'

'I don't understand.'

'For the taxi. I told him you'd pay. Will you? Please?'

'Who are you? What are you doing here?'

'Don't you recognise me? From the photographs? I'm Yito.'

I paid off the taxi-driver who had driven her the twenty miles from Swindon train station, then I returned to the roughly tiled and weed-infested patio. 'You haven't changed,' Yito said to me as we stood, both awkward. 'Those photographs I took of you nine years ago. You look just the same.'

'But you've changed,' I said, fairly ridiculously. I offered her some wine, which she accepted but scarcely touched as she talked.

She had just finished her A-levels, she said, and in the autumn if her grades were good enough she would be going to a College in Devon to study photography. Then she explained why she had so suddenly arrived on my doorstep. 'You told me in one of your letters that you'd been to Inchfield Park. I was born there, you know. And my father – John Doberfield? – he died there. Alice took me once when I was eight and I took some photographs. I want to go there again and take some proper ones. It's such a beautiful place. I wondered if you'd mind taking me. You're the only person I know who could.'

'There's your mother? Oh... Maybe... Is she still in jail?'

'No. She's dead. She died in the prison hospital.' There was no sadness in her voice, no hint of loss. 'I never saw her after she was arrested. She wouldn't. She blamed me, you see. She always told me to give all the photos to the men but – I wanted to keep a few. Then, like an idiot, I showed one to my best friend...' There were a few moments' silence. Yito was being so disingenuous, so innocent, so charming... 'So is it all right? Will you take me to Inchfield Park? Maybe tomorrow?'

***

'Do you notice anything?' Yito was breathing fast. At the centre of a clearing was a majestic beech tree, its girth huge and its bark grey and smooth, the trunk pocked only by the scars of branches from its younger days. The lowermost branches now were at least six metres above the ground.

I recognised it immediately. 'Not really. What?'

'Suppose you wanted to kill yourself there. How would you do it?'

'Climb to that lowest branch, I suppose, tie a rope to it, put a noose around my neck, and jump.'

'So would I. So now do you notice anything?'

'No. Sorry.'

'Could you climb that tree?'

'Mmm. I see what you mean.' I looked round at other trees. 'Almost any one but this one.' We discussed other possible methods of hanging oneself from the beech tree, but found a problem with them all. 'So what are you saying?' I asked her. 'That somebody helped him?'

She shook her head. 'That he was lynched. I think that somebody – probably a gang – threw a rope over the branch and tied it round his neck. Then they hauled him up and left him hanging there until he was dead.'

***

While Yito took a roundabout route, looking for photo-opportunities which she said she saw better alone, I went straight to the mansion. And after crawling through a window I began re-exploring, settling finally in the room from which I had seen the naked temptress. My gaze fell on a large grey feather poking incongruously out from between lumps of fallen stone. I clambered over the rubble to investigate, fully expecting to find the feather still attached to the skeleton of a long-dead bird. But it wasn't; it was free and pulled easily. I twirled the feather between my fingers, wondering why the tip was stained black – except, looking closer, I saw it wasn't the tip. The end had been cut to a shape, an oblique chisel, and slit in the middle. My pulse began to race. Could a feather last that long?

The quill had been near the corner of a piece of furniture almost entirely buried by ceiling debris. Tentatively, I began moving the stones one at a time; some were small, others almost too large to shift. Bit by bit there emerged what looked like a writing desk, it's top although cracked and splintered looking as though it would lift if only I could free it completely. The process was slow and increasingly dangerous as I undermined the pile of stones that had crushed the wood and then protected it from the elements. Moving a slab from the right hand edge of the desk, I saw a piece of paper jutting out from between lid and side. When I pulled, the paper tore, or maybe it was torn already, leaving me with just a fragment from the edge of a page. On the fragment were a few words, written in the beautiful italic hand that I had seen before.

Abandoning caution, I threw and brushed to one side the debris that stood in my way, but still the lid wouldn't lift. I pushed, then pulled; nothing moved. I shifted my stance on the stones and tried again. At last something was giving. At the risk of rupture I turned sideways and pulled with all my strength. Suddenly, something snapped and the lid jerked upwards.

As I fell backwards, I caught a fleeting glimpse of the desk broken and falling, spilling out a pile of ripped up sheets of paper. I landed heavily on the uneven rocks, then tumbled to the side. Seconds later the whole pile of rubble collapsed, falling and bouncing on top of me.

Chapter 11

I was lucky. No large stones landed on my head or torso, no bones cracked in my legs, and when everything had settled I wasn't trapped. But the pain in my left arm was so bad that at one point I passed out which, so she said later, made Yito panic when she found me.

When I came round, I was disoriented – but not enough to forget the prize that I had been seeking for years. Before we left, Yito stuffed every piece of paper she could find into her rucksack, scattering rocks and debris left-and-right in her search for more.

As we climbed up through the forest, I had to use my right hand to support my now swollen left arm. Fortunately, Yito could drive and eventually we found a hospital with an Accident and Emergency Department. An X-ray showed a simple ulna fracture in my left forearm, not needing surgery just a plaster cast.

'Can we talk?' Yito asked after driving me home and settling me in a chair with a glass of brandy. 'I've got a proposition.' She was looking nervous.

'Sounds interesting. Go on.'

'Well, how about my staying and working for you over the summer? I was going to ask you anyway, and now… I mean, you're going to find it really difficult to cope on your own until your arm is out of plaster. You know, driving, shopping, house-work, cooking.'

I took a gulp of pain-killing brandy.

'I suppose I am.'

'And I'm really good at DIY. And gardening too. We did a lot at the children's home. I enjoy it. And, not being rude, this house and garden could do with a big dose of TLC. How about it?'

My hesitation seemed to agitate her. 'I'm not asking you to pay me or anything. Not a wage anyway. Just feed me. Maybe buy me a few clothes if I get desperate. But mainly just film and chemicals, which you probably would anyway, wouldn't you? I won't be expensive, I promise. And, oh, I can't tell you what it would mean to me, instead of going back to the home. To live here, in a place like this, all summer. To have that woodland right outside the back door. To be able to talk to you about photography face-to-face, instead of by letter.' She paused for breath. 'And I can help you with your work too. How are you going to start putting the manuscript back together with your arm in plaster? Go on. Please. Say I can stay.'

'I'm not sure Yito. Have you really thought about this? About what it would be like, just the two of us? You know absolutely nothing about me.'

'I know that you've always been kind to me. Why? Are you saying I shouldn't trust you? Because, if you are, I don't believe you.'

'Really? You're eighteen, very pretty, and I've been very short of female company recently. I'm not made of stone, you know.'

Her dark eyes began to sparkle. 'I never thought you were. So – what? The first time I wander around the house naked, you'll ravish me. Is that what you're saying?'

I laughed. 'You spend a lot of time wandering around houses naked do you.'

'Well, let me stay and you'll find out, won't you? So... Is it a deal? Can I?'

I finished my brandy. 'OK, you've talked me into it – and I suppose I will need somebody to help dress and undress me.'

It was Yito's turn to laugh, her face then settling into the most wonderful smile. 'That's so brilliant. You won't regret it. I promise.' But then slowly she began to frown. 'Actually… We were joking around just then, weren't we? Because…' Suddenly, her young face was stern. 'You know my history, so you might think… But I have to tell you: the last time I had proper sex… Well, I was thirteen. And the thing is, it's never happening again. It can't happen again. Not with you, not with anybody.' She stopped and studied my face. 'We were joking, yes? I can still stay, can't I?'

***

In between chores and helping me sort, scan, catalogue and print backup copies of the manuscript fragments, Yito still found time to plan and take endless photographs which we would then pore over and discuss long into the night. 'I've never been able to do this with anybody before,' she said one midnight. 'It's brilliant.'

Her interest in her art centred mainly on nature: moody, light-driven shots of trees, flowers and animals. But when she had willing models, such as myself, she also photographed people, always naked: 'Stop clenching your bum like that, Red. You're ruining the line.'

'But this goldfish pond is freezing. You should try it.'

Easily her best was an exquisite series of Gemma early in August floating amongst water lilies in one of the Inchfield lakes. But Yito was very critical. In her opinion, absolutely anybody could take a passable picture of a nude out of doors.

'I want to go further,' she said. 'I don't just want to show the human body in nature, I want to show it as part of nature. I want to merge it with other living things. Set it in nature's context. Show it evolving, and devolving. Strip the erotic and obscene from genitals to make them objects of beauty. Because they can be, can't they? And fun too. I want to turn pornography into simply biology. Voyeurism into – I don't know – something else. I want...' I could see her becoming exasperated. 'Oh, I don't know. I can't put it into words, but one day I will put it into pictures.'

We both laughed at the passion she had just shown, her self-consciously, me with amused affection. 'Where did all that come from?' I asked. 'What have you been reading?'

'Reading? Loads.' Then her smile gradually faded. 'But... Maybe... More than anything, it could be my way of making sense of my childhood, don't you think?'

***

My sheer joy at having Rebecca Downing's memoirs in my hands at long last was tempered by the enormity of the task of reconstruction. Whoever had torn up the sheets had done so thoroughly. Although the occasional fragment was large enough to contain the best part of a paragraph, many pieces were so tiny they bore only a few words. The very smallest pieces we just dumped in a large envelope which I filed away in my office filing cabinet. The rest felt like starting a 20,000 piece jigsaw but without a picture to work from, knowing that many pieces were missing.

I began with a nearly complete paragraph containing the word 'Matilda's'; Yito began with a smaller fragment containing 'John Dob'. And slowly, very slowly, our respective pages grew.

Mine was readable first:

> Just one man appeared, an utterly nude [...] arrying a bow that was quite as tall as himself. With great agility he ran [...] he four bodies and prodded each in turn, as if he was investigating them for s[...] life. Then he placed a dirty bare foot on Matilda's chest and heaved out the arrow. I saw no signs of compassion on [...] ce as he went from corpse to corpse; it was totally transparent that retrieving [...] s was his only and unpleasant concern. Lifting my Aunt's skirts a[...] oats with his bow he gazed for an age at her bloomers, whi[...] look bloated and white. Then he looked at me and with a cross express[ion on his] oval, brown face he began to advance. Wings seemed to flutter inside me as he lodged a long, long arrow in his bow.
>
> He stood before me, his sharp arrowhead only a yard from my chest. I begged him not to kill me. I told him my name and explained that I meant him no harm. I spoke in English, then in Spanish, and in desperation French – but when the man spoke, the words of his sing-song clucking voice formed no language that I had ever heard. I tried to be defiant, British, brave and strong but in the face of death my will failed me, and I began [to] blubber. Slowly he lowered his bow and quietly walked away.

***

I've got to stop,' said Yito, cupping her face in her hands. 'I'm going cross-eyed.'

It was past midnight and we were in my office. While Yito had been trying to make sense of her page about 'John Dob', I had been rummaging through her boxes of slides. 'So... Shall we call it a night?' I said.

She smiled at me, the corners of her mouth twitching slightly. 'Look... Say if you think this is a really bad idea but...When the College term is over... Can I come back here? Spend Christmas with you? I haven't really got anywhere else to go.'

'Of course you can.'

A look of relief spread over her face. 'Thanks. It's worked well, hasn't it? For me, anyway.'

'Me too. The house and garden have never looked so cared for. And apart from your terrible early attempts at cooking…'

Laughing, she picked up a cushion and threw it at me.

I caught it and threw it back. '… and your broken promise…'

She paused in mid-throw. 'What broken promise?'

'You know. To walk around the house naked all the time. I'm really gutted. You've seen my bits from just about every angle imaginable for your photographs – but have I seen even a glimpse of yours?'

Her expression became pained as we lapsed into an awkward silence, which I rushed to break. 'Talking of naked women, who's this?' I handed over a slide of hers that had intrigued me. It was yet another woman floating in the lake at Inchfield but whoever she was, she clearly wasn't Gemma.

Yito examined, then dismissed the picture. 'Oh her. It's crap. I so need a telephoto lens. This shot doesn't even begin to capture the aura there was about her.'

'Who is she?'

'No idea. I didn't get to speak to her. And she didn't stay long. It was that day you broke you're arm. One moment she was there, and the next she was gone.'

'Without her clothes?'

'Actually – I didn't see any clothes.'

***

By the time Yito left Wiltshire for Devon to begin her first term at College, the piece about her father was just about readable:

CABALLITO

At heart John Dob[...] kind and trustworthy man. But he grows ill-humoured far too easily, especia[...] e is the worse for drink. I once found him arguing quite unpleasantly with [...]sa. And the reason? Nothing more than feeding 'rights,' as if there ever [...]e such a thing. 'Do have an open mind,' I told my grandson. 'At least listen to [...]ur teacher. But as usual my headstrong Mariposa became vexed with me, grabbing a handful of gr[...]s and shaking the heads in my face.

'These are seeds, Gran[d]mother,' he said. 'They are the means by which a spirit takes root to become grass. That much I believe from that man's twisted words, but nothing more. How can liquid be a seed? [...] runs away. How can an animal? It runs away, too. Neither can take root in [...] and grow. So how can that so-called teacher try to tell us otherwise? Thi[s is] no reason to stop a brother feeding his sister. The man is a fraud, Ipomoea. He has fooled you. All he and his Wicc[a] want is your money. Our money. If they spend it all, how will we ever retu[rn]

Chapter 12

Almost in rapture, Yito gazed out of my kitchen window. A thick layer of freshly fallen snow was giving our corner of Wiltshire a Scandinavian look. She turned to face me. 'Can we go to Inchfield? Please? The valley will look brilliant.' And after three months without her, I couldn't say no.

We set off soon after breakfast, driving along freshly gritted-and-salted country roads. The cold solstice sun, low in the sky, reflected off the white fields. Occasionally, a large dollop of ice would fall from overhead branches onto our windscreen. 'So, tell me what you've found out about Rebecca while I've been away,' she said as we drove. 'Start at the beginning.'

'At the beginning? OK. Well, she had no interest in missionary work for a start. Just adventure. So when her uncle told her that the forest Indians were – as he put it – "the most barbaric and the most difficult to tame", she decided she had to meet them.'

Yito's dark eyes peered at me from beneath the rim of her knitted grey bobble hat. 'Did he say anything else about them?'

I chuckled. 'Quite a lot, but he wouldn't get points for political correctness nowadays. He said things like, "Their capacity for reason is so low, they are more like animals on two feet than men with a soul." And another gem was, "Worst of all, they have no shame. The creatures go everywhere naked, and openly fornicate".'

Yito smiled. 'They sound just like the lads on my course,' and for a while we couldn't speak for laughing.

'The thing is,' I said eventually, 'Rebecca knew nothing about men or sex…'

'Really?'

'Really! She wrote that, before seeing that first Indian, she'd never seen a man naked. And you can tell, she had absolutely no idea where babies came from.'

'Surely not all women were so naïve back then?'

'Rebecca was a special case. Her mother died giving birth to her and her father wanted her to become a nun. She was raised by her Aunt Matilda, educated by a devout governess from Roedean, then went to a residential Convent School. Mainly she knew about the scriptures and languages. But plants too, and not just from England. She even owned a microscope. Anyway, at the last minute she refused to become a postulant and insisted on going to Newnham to study Botany, though she doesn't say how she persuaded her father.'

'Didn't Newnham teach her a thing or two about life?'

'She wasn't there long enough. Matilda chaperoned her and reported back that Newnham was "evil." Rebecca's father took her away immediately. Next stop, South America and her uncle's Mission.'

'So how did she get away from there?'

'Easy! She told her uncle that God visited her in a vision to say that she had been chosen to save the souls of the forest hunters. And her uncle must have bought it because he sent her and Matilda with three bearers upstream to the next Jesuit Mission, much nearer to the forest tribes. But if Rebecca hadn't deliberately sunk the canoe, I daresay they would all have arrived safely and she still would never have met an 'untamed' Indian.'

Yito sighed. 'My tutor has got American Indian blood in him. But he's from the north. An Apache, I think. He's called Cochise. About your age, I'd say. Honestly, he is so good-looking. And he is definitely untamed. All the girls are lusting after him.'

'Are you?'

She gave a coy smile. 'Maybe a little. But, you know…' Then she fell silent again.

***

There was already a car parked in the 'passing-place' near Inchfield Park: a battered dark-blue Ford Prefect. And as we crunched across the cow fields with their thick covering of snow, we tracked booted footsteps. Wearing warm fleece-lined winter coats and waterproof boots, we were both well insulated against the cold as we slipped and slid down the badger track and onward to the valley bottom. In places we had to hold hands to stop each other from falling. I was so preoccupied with keeping my balance, I only faintly registered the column of smoke slowly rising from the trees high up on the far northern side of the valley.

The lakes looked wonderful, so glass-smooth that they reflected the blue sky and snow-bedecked trees perfectly. As we approached the run-down boat house, a figure emerged wearing a black oilskin. It was Hood. Startled, he looked from me to Yito and back again. His breath had condensed on his long beard and frozen among the hairs. I reminded him of our meeting nearly five years before. He briefly nodded his head in Yito's direction.

'She's a bit young. What's your secret?'

'Just a friend. This is John Doberfield's daughter.'

'Is that right?' he said, studying her closely. Then he looked back at me. 'Reckon if you believe that, you'll believe anything.'

'What do you mean?' Yito said.

Hood took a deep breath and his expression relaxed. 'Not for me to say. He wasn't exactly popular, round here, John Doberfield.'

'Why not? What did he do? Did you know him? Can I talk to you about him? Do you know anything about his death?'

Hood shook his head and tugged ice from his beard. 'Tell you what. I'll do you a deal. I won't tell anybody who you say you are, if the pair of you just bugger off and leave me to do my fishing. Fair enough?'

I shrugged and began to usher Yito away, but then I noticed the smoke again, curling it's way upwards in the still air. 'Who would make a fire in the forest on a day like this?'

Hood looked at me as if I was stupid. 'Winter Solstice! They'll be burning a Yule log. From an Ash tree, shouldn't wonder.'

'Wiccans?' said Yito. 'I thought they'd all gone from the valley.'

'Maybe they have, maybe they haven't. But I wouldn't go over there to find out if I were you. Whoever they are, they don't take kindly to anybody climbing that slope. They've taken a pot shot at me more than once.'

I would have taken Hood's advice and stayed in the valley bottom but there was no stopping Yito. I either had to let her go alone or keep her company. It wasn't easy clambering up the steep slope in the snow. Climbing itself was difficult enough; climbing quietly was impossible. 'There's nobody there,' I whispered when I first glimpsed the distant fire through leafless branches.

Yito fumbled around in her camera bag, found her new telephoto lens and attached it to her camera. 'I think there are people there,' she said, focussing. 'At least two. But they keep disappearing amongst the smoke.' She took a few photographs, then turned to me with a broad smile. 'It's a man and a woman. True Wiccans – they're naked.'

'They can't be. Not in this.'

'Let's get closer.'

'And do what?'

'Talk to them, of course.'

But by the time we reached the clearing, nobody was there. Just a large log smouldering in the centre of a flaming bonfire. We could feel the heat from yards away, and a flat area around the fire was free of snow. It was wet, though; and muddy. 'Somebody was here,' said Yito from the far side of the fire. A skinned and gutted rabbit was cooking on a spit above ashes. 'And look… Cloaks. And masks.'

'Maybe they were expecting more people. Perhaps the weather put the others off.'

'They must have seen us coming.' She was pointing at two sets of parallel footprints heading uphill in the snow. 'And they were barefoot. Look! Toe prints.'

'That's ridiculous. So where are they now?'

We gazed around, looking for figures – or movement – but saw nothing. Then we heard something heading towards us. Not exactly a whistle, more a rush of air. The missile thudded into a tree behind us, a metre or so above our heads. Scarcely had we registered what had happened, than another arrow buried its head into the same tree, but this time lower. I didn't wait for a third arrow; just grabbed Yito's hand, dragged her away from the fire, then ran downslope with her. Occasionally, we stumbled, Yito desperately clutching the bouncing camera round her neck and camera bag over her shoulder. But after thirty metres or so she stopped, her free hand grabbing an icy tree-trunk, supporting herself, preventing herself from slipping further down. 'No! Wait! I might never get another chance.'

Breathless, hands on knees, I told her it was too dangerous. But ignoring me, and turning to face upslope, she made a megaphone with her hands and shouted: 'I want to talk to you. My father was a Wiccan High Priest. In this valley. He died. You might have known him.' Disturbed by her shouts, a flock of rooks and jackdaws flew from the treetops. Cawing loudly, maybe forty black shapes circled in the blue sky above the trees. Gradually they settled and silence fell as Yito waited for an answer.

The response came: another arrow, thumping into the tree trunk by her side. I grabbed her hand again and pulled her further down the slope, keeping her moving, not letting her stop or turn until we reached the valley bottom.

Chapter 13

Yito breathed on the window pane in my office and idly drew an arrow with her finger tip. 'Those arrows yesterday...' She turned and rested her back against the wall. Her clothing was scruffy: jeans and a misshapen blue sweater. 'Did they remind you of Rebecca's story?'

'I suppose they did. And so did you. Your determination, lack of fear. Just like Rebecca.' I walked over to my desk and rummaged for a printed sheet of italic writing. 'Listen to this: "He had spared me... but others might not. He had a weapon but I had not. He knew how to find food..." and so on... "So I shouted and ran after him." And this was the guy who had just murdered her Aunt.'

Yito's long glossy black hair was tumbling over her shoulders and her dark eyes were full of life and excitement. 'Go on.'

I cleared my throat. '"He turned to face me and raised his bow in threat. I asked him – in Spanish – to take me with him, but he simply walked away again. Undaunted, I tried a second time. On this occasion he stared at me as if I was a troublesome dog and gestured at me to go away. When I would not, and kept following him... a third time he raised his bow and this time he shot."' I stopped, and held the sheet out to her. 'Why not read it yourself.'

Yito gave me a man-melting smile. 'No. You. Please. I like listening to you.'

'OK, but I'll paraphrase. It all gets a bit... You know. Anyway, it wasn't her he'd shot at. It was a monkey, a Capuchin. He's killed it, and goes to collect it from where it fell. Then... Oh, wait. There's a good bit here: "With a growing and profound uneasiness, I watched him sink to his knees and reach under the branches. Even to this day, I remember how grotesque the sight seemed that first time; how my sheltered sensibilities were so outraged. His buttocks parted to reveal a horrendous sight, pink-centred and ringed with a halo of corrugated brown skin."'

Yito grinned. 'Does she mention his other bits? She must do, if she's never seen a naked man before. Were they "grotesque" too?'

'She calls them "a growth" on his groin. "Like a brown slug crawling over two walnuts." It's not until she sees the whole tribe, later, that she realises all men are like that. I'm sure she expected them to have only hair down there, like herself. She really had no idea.'

'A slug over two walnuts,' Yito mused. 'Now there's a picture to take. Anyway, go on. I know she doesn't die – but what happens next?'

'Oh, she lost him. He ran off with the Capuchin and she couldn't keep up.'

Yito stood in front of me – so close I could smell toothpaste on her breath – and took the sheet from my hand. 'Do you know what happens next?'

I nodded.

'Then tell me later. I must get started. What time do they arrive? You have so let this house and garden get in a mess while I've been away.'

'Some time this evening. But there's no need. They won't care.'

'Yes there is. It's a matter of pride. But it's OK,' she said, catching my expression. 'You go and work. I don't mind. That new book-deal of yours is fantastic, but they haven't given you much time, have they?'

***

Our Christmas guests were to be Gemma and her three children, but not Leo. And I felt partly to blame. 'You don't have to put up with it all,' I said to a tearful Gemma back in October after she confided her latest suspicions to me.

'Yes I do. How else can I hang on to him?'

'Then don't "hang on." Tell him where to go. Or don't just threaten to leave him – do it. He'll soon be begging you to come back to him.'

'I can't risk it. And before you say anything it's not only because I'm trapped by the kids, or don't want to upset my parents, or because I'm too lazy to work.'

'Why then?'

She gave a big sigh. 'It's because… Oh, I don't know. It's not all his fault, you know. He never hid what he was like. I knew exactly what I was letting myself in for.'

'Well at least show him what it feels like to be cheated on. Have an affair yourself.'

She laughed. 'What! And lose my leverage?' A broad smile spread across her face and she placed a hand on my chest. 'Besides, you know there's only one man I've ever lusted after apart from Leo – and he's hung-up on some stupid friendship thing.'

But by her Christmas visit, something had changed. 'So what was so different about this one?' I asked.

'She was only just sixteen. And somebody thought I should see a photo of them together.'

'What have you told Solymar?'

'Oh, Solymar knows. She's bearing the brunt of it – it's all round the school. But the boys… I've told them that their Granddad is ill, and Leo has to spend some time with him.' She looked at me with her clear blue eyes, then gave me a platonic kiss on the cheek. 'Thanks for letting us come here. The kids will have much more fun with you and Yito than just with me at home. And so will I.' She peered at me, her head slightly cocked to one side. 'Have you got Yito into bed yet?'

***

'But you must have a drink. It's Christmas,' said Gemma, who had already finished one bottle of Chardonnay and was fumbling to open another. It was Christmas Day evening and Gemma was talking to Yito, not to me; I needed no such encouragement. But Yito still hadn't touched a drop of anything stronger than orange juice.

'I really shouldn't.'

'No argument,' slurred Gemma. 'Keep us company. It's Christmas.' And at last, smiling in resignation as we settled down for an evening of playing cards, Yito gave in.

Gemma's three children were sitting in front of the fire, watching one of their Christmas videos and occasionally squabbling over who had the right to this or that chocolate. Perhaps distracted by the cards, the video and the squabbling, Yito seemed not to notice Gemma surreptitiously topping up her wine. She was just showing signs of flirtatious animation when she began to look uncomfortable.

'Is it too hot?' I asked. Her normally olive complexion was looking distinctly pink, as if she were blushing. Her breathing sounded tight.

'Shall I open the window?' said Gemma.

Yito shook her head. 'No, it's the alcohol. This is what happens. Suddenly, my stomach feels like a balloon, and my heart races. It's crazy. My mother could drink gin like water.'

Gemma began taking Yito's pulse. 'Races! It's going mad.'

Now Yito's face was bright red. So were the bits I could see of her neck, chest and shoulders. Her hand went to her mouth. 'Sorry... I think I'm going to be...' and to our consternation she stumbled quickly from the room. The three children watched her go, then turned back to the television.

'I'll go and check on her,' said Gemma – and when she returned, she was alone. She had put Yito to bed, she said, and blamed me for persuading 'the poor girl' to drink against her wishes. 'Don't do it again,' she ordered. Because, in her opinion, Yito had a genetic intolerance to alcohol. The symptoms were classic. 'She must have inherited it from her father,' she concluded.

***

On my way to bed, I looked in on Yito, opening her door just a little. She was asleep, her sheets pushed back as if it were summer, her top half exposed and naked. But she was so poorly lit from the landing that I had to imagine rather than see the details of her body. She needed covering and tucking in. I hesitated, maybe for a full minute, just peering into the room. Then I gently closed the door and ambled on to my own ice-cold bedroom.

Chapter 14

'Her nights sound terrible: huddled under bushes trying to shelter; clothes soaked to the skin; convinced she was going to be attacked. She didn't dare sleep.'

With our arms linked for warmth, Yito and I were strolling through the woodland behind my cottage. The ground was frozen, the carpet of fallen leaves crunchy underfoot; frost whitened the bushes and our breath hung mist-like in the air.

'Did she say what frightened her most? Animals? Indians?'

'Animals, mainly. Despite what happened to her Aunt, she still saw the Indians as her main sanctuary. A legacy from the Isabel Godin story, I suppose.'

'What was she living on?'

'Not a lot. Just nibbling anything that looked edible but forever scared that she was poisoning herself. But she was a sensible girl. When she came across a corral of brushwood with traces of old fires and a few shelters she decided to stay put. Save energy. And hope that an Indian would visit again. Find her before she died.'

'Shelters? You mean huts.'

'Nothing so grand. Just woven leaves to keep off the rain. Huts are for people who stay in one place.'

'So how long before she was found?'

'Five days. Just a small group, and it all sounded very touch-and-go. She said the men seemed to want to shoot her, but the women wouldn't let them. But even the women wouldn't share their food or their fire with her. Just kept shooing her away. Until Ángelita stepped in.'

'Ángelita?'

'That's what Rebecca called her. She was beautiful, Rebecca said; about eight years old with "the face of a little angel." Wonderful sloe eyes, white teeth, a few gaps. She sounded just like you that day I met you in Wales. But one of her legs was misshapen, hardly any muscle. She could walk, but with a limp. Anyway, Ángelita brought Rebecca a few tit-bits of food after the others had eaten. Rebecca said she felt like a family dog being thrown scraps.'

'So the women didn't fight over her clothes? Or the men over her body?'

'Seems not. They just wanted her to leave them alone. But from then on she followed them around at a distance, and this time she could keep up. Guess why?'

Yito pondered for a few moments. 'Because Ángelita couldn't walk very fast?'

I smiled. 'According to Rebecca, it was Ángelita who saved her life.'

We arrived at the fallen elm tree and rested there awhile. Two Robins began chasing each other in and out of a frosty thicket. 'Reading all this...' said Yito. 'Has it got to you at all? It must have done a little.'

'Got to me how?'

'You know. That dream of yours. To live in the Amazon. Share the lives of people like these.'

'Oh that. No, not really. Well, maybe a little. But I resigned myself to that never happening ages ago.'

'No, you shouldn't. Don't give up. It still might happen. Who knows? Maybe even on the back of this book.'

'Well...' And I left it there. My pride wouldn't let me say more.

Arm in arm again, we began to walk back to the cottage. 'So how did Rebecca lose her clothes?'

I chuckled. 'To a Caiman.'

'A Caiman! You mean one of those South American alligator things?'

'Exactly! Whenever Ángelita's group camped near a stream, Rebecca used to coyly slip away to bathe and wash her clothes. But one day this Caiman dragged her pile of clothes into the water and attacked her boots as if they were alive. Everything either drifted downstream or sank. Suddenly, she was as naked as the Indians.'

'And...' her dark eyes looked up into mine.

'When the Indians saw her without clothes, their attitude changed completely. From that moment, she became one of them. Ángelita's grandmother – Rebecca calls her Abuela – more or less adopted her. And after a while... Well, when we get back I'll show you the bit I'm working on now.'

realisation first dawned that I should never leave the ... sibly find my way back to my Uncle's mission. Nor did ... the forest in pursuance of such a quest. And of course, ev... a year, I did not know how to ask somebody to ... the time m... command of the language finally ... wish to leave the forest anyway. I had learn...d to ... tions and discomforts ... the insects, the bites, the lack of privacy. ... had learned to respect deeply, but no lon... ally to fear, the animals and the ... gers that lurked all around me. But ... ove all else, I had grown used to the ... of actually being valued, for myself, as an equal, by men, women ... ngle, I was blissfully free to do absolutely whatever I ...

...nham ... why should I ever want to return to ... ated by men like my 'father?' Or a 'husband?' To be terrified and tyrannised by Catholicism? To be strangled by those awful corsets? In heaven's name, why?

***

Shortly before Yito returned to college for the spring term, she and I put together a section which told how Rebecca met John Doberfield.

Now calling herself Ipomoea, Rebecca walked with six grandchildren into a village on the banks of the Río Envira. The next few months were both difficult and harrowing. Claiming British citizenship but without money, Ipomoea and her family were dressed by the riverside missionaries, then ferried unwanted from place to place downriver until they ended up, just like Pierre Godin two centuries earlier, in French Guiana. There the Honorary British Consul in Cayenne recruited a local young teacher of English to help sort out the documentation for Ipomoea and her grandchildren, and to help her relocate. That teacher was Yito's father.

Ipomoea writes that while in Cayenne she "came to yearn" for the peace and quiet of her childhood home in Inchfield Park which "in ambience" was so much nearer to the forest home she had just left than were the "noisy, smelly, filthy and dangerous" villages, towns and cities along the Amazon that she had endured during her journey. So when John Doberfield discovered on her behalf that not only was her family estate in Gloucestershire still intact but also that her father was still alive, it was arranged that she should return with her grandchildren to England. And at Ipomoea's request, with the promise of a generous payment as soon as she had the means, John returned with her to help them settle. Intrepid though Ipomoea was, she refused to fly and instead crossed the Atlantic by ship.

'Do you know yet why she changed her name to Ipomoea?'

I nodded. 'The Indians named her after a climbing plant with big white flowers – white like her skin, they told her. The flowers only opened at night and she recognised it as a Moonflower.'

'So why "Ipomoea"?'

'She says that's the Moonflower's scientific name.'

Yito frowned at me. 'So why, Red? Why, after fifty years of "freedom", did Rebecca – Ipomoea – suddenly decide to leave the jungle? And why only with her grandchildren – not her children?'

Chapter 15

'When are the results due?'

'Three weeks time. After Easter. Just before I go back to College for the summer term.'

'And the prize?'

'Oh, it's brilliant. A thousand pounds worth of digital camera. Absolute top-of-the-range. Can you believe it? Plus the top five contestants are promised a gallery exhibition in July.' Yito's expression became soulful. 'No harm in dreaming, eh?'

'So what's the picture? Can I see it?'

She shook her head. 'Not until the results come out.'

'You? Superstitious?'

'No! Of course not. It's just…'

I laughed. 'It's OK, you don't have to – but at least tell me what the picture is.'

'Lots and lots of bright-blue damselflies. Doesn't sound much, does it? But the lighting is just so… And the composition, too. They're all in pairs, all mating – and there's a couple of surprises.'

'What sort of surprises?'

'Well… Don't laugh, but I took some pictures of Leo and Gemma then manipulated them on the computer – you know, made them bright-blue and stick-thin so they looked like the damselflies. Then I pasted them amongst the real ones. What do you think? Good idea? Or what?'

***

'I really don't get it, Red. They're arguing about 'feeding' again. Really angrily too. Something about Mariposa and his sister. What's to argue about?'

I heard Yito rise at five o'clock while it was still dark, and a couple of hours later I followed her downstairs. Now, with the early morning sun streaming through the office window, and with both of us wearing dressing-gowns, she was sitting facing me on the computer chair. She crossed her legs, showing a silky light-brown thigh. I couldn't see underwear.

'Actually... They're arguing about sex, not food. Your father will be telling Mariposa he mustn't have sex with his own sister, and Mariposa doesn't like it.'

'Feeding means sex! How do you know that?'

'From these. I'll show you.' My most recent pages of Ipomoea's text were in the top drawer of my desk; I leaned across Yito to rummage for them.

'Oh, hello,' she giggled. 'And good morning to you, too.'

Occasionally laughing at myself, I found the sheets of paper, straightened up, then re-wrapped and re-tied my dressing-gown. 'Sorry!'

She grinned. 'Sorry? Why? Hardly a stranger, is he? How many photos is he in now? So... Is it me causing that? Or is it just one of your Morning Glories?'

'A bit of both, I guess.' As I began scanning Ipomoea's words, I cleared my throat. And when I finally spoke it was in my long-unused lecturer's voice. 'Don't forget, none of the old hunter-gatherer animists made the link between sex and babies.'

Yito was still grinning at me and my condition. 'I know. You've told me. But I'm still not sure I believe it?'

'It's true. They knew nothing about eggs or sperm. As far as they were concerned a baby arrives at the first twitch, not during some routine intercourse ages earlier when the woman feels nothing. They thought pregnancy lasted about six months; moon-months, that is.'

'Routine, eh? Feels nothing.' She chuckled then uncrossed her legs, pushing her dressing gown between them to stop it gaping. 'Arrives? But how if not by sex? You never told me.'

'Surely I did. It's spirits. They're bumping into women all the time – at least that's what these tribes believe – and every so often, if a spirit likes the look of a woman, it goes inside her to grow into a baby, and that's when she feels the first twitch; as it enters and settles down inside her.'

'Spooky! But what spirits? Where from? Dead people?' The top of her gown was beginning to gape; her belt loosening.

I should have told her, but didn't. Just cleared my throat again. 'No, from anywhere. Everywhere. That's what Animism is all about. Every plant and animal contains a spirit. So does every rock, cloud, raindrop, the sun whatever. And the air is full of them, all travelling around, going from one resting place to another. Often a mother would name her baby after where she thought its spirit had been before.'

A quizzical look spread over Yito's face. 'I wonder if that's where Alice got the idea for my name? From the Inchfield Animists? She always said she first felt me kick while surrounded by Damselflies.'

'Damselflies? I thought Caballito was Spanish for little horse.'

'Well... It is. It's both. Though strictly Damselfly is "Caballito del Diablo"; little horse of the devil.' She laughed at my expression. 'Don't look so shocked. Wiccans don't believe in the devil, and they're scornful of Christians because they do. It's all a bit of a joke. Alice used to tease me about the Diablo bit of the damselfly name, especially when I was being naughty.' She leaned forward to brush something off her bare foot; briefly a shaft of sunlight spotlighted a dark-brown nipple. When she sat back, resting her head against the high back of the computer chair, her dressing-gown no longer quite met, her belt almost undone. I glimpsed the crease of a groin; a strand or two of black hair. 'Strange memories,' she murmured, her dark eyes gazing up into mine. Gradually, her reverie faded. 'But where did they think fathers fitted into all this? Or sex?'

I couldn't answer, wrestling instead with my strongest ever compulsion to hold her beautiful face between my hands, to kiss her parted lips, to taste her mouth – to throw off my gown and pull open hers. 'No!' she said, leaping to her feet, turning her back on me and moving away. At a safe distance, she faced me again, pulling her gown tight around her. 'Don't look at me like that.'

'Like what?'

'You know "like what." Your hard-ons are one thing. They come and go, and I know they mean nothing. We laugh about them. But just then, that look in your eyes... That's a first, and oh, boy, do I know that look. Once a man crosses that line...'

We stared into each other's faces for an age, not moving. 'Look, I'm sorry,' she eventually continued. 'I know this is difficult for you, and I really admire how you're coping. But it's difficult for me too, you know. You're an attractive man. I love your body, and not just for photographs. We have fun. You're kind to me. Gentle. Tolerant. Supportive. Clever. Everything I would want and need in a man. Believe me, if it was possible, I would have been in your bed ages ago, clinging on to you for dear life. But I can't. I really can't. You have to believe me.'

'Can we still not talk about it? Maybe find a way round whatever it is.'

'There is no way round. And no. We can't talk about it. I'm sorry. You just have to trust me on this, Red. Please… Don't spoil what we have here; it's wonderful. And please don't force me to leave – because I will if that's the only way.' She hesitated. 'You really scared me just then.'

I sighed. 'I know I did. I'm sorry. I scared myself too. But it won't happen again, I promise.'

It seemed an age before she smiled, but soon after we were both grinning and shaking our heads. 'Go have your shower,' she said gently. 'Get dressed.' Then, holding out her hand she added, 'And give me the sheets. I'll read about sex and fatherhood for myself.'

***

'So Ipomoea's Indians really thought that a man's balls are small breasts that produce milk. And that his cock is a nipple…'

I nodded. 'A "man-nipple", Ipomoea calls it.' We were both smiling and chuckling.

'It's so funny. Just imagine. Men are there to feed others. That's all they do. Catch meat to feed people through their mouths. Produce "man's milk" to feed to women and girls through their cunts. I can't get over it. They actually thought that sex is a form of feeding. And important feeding too. Like… Grown women need the milk to stay healthy. Young girls need it to grow breasts and pubic hair.' Her smile became mischievous. 'No wonder I hit puberty so early.'

We were outside at the patio table, finishing our earlier fraught conversation over a coffee. The first Cuckoo of spring was calling in the copse, and early Swallows were hawking insects around the trees; the air was cool despite the promise of April sun.

'I love the way that Ipomoea describes the evening routine,' Yito continued, wrapping her hands round her steaming coffee mug. 'You know... The lighting of the fire, cooking of the meat, sharing it out, eating... Then sex. Women approaching men. Men, women. Checking out who's 'hungry', who 'has milk'. Then just doing it, there and then. No big deal. In full view.'

'Because they thought sex was just something to do. For fun and food. No bad consequences, only good. There was nothing to hide.'

'Amazing, yes? That's just how Ipomoea describes it. And that's why they didn't really care who they did it with.'

'Well... They still had their favourites.'

'I know, but still. That didn't stop a 'hungry' woman – I love that phrase of hers – being fed by as many different men as she could get, one after the other. Yet if a woman – or a man – says "no"... Well... They're left in peace. I really never knew that some tribes were so free-and-easy over sex.'

'The theory is that – oh, for ages; tens of thousands of years – all of humanity used to behave like this. I just never thought I'd read a first-hand account of it in action. This manuscript of Ipomoea's is brilliant. A gold-mine.'

Yito took a sip of her coffee, looking thoughtful. 'But what about disease? They're so promiscuous. Surely it would be rampant?'

'No, you see. That's the point. Isolated tribes don't have STIs. Unless you count crabs. You know... Pubic lice.'

'Really? The lucky buggers.' She looked thoughtful again. 'But what about emotions? Love? Jealousy? Sense of betrayal?'

Without an answer this time, I shrugged and moved on. 'The bit I liked,' I said, 'was the first time Ipomoea said 'yes.' She sounded so relieved that a man had offered at last. "He knelt before me, his man-nipple turgid, promising milk. It would have seemed ungracious to say no." And afterwards, "the sensation wasn't at all unpleasant." And – did you notice? That man was the Indian who killed her Aunt. The man she called Capuchin.'

A few heavy drops of rain fell from a scudding cloud, then within moments the patio was bright with sunlight.

Yito gave a tiny smile. 'My favourite was her description of the way the children copied the grown-ups over sex. Even from being toddlers. The way they used their fingers, and the boys their little cocks, to poke and prod each other – and the adults let them do it. Let them do it to them too. Taught them what to do. How to do it properly. All part of their childhood. All in public. All in total innocence.' A new cloud passed across the sun, and another across Yito's face. 'If only I'd lived there, Red. I'd have been spared being made to feel the freak that I have here.'

'Here? By who?'

'By all those social workers. All those bloody psychologists. Every one of them absolutely determined I was going to be scarred for life. My God! If anything was going to scar me, it was them. I didn't need counselling. I just needed to be treated like a normal person. The way you do.' She took a sip of her coffee. 'Something else I'd have been spared too. I wouldn't have spent my life thinking about a father I never knew. Because "father" would have had no meaning, would it? It couldn't have. All Ipomoea's Indians knew about was mothers.' A sadness had gripped her. She seemed about to say something else, but she didn't.

***

As she knelt on the damp and un-mowed lawn, Yito was crying. I watched from the house for a few moments, her sadness reaching me and making my own eyes water. After crossing the lawn, I helped her to her feet. 'What's wrong?'

'Just hormones,' she said, sniffing; wiping her eyes and nose with her hand.

I gave her a handkerchief. 'It's more than that. I hear you sometimes. In the middle of the night.'

'Really? I'm sorry. It's nothing. Just part of being me.' She took a deep breath. 'And, I suppose, I'm also worried about the competition. I've just decided I made a huge and horrible mistake. What I did with Leo and Gemma…? The judges will think it's just a meaningless gimmick, won't they? I should have left it just damselflies. My big chance – and I've blown it.'

Chapter 16

'What time again?' asked Gemma, soon after arriving with her family.

Yito was looking pale. She hadn't slept well for nights. 'The judging panel meets at four. So Cochise says any time after five.' Her tutor knew some of the judges, and Yito had given him my contact details.

Time dragged and conversation stuttered. Gemma visited the toilet, then ten minutes later visited again. At 5:30, the phone rang. We all looked at each other as I picked it up. But it was only Leo, from work, asking if we had any news yet. He didn't know Gemma was with me, their separation now permanent. 'I'll phone you. Soon as.'

'Why don't you phone Cochise?' Gemma asked Yito fifteen minutes later.

'No. We had an arrangement. I've just got to be patient.'

An e-mail arrived, then a text. Both junk. Gemma's two sons began complaining they were bored with colouring and started to throw pencils at each other instead.

At 6:10, the phone rang. It was Leo again, now in a pub.

'I'll phone you,' I repeated.

For the third time, Gemma went to the toilet – but this time when she returned, she wasn't alone. 'You've got a visitor,' she said to Yito.

Yito looked up, gave a shriek of delight, scrambled to her feet and almost leaped into the man's arms, there to jump up and down and hug him at the same time. She stepped back and looked into his face. 'Really! Have I? You wouldn't be here if I hadn't.'

He gave an easy smile and a nonchalant nod, signals for yet another shriek and long hug from Yito. Eventually she calmed down. 'Red. Gemma. This is Cochise. I've won! Can you believe it? I've actually won.'

***

Gemma's judgement on Cochise was immediate. 'He's absolutely gorgeous.' She and I were working in the kitchen to accommodate the unexpected visitor who at that moment was lounging on the settee in the sitting room, drinking the champagne I had been saving 'just in case,' and enjoying Yito's very excited and tactile attention.

Cochise had thick black shoulder-length hair, olive skin, dark-brown eyes and a slightly aquiline nose. He was beardless with a firm jaw, good shoulders, narrow hips and absolutely no sign of flab. His denim jeans looked expensive, and so did his trainers. His single, gold earring probably wasn't cheap either.

'Why didn't you phone?' I asked him at the first opportunity

'And spoil the surprise? Besides, it's less than an hour from London to here in the Porsche.'

Despite the full house, I had no choice but to invite Cochise to stay overnight. Yito wanted to photograph him at Inchfield Park for her winners' exhibition in July. 'And what better opportunity than tomorrow?' she said to me.

'But why Inchfield? And why Cochise?'

'I've got this idea for a picture built round my father's death. Me at the big beech tree. Naked, vulnerable, alone… Because I was robbed of my father, yes? Then hanging from the branch where my father was found I want to cut-and-paste this ghostly naked image of Cochise with a noose round his neck. In the background, I want a whole load of shadowy figures.'

'Who will you use for them?'

'Oh, I'll just do multiple pastings of Cochise. He'll be too dark to identify. It's mainly his eyes I want, in the shadows. Cochise also thinks that my father should have a stiffy – good idea, yes? To symbolise that almost my father's last act was to produce me.'

'A stiffy! Christ! You'll never be allowed to show it. Not to mention you'll be suggesting publicly that your father was murdered. And I still don't see why your model has to be Cochise. Why not use me?'

Yito gave a tiny laugh. 'Don't be offended, it's nothing to do with the stiffy. And don't take this the wrong way but… Well… Look at my mother and look at me. My father had to look a bit like Cochise, don't you think? More than like you, anyway.'

I grunted. 'You know… I've always thought it strange that you don't really know what your father looked like, except from Alice's description. That you've never seen a photograph.'

'My mother said she never had one. I was hoping Ipomoea would describe him in her memoirs, but she hasn't yet.'

***

Cochise eyed me over a glass of my best Merlot which he had found in my wine-rack. 'I'm sure I read one of your papers once, Red. I thought it was excellent.' His voice was deep and silky-smooth. With Gemma's children in bed and the champagne all drunk, hardly any of it by me, the four of us were sitting round the dining-room table.

'Thanks. Which one? Can you remember?'

'Of course. It was a computer model. Something about the influence of bison ecology on Apache lifestyle. Was it yours?'

I nodded.

He gave a relaxed smile. 'Don't ask me what you concluded, but I remember being most impressed.'

I thanked him again, but with him clearly unable to remember anything further, the topic floundered to an end.

'"Cochise." What a name!' said Gemma. 'Is it Apache? Does it mean anything?'

'It means 'firewood.' Strong, explosive, fiery – like me. The most famous Cochise was a chief of the Chiricahua Apache in Arizona; a large muscular man. Classical features, long black hair – just like me. He led an uprising against the Americans in 1861 and was shot several times, but still lived to die of natural causes.'

'Is there a Mrs Cochise? I mean for you, not the chief.'

Cochise reached out and patted Gemma's hand. 'Property is theft, Gemma. How could I enjoy sitting here, lusting after two beautiful women like yourself and Yito, if I had a woman waiting for me at home. I'm a wandering spirit. How else would a part-Apache be teaching in Devon?'

'So, no children then.'

'Five that I know of. With five different women.' He looked at me. 'And before you say I'm irresponsible, Red, I'm supporting them all, and have been ever since each paternity test said that I should.'

'My name's not really Red.'

'I know, but Yito talks about you a lot and it's kinda stuck.'

'And if anybody's going to criticise you, it's Gemma, not me.'

Gemma almost flustered. 'No! No I'm not. Not as long as you're paying to maintain them. Each to their own is what I say.'

***

I took solace in Merlot and cared little that I was beginning to slur my words – because Cochise, now on brandy, was beginning to slur his words too. And pontificate. 'There are photographers and there are photographic artists, like me, and my Yito – my prize-winner.' He raised his glass of Cognac and for about the tenth time clinked glasses with her. She had been drinking water and her glass was empty, but still she indulged him.

'Artists need vision, determination, imagination. They must have no shame. No inhibitions. Just like Yito.' He looked into Gemma's eyes. 'A model just bares her body, Gemma. A good photographer lays bare her soul.' Now he looked at Yito. 'Just like my Yito.'

She gave a coy smile.

Cochise swirled his glass, smelled the bouquet, then took a long swig. He glanced at Gemma again as if to make sure she was watching him. He needn't have worried. She was wide-eyed. 'What I'm saying, Red, is that nobody, man or woman, can bare their soul without first baring their body. Some students won't, you know. They're a waste of my time. But Yito here is a natural: a harlequin soul inside an exquisite body, and totally uninhibited. She's my most exciting protégé ever, I know it. You should hear what we've got planned for her exhibition in July.'

'What?'

'Sorry, it's a secret. But it is going to be so shocking, so controversial, so beautiful... This exhibition will be the making of her.'

Chapter 17

'Of course you were bloody arrested. I just can't believe those photographs you showed. As if one of Cochise with a stiffy and being lynched wasn't bad enough. That full frontal of Solymar draped over a fallen tree was just asking for trouble. She was only eleven, for Christ's sake. And how old were you in those photographs with the snails and worms?'

'I was nearly sixteen.'

'"Nearly!" Jesus, Yito. As for that last picture, *Mother & Daughter*... Those two Polaroids of your time in Wales... What the hell did you expect to happen? You can't go showing the country's Press close-ups of the groins of a woman and a pre-pubertal girl each impaled on a dick and not expect to be arrested, especially with Blakely and his Child Protection Unit crawling all over the place. What the Christ were you all thinking? Yito? Cochise? How the hell could you make her show those pictures?'

'He didn't make me.'

'OK, encourage, pressure, even allow, whatever. It was unforgivable of him.'

The pair had arrived at my cottage following Yito's release on bail. It was growing dark, but for once the July air was warm and humid. Outside, on the patio, we were drinking wine or water, eating peanuts, and squashing the occasional mosquito. And I could quite happily have squashed the man across the table from me as well. 'My God, Cochise. You and all those anti-censorship friends of yours must have thought it was bloody Christmas when you found Yito in your group of students and learned her history.'

Cochise leaned forward, both fists on the table. 'Who better than Yito to push back the boundaries? For her, *Mother & Daughter* is reportage. A record of her life with her mother; an essay on what shaped her. Part of her soul. And whatever anybody says it is art: those skin tones are wonderful; all that shadowy merging of white and black. And it is funny. Each cunt has swallowed a man, just spitting out his balls. Empty your mind of prejudice, Red, and you'll see the humour.'

'Humour!' I groaned. 'Please don't tell me you "encouraged" Yito to say that to the police?'

'Of course. And now she's here, not charged.' He sat back, still so calm I wanted to throw my wine over him. 'Just think of the notoriety she achieved,' he continued. 'And the questions she raised about censorship? The whole photographic world will thank her. She will be a martyr.'

'Fuck censorship. And that notoriety you're so proud of may yet get her a criminal record. Who wants to be a martyr in jail at her age?'

***

We were sitting in a beer garden on the edge of the Marlborough Downs. Yito leaned back and gazed up at the evening sky. The air was full of Swifts, flicking their stiff black scythe-like wings while wheeling, diving, and screeching at each other. Cochise wasn't with us; a text message had sent him scurrying with a worried frown back to Plymouth. All talk of the exhibition and its consequences had been banned for the evening, which meant we were struggling for things to talk about.

'You haven't mentioned Ángelita and Abuela for a while,' Yito said to me. 'What happened to them? Does Ipomoea say?'

'She does, but I'm not sure you want to know.'

'Of course I do. Tell me.'

I looked around, checking that nobody else would hear. 'OK... They were executed, both of them.'

'Executed! A frail old lady and a lame child. What could they possibly have done?'

'Become too frail. And too lame. They couldn't feed themselves, they couldn't keep up and they couldn't be carried. In the end, Abuela was given the choice: to be left behind on the trail or to have her spirit forcibly "moved on."'

'Oh my God. But what about Ángelita? She was only – what? Ten? Eleven? How could she make a choice like that?'

'She wasn't given a choice. Seems it's a tradition that when an old woman is killed, the weakest of the children is also killed and buried with her – so that their spirits can move on to their next lives together.'

'That's horrible. How did they do it? With an arrow?'

'A long heavy club. Back of the head. Abuela's last words to Ipomoea were: "Please don't think badly of them. This is our way."'

Yito stared for an age over the distant undulating hills. 'Well that's my appetite gone.'

The waitress brought out our food and for a while we busied ourselves with cutlery, condiments, and the pouring of more drinks. It was Yito who eventually broke the subdued silence.

'Did I tell you? That disgusting man Blakely knew about the investigation into my father's death. He knew it was recorded as suicide.'

'Really? But how did he know? Was he part of it? The investigation, I mean.'

'He wouldn't say, but he could have been, couldn't he? Twenty years ago? And weren't you told he started in Gloucestershire somewhere? That time he arrested you?'

I nodded. 'So what did he say about it all?'

'Say? Nothing. Just asked me questions about that picture of mine in the exhibition. You know, the lynching, the one of Cochise. And he was really aggressive about it. What made me think my father was murdered? How? By whom?' She looked across at me, her dark eyes piercing. 'I really hate that policeman.'

***

My mobile phone rang. 'Oh Red...' Yito was in London, checking in at a police station as required by her bail.

'What's wrong? Has something happened? Is Cochise with you?' As Yito's guarantor, Cochise usually accompanied her.

'He has to go back to the States. Urgently. His mother's seriously ill. But there's more.' She was gabbling.

'Try to calm down. Deep breaths. What else?'

'The police have brought charges after all.'

'Oh my God. You're not in jail, surely?'

'No. Not yet. They've allowed me bail again. But my trial's soon, Red... And jail is where I'm going, I know it is. Blakely told me.'

***

The courtroom began to fill for the verdict. Yito was escorted in and gave me a weak smile as she took her place in the dock. After what seemed an eternity, the three Magistrates filed in and took their seats. The owlish Chairwoman held a sheet of paper in her hands but scarcely looked at it, peering over her glasses at Yito.

'Miss Doberfield. You are not the first photographer to challenge the borderline between decency and pornography and I am sure you will not be the last. At least, in your case, your photographs show talent. They also show an unusual maturity for someone so young, doubtless a result of your unique history. You have drawn strength from, not sought excuses in, your childhood horrors and that can only be applauded. Some of your photographs are breathtakingly beautiful, others force us to contemplate the vulnerability of life. How most of them could incite anything other than admiration I can't imagine, and banning them all would be censorship gone too far. It is our belief that if we are not careful, our society will end up being so censored that there is nothing left to make us think and argue. But as the law stands, you are going to have to restrain yourself, because some of your photographs involve children, notwithstanding one of those children being your younger self. And whereas we three find some of your images beautiful and meaningful, they tread a very fine line.'

'*Mother & Daughter* though does not tread any line. It is neither beautiful nor meaningful. We have debated your right to have that photograph in your possession, given its history and that it is part of a factual record of your life with your mother, but we are not unanimous. So, as I gather all copies have now been destroyed, we are erring on the side of leniency and are not referring that particular discussion to a higher court. But…'

Now the owl's face became stern.

'… there can be no debate over your attempt to publish the image. You projected the picture onto a screen in a Press Conference and had every intention of exhibiting to the general public. Anybody could then have seen the content, and who knows what consequences you might have had on your conscience. It was a very silly – and criminal – thing to do.'

The Chairwoman glanced at the other two magistrates as if asking if they had anything to add. Both looked solemn, both pursing their lips. Yito glanced at me, visibly shaking. Leaning forward, I was gripping my hands together so tightly they were white. The Chairwoman sat up straight and looked directly at Yito.

'In deciding your sentence we have accepted that you received bad advice – even pressure – from people whose opinions you valued and who you probably trusted to put your interests before their own. We have taken into account your age and your unfortunate history, and we have also acknowledged that you had the honesty and good sense to change your plea to 'Guilty,' even if it was at the very last minute. In view of all this, we have decided that the appropriate penalty is a term of six months' imprisonment…'

Yito's hands went to her face. Briefly, the Chairwoman paused.

'… this term to be suspended indefinitely, on the condition that you never again take, possess or publish an indecent image of a child.'

Chapter 18

The evening air was stifling, and upstairs Yito was taking a cooling shower. A moth flew in through the kitchen window and joined others in circling the wooden chandelier. Suddenly, sounds of hammering and shouting thundered through the cottage. A shiver ran through me as I pulled on and tied my bath robe. 'Who is it?' I shouted.

'Police! Search warrant.'

I opened the door as far as the security chain would allow, but the visitor's hefty shoulder proved both the uselessness of the device and the frailness of the door. DI Blakely staggered in, leaving a trail of whisky fumes hanging in the air. Caught off-guard I was momentarily speechless. He turned and peered into my face, breathing over me. 'Where is she? Get her here. Now!'

'I'm on my own. Where's your warrant?'

'It's a private call. I don't need a warrant. I've got things to tell her. Things to her advantage. Where is she?'

'I told you. I'm on my own.'

'Don't fuck with me. And don't think I've forgotten who you are – Red! Now where is she?' He walked into the kitchen. On seeing a bottle of whiskey and glasses in the corner, he helped himself, and after downing one shot, he poured another. 'Well what are you waiting for? Get the witch in here.'

'How many times? She's not here.'

He pushed past me out of the kitchen, stood swaying at the bottom of the stairs and shouted up. 'Want to know how John Doberfield died? I'll tell you. See what you think of your precious 'father' then.'

'Get the hell out of here, Blakely. Or I'm calling 999.'

His glance was full of contempt, and before I could stop him he staggered upstairs and pushed open the bedroom doors, one after another. He found Yito hiding under the duvet on her bed and yanked back the covers. She was at least wearing her dressing gown as she cowered there, even though it covered little when he first saw her.

I grabbed Blakely by the shoulders and pulled him away, then stood between him and Yito as she sat on the edge of the bed and pulled her gown around her. I was taller and perhaps more agile than him, but he was heavier. His face and shaven head were blotched with red and sweat. So was his iguana neck. Swaying, he reached out to steady himself on the bed's footboard. 'Want to know why I joined the Child Protection Unit?' he slurred. 'To fight against degenerate scum like you, your mother and Doberfield. Do you really want to know what he was like? Teacher, my ass. Not content with just fucking young girls, was he? Stood there naked in front of his whole class, bold as fucking brass, tossing himself off. Made them look at his stinking sperm down a microscope. Then he got his grubby hands on that poor little orphan girl... My Christ, she was just eight years old when he kidnapped her. He raped her, he tortured her and did God knows what else to her 'til she couldn't take any more. Then he just dumped her tiny body in one of the lakes. The only decent thing that deviant bastard did in his whole fucking life was to top himself. If I were you, I should pray to God that he wasn't your fucking father.'

'He was my father. Alice told me.'

'"Alice told me."' he sneered. 'Alice didn't have a clue.' Visibly streaming with perspiration, he took off his coat and threw it on the bed, then he leered past me at Yito. 'Like mother, like fucking daughter, eh? She'd open those filthy legs of hers for anybody with a dick. Didn't matter what age they were: seventy; twenty; ten. They were all the same to her as long as they could get it up and stick it in?' He unbuttoned his shirt, then pulled it free at the waist and wafted it as if to cool himself, never once taking his pig-eyes from Yito. 'You didn't stand a fucking chance, did you? No wonder you've ended up just as evil as her. All that pornographic filth of yours. It drives me crazy, the way it just goes on and fucking on. People like you have got to be stopped before you produce the next generation of perverts. And by God am I the man to do it.' Drunkenly angry though he was, he stepped up a level and began jabbing his finger in Yito's direction. 'You just keep looking over your shoulder, witch. Because I'll always be there. You so much as point your camera at another child and I'll have you in jail before you can even press the fucking button.'

Yito was standing half-behind me, gripping hold of my arms, her hands quivering. 'You're lying. John Doberfield was a good man. Kind. Trustworthy. People have told me. And he was my father. And he didn't commit suicide, he was murdered. So instead of victimising me why don't you find out who killed him.'

'Victimising you? You were as guilty as hell, yet those soft fucking idiots on the Bench let you off scot-free. Well I'm damned if I'm going to do the same.' He glared at me. 'Lose yourself, Red. Go write a book. I'm just in the mood to fuck out some justice.' After pulling off his sodden shirt he threw it on the bed. With his whole chest glistening and streaming with sweat, he had more muscle and less fat than I'd expected – except on his pectorals, which were almost breast-like, with nipples that were large for a man. Incongruously, between his 'breasts', was a thick mat of wet black hair which, stretching on down to his navel, looked like a map of South America. Yito gripped my arms tighter, her nails digging into me.

'Don't you threaten her, Blakely. Breaking and entering. Harassment. Now what? Attempted rape? You'd be finished.'

'Attempted? I never fail at anything. But I don't do rape, OK? Or fuck around. Some of us have principles. A firm hand, that's what she lacks, that's what she needs. And I'm just the man to show her one. She'll behave then, I guarantee. As for you, you pathetic bastard, I've screwed your life once already. Just give me half-an-excuse and I'll do it again. Maybe I'll frame you for beating her up. Now lose yourself. This is between the witch and me.'

Yito bolted for the door, but not fast enough. Blakely caught her by the arm of her dressing gown. I grabbed him from behind by the shoulders and tried to pull him away, putting my arm round his pulsating throat. 'Go!' I shouted to Yito. And after struggling free, leaving Blakely holding her gown, she ran down the narrow stairs.

Blakely and I collapsed in a wrestling heap on the floor of the landing. A moment later we began rolling slowly down the stairs from one step to another, struggling with each other all the way, each trying to land punches, each trying to defend himself. At one point I was upside down and under him; at another the right-way-up and on top. But when we finally left the bottom step and landed on the carpeted floor, I was underneath, winded by his weight. Leaving me on the ground, Blakely staggered to his feet and stumbled out of the door into the night, shouting after Yito that there was no escape.

By the time I scrambled outside, both of the others had disappeared, so I ran indoors again, sprinted up the stairs then opened the back bedroom window. I cupped my hands and shouted in the direction of the trees. 'Blakely! I've dialled 999. Said I've got a drunken intruder. Leave before they arrive and I'll say it was a mistake.'

I repeated the message until I saw movement in the shadows. 'Here's your coat...' which I threw out of the window to the ground beneath. '... But I'm keeping your stinking DNA soaked shirt as collateral. You've got five minutes max.'

The security light came on as the shirtless figure retrieved his coat, uttered threats and obscenities, then staggered hurriedly down the path. A couple of minutes later, a car started in the distance, lights became visible through the trees, the sound of an engine gathered pace and then was gone. It was another five minutes and the moon had struggled from behind clouds before Yito appeared in the faint silver light. I met her at the door with her dressing gown.

'Have you really called the police?' she asked, trembling.

***

Yito was in shock and with the cottage door broken and insecure asked if we could share a room for the night, even wanting us to pull a large wardrobe across the bedroom door. It was our first time in a bed together and with her distraught and myself wrestling with guilt from almost unbearable arousal, neither of us slept. Bathed in the pear-drop smell of her tears and breath and occasionally kissing her hair, her forehead, her eyes, I held her body in my arms and tried to discipline myself to think only of comforting her. 'It's OK,' I said. 'He's gone. He wouldn't dare come back.'

'Oh, Red... It's not just him. It's everything. It's my father. It's us. This. Things you don't know. Things that you don't want to know.'

'Of course I want to know. I want to know every single thing about you, whatever it is. Nothing will change anything, I promise. Come on, Yito. Tell me. Tonight. While we're like this. We can never be closer. Let me help. Please. I want to understand. What don't I know? What makes you cry at night? It can't just be your father.'

She raised her head in the darkness. 'Do you really not know already? Have you really not guessed?'

'How could I? Yito… Just tell me. Share it with me, please.'

After falling silent for a while, she eventually groaned, sat up, and switched on the bedside light. Then raising her eyes to the ceiling she wailed, 'Oh God! I could so regret this…'

Chapter 19

I stared at her, my lips parting then closing as every half-formed response to her news stalled as inadequate. 'No,' I forced out at last. 'No, you can't say that. Not soon. Not even ever. The drugs are improving all the time. You are on drugs, yes?'

She shook her head. 'They don't start treatment until some chemical in your blood drops below a certain level.'

'And yours hasn't yet? There. You see. You can carry HIV for twenty years before developing AIDS. Longer. When did you last have sex? Thirteen? Maybe it was him. Add twenty years, that's thirty-three. That's another fourteen years. 2016, for Christ's sake. At the earliest. They'll have a cure by then. They must have. You won't die, Yito. You can't.'

'But I didn't catch it through sex. I caught it from my mother, at birth. She had a blood transfusion. In 1983? People had hardly heard of AIDS then. And guess what? It took eleven years for anybody to track her down and break the good news to her, and she didn't tell me until she was in jail, dying of it, a few years later. And even then she told me in a bloody letter. Can you imagine? So I've had HIV for nearly twenty years already. Changes things a bit, eh? So no, I didn't catch it from a man, but oh boy, how many men have I infected? Me and my mother together. Mother and daughter. How do you think that makes me feel?' While kneeling on the bed and facing me, she forced a weak and tearful smile. 'That day you visited my mother. I would have had sex with you, you know – for your camera. Doing it meant that little to me. Lucky escape, eh? I might have given you HIV.'

'You shouldn't have waited so long to tell me. All this time you've been suffering. All those tears. I could have helped.'

'I was afraid it would scare you off.'

I reached out and pulled her down to my side, wrapping my arms around her. 'Then you obviously don't know me. Or how much you mean to me. It would take more than a life-threatening virus to drive me away from you.' I kissed her on the nose. 'But is that really the reason you've given up sex? Because you're worried about passing on HIV to even more men?'

'It's one of the reasons.'

'But what's wrong with condoms?'

'Everything. It's not just the HIV. Pregnancy, too. It would totally destroy me. I couldn't have an abortion, but for a child of mine to go through the same hell as myself? I just couldn't cope with that decision.'

'But condoms...' I began.

'Aren't reliable enough. They come off. They split. They burst.' She gave me a gentle kiss on the lips. 'I get horny too, you know. But a few minutes of pleasure? It's just not worth it. I had enough sex when I was little to know it's overrated.'

'But that was then. You're grown-up now. And there doesn't need to be penetration.'

She tilted her head to look me in the eyes. 'I know, but give me time, eh? Please? Just telling you has been a huge step for me. Let me adjust. For now, just this. Being held, being close. For me this is perfect.' She hesitated. 'Can you cope?'

'I can try. But, you know... They'll be able to stop HIV passing from mother to baby completely soon.'

'I know. But I'm expecting to be dead by then.'

Chapter 20

We gave up on trying to contact Cochise. He hadn't answered his mobile phone since a few days before Yito's trial, and the phone number he gave us as his parents' in Arizona seemed not to exist. But wherever he was, his legacy stayed with us. Increasingly, e-mails arrived from the agent he had recruited for Yito; and every day Yito grew more excited and nervous as media interest in her photographs and personal history increased. 'Journalists, OK. But radio? And television? I couldn't. Could I?'

Yito had already decided not to continue with her degree, and given the ever-present spectre of her HIV all I could do was agree. Rightly or wrongly, she still felt overwhelmingly that time was not on her side.

'OK. I still don't agree, but suppose you really don't have that long,' I whispered to her during a tearful hour one middle-of-the-night. 'Tell me what's important to you and I'll do my damnedest to help.'

Yito hugged me and nuzzled her head into my neck. 'I know you will, and I have thought about this, trying to make sense of it all. But everything sounds so trivial. Like I want to make pictures, really memorable pictures; images from my brain to live after me. And to learn the truth about my father, that's important too – so is bringing his murderers to justice, whoever they are.'

'You don't believe Blakely then. That John Doberfield might not be your father – and that he really did commit suicide.'

'No, of course not. Do you?'

***

'Did you hear that?' I asked quietly. 'That splash?' Yito shook her head.

Picnic finished, we were lying on flattened grass and staring up at a clear blue sky. A gust of wind blew hair about my face and bowed the tall teasels and willow herbs surrounding us; we were at Inchfield Park.

In such a magical place, unconstrained lovers would have indulged themselves more than once, but we were contenting ourselves with companionship, tranquillity, and communion with the past. We had imagined Ipomoea's naked grandsons with their bows hunting rabbits, squirrels, pigeons, even deer, and maybe spearing fish in the lakes. We pictured the women and girls scouring the forest and shrubbery for edible fruit, nuts, roots, leaves and shoots. 'But what about winter?' Yito had said. 'Surely they had to wear clothes then. And buy their food. And where did they live? Not the old Mansion?'

Certain that I had heard something, I stood to peer over the vegetation; to survey the lake down-slope from us. 'Look, ripples, going out from the bank.'

Yito stood to join me, placing her hand on my shoulder to help her stand on tip-toe. 'Aren't they just the wind?'

'Too concentric.'

'A duck dived?'

'Too big a splash.'

Confused, we glanced at each other, but when we looked back at the lake we saw the answer: a naked woman floating in the water, staring up at the sky. It was Yito's vanishing nude, maybe the woman in the snow – even my ghostly temptress. A chill passed through me, but the woman wasn't dead. 'How did she get there without us seeing?'

'Underwater?'

'I'm going down,' said Yito. 'Try to talk to her. You stay here. Take as many photographs as you can. Zoom right in.'

'Shouldn't you put some clothes on first?'

Yito laughed at the suggestion then left, stooping for cover from the tall plants. I lay down, elbows on the ground, and cleared a corridor through the vegetation to see and photograph without being seen. Sharp stems of grass pricked my belly, groin and thighs.

The woman was facing away from both me and the direction Yito would approach as she began wading into shallows, a lagoon amongst rushes. Her skin was a uniform dark olive; she was no stranger to nudity. She reached back to squeeze the water from her long dark hair.

With Yito's prize-winning camera on full optical zoom, I took photo after photo. Yito was approaching the woman, swimming gently, quietly – and so far undetected. But as soon as Yito stood and began to wade, maybe even to speak, the woman spun round, panic in her posture.

Something began wriggling between the grass and my genitals. A worm? A beetle? In the distant lake, Yito stumbled and collapsed sideways into the water. Between my legs, something jabbed a burning hypodermic into my scrotum. Writhing, I brushed away the wasp that had been trapped beneath me, and collected another sting this time on my hand.

When I looked back to the lake, the woman had gone.

***

Yito had little sympathy for me, or herself. 'She was just beginning to talk to me. If only you'd seen where she went. What's a tiny wasp sting?'

'It wasn't tiny – and I know where she went, even if I didn't see her.' I was clutching myself, which at least made Yito smile. 'She frightened a Woodpigeon from the trees over there, made a couple of Blackbirds give alarm calls along there, and then scared Jackdaws from the trees up there, near where we saw the fire in the snow. Did she say anything? How old would you say she was?'

'Difficult to tell. Maybe forty.'

'Did you ask where she lived?'

'Around here, that's all she'd say.'

'Anything else?' With a groan, I squeezed myself harder as the pain escalated.

'I tried asking about the commune, but she clammed – and that was when I fell. But she did tell me her name. Well... Sort of. Not her real name – she said I wouldn't be able to pronounce that. But it seems she sometimes calls herself Nubes, and her friends...'

'Call her "Noo",' I interrupted with another groan. 'She's one of Ipomoea's grandchildren. Your mother mentioned her.'

Yito's mouth fell open and her eyes lit up with excitement. 'Really! Are you serious?' She glanced around, as if expecting the whole family to appear, then grabbed me, scarcely able to contain herself. 'We've got to talk to her. Properly next time. We must move nearer. Lodge in one of the local hotels. Come here every day until she appears again. Oh my God, Red. Just think. One of Ipomoea's grandchildren. That's just so... She can tell us what really happened to my father. And all about Ipomoea.'

Chapter 21

We chose a surveillance site high up on Inchfield's southern slope. A thick stand of trees shielded our backs while in front we had a good view both across and along the valley. The only drawbacks were the bum-slide to get down to the place, and the ungainly scrabble upwards to leave. But despite being the ideal vantage point, the site gave us little reward. Over the course of six days the only person we saw was Hood on his Saturday fishing trip. Otherwise, apart from ten foxes, one badger, and one Muntjac deer, we saw nothing else of interest: no headless horsemen or their ilk, and definitely no naked temptress.

'We're being stupid,' said Yito over dinner at our hotel on the sixth night.

'We are?'

'If that really was Noo at the winter solstice… If she really has converted from Animism to Wicca… Then we already know the next time she'll be in the Park.'

'We do?'

'Of course! The next Full Moon. It's even August, so it's a special Full Moon. Corn, I think. I'll check. But if Wiccans still meet at Inchfield, they ought to be holding some sort of ritual that night. And if they do, and Noo's amongst them, the rest is easy.'

'But we can't just walk up to her and ask to talk in the middle of a ritual. We need to corner her. On her own. Stop her running off.'

***

'A Full Moon Ritual is called an "Esbat",' Yito told me as we spread out a blanket at our Inchfield site. It was mid-day and the temperature was already in the high-twenties Celsius with the promise of a warm, sticky night and clear skies.

'I know, you told me.'

'Did I? Sorry! But did I tell you that the idea is for the High Priestess to draw the Great Mother Goddess down from the moon; to absorb her energy from its light, then use it?'

I chuckled. 'Yes.'

We couldn't see the whole valley from our vantage point but we could see enough, not least the place where we had seen the woman we now thought was Noo with a man at the Winter Solstice. This glade was on the opposite slope and slightly below us, perhaps 200 metres away.

In the midday heat, I stripped to the waist, no further. 'But they will be sky-clad,' Yito predicted. 'It's the Wiccan way – to remove all traces of social status before worshipping.'

***

'Here we go. There's someone in the glade.' Yito had rigged up her camera on its sturdy tripod, leaving the telephoto lens zoomed right in and pre-focussed on the distant clearing.

I picked up my binoculars. 'It's a woman – and you're right, she's already naked.'

'Is it Noo?'

'It could be.'

'Is she alone?'

'I think so.'

The woman began placing things on the large stone table that we had first noted at the Winter Solstice. I began a commentary. 'A basket of something, I think. And maybe a bottle too, from the way the sun's reflecting.' Most of the glade was in dappled shade, with occasional broad shafts of sunlight. The naked figure disappeared among the trees at the back of the clearing.

'So that table is their altar,' said Yito. 'And she'll be bringing autumn stuff. Apples, corn, nuts – anything. Wine or cider, too. Maybe they'll be doing a "Cake & Ale" ritual as part of it.'

I chuckled. 'Cake & Ale? That doesn't sound very sexy or sinister.'

'You still don't believe me, do you? Sure, they use spells and magic – but because every act for good or bad is supposed to return to them threefold, it rather puts a brake on "sinister" don't you think? To harness nature's energies, that's their aim. Then to use it to empower themselves and others.'

'Sex is part of Wicca, though. You've said so.'

'But mainly in Spring. You know – fertility, re-birth, all that.'

After about thirty minutes, the woman returned to the glade carrying two more baskets and placed their contents on the altar as well. Every so often, Yito took a photograph.

'I'm almost sure that's Noo,' I said. 'The colouring. The hair. But… Hasn't she arrived a bit early for a Full Moon Ritual? It's still six hours to sunset and moonrise.'

Yito shrugged. 'There's lots she could do. Purify the area. Mark out the circle. Maybe there's only her and the guy we saw at the Winter Solstice – and she has to do all the preparation.'

Still naked and barefoot, the woman began moving downslope from the clearing; mainly she walked, sometimes she nimbly skipped, and occasionally she slid on the loose soil and leaves. Once she had reached the valley bottom she made her way to the side of the lake to dive in where we had once seen ripples. Then after swimming to the shallow lagoon surrounded by reeds, she began to bathe herself – just with water, no soap – working on each part of her body so precisely and in such a sequence that Yito said it had to be a ritual. Through the binoculars, we could see her plainly. It was Noo. And when she left her bathing site, she followed the same route I had once surmised from bird noises, eventually making her way back up to the 'Wiccan Glade.'

If she was always so predictable…

***

'Just think,' whispered Yito when we saw the ceremony starting that evening. 'This used to be my father's coven.'

With six men and seven women, the group was larger than we expected. And the 'Esbat' was longer, starting soon after moonrise around nine o'clock and ending past midnight. We saw a great deal of choreographed posturing: facing the moon; raising arms; placing arms across the chest; passing of food and chalices. There was also a frequent chanting that by the time it drifted across the moonlit valley had a gloomy and plaintive quality. But apart from the outdoor setting, masks, and nudity, the essence of subservience and awe seemed little different from the rituals of more mainstream religions. 'I was expecting something a bit more dramatic and different,' I said as, with the coven dispersed, Yito and I curled up together on our blanket to wait for daybreak, not even attempting to scramble out of the Park in the moonlight.

'What you mean is,' Yito chuckled, 'you were hoping to see an orgy.'

***

The moonlight, general haziness and the slightly blurred sky-clad figures gave Yito's photographs of the event an ethereal, supernatural feel, all accentuated by smoke from the large red, yellow, green and blue quarter candles and the large white Moon candle on the altar. The final touch was provided by the brown masks worn by the men and the white masks by the women; half-masks, covering eyes and cheeks but leaving the nose and lips exposed. One man, the High Priest, also wore a brown cloak.

'That one's not bad,' said Yito as we scrolled through the set on my office computer.

'The start of the kiss, yes? Zoom in a bit?'

The High Priestess – Noo – was standing, arms across her chest, while the High Priest knelt to kiss her feet; step one of what Yito had called the "Fivefold Kiss." 'After the Priestess draws the moon goddess into her, the Priest kisses first her feet, then her knees, her womb, her breasts and finally her mouth. He gives a little chant between each kiss. Quite sexy, eh?' She had photographs of all five steps.

'I wonder how Noo ended up being the High Priestess of a coven?' I mused. 'And who that High Priest is?'

'My father's successor,' muttered Yito as she zoomed in on him in a rare shot with his cloak gaping. A moment later her hand went to her mouth. 'Oh – my – God!'

'What?'

'Can't you see? Look at his chest, and that hair.'

I peered intently, then nearly choked with astonishment. 'Jesus Christ! It's South America! It's bloody South America.'

Chapter 22

The thought that DI Blakely might be the High Priest of the Inchfield coven did nothing to deter us from our plan for Noo; on the contrary, we decided the knowledge gave us some insurance if anything went wrong. So, around midday on the Harvest Full Moon, 21 September, we took up positions either side of the path that Noo had used previously after her ritual visits to the lake. The track, snaking through tall vegetation and between bushes, was a series of half-buried rocks that formed a virtual stairway from the water's edge up to the main path.

At around three o'clock we saw Noo wading into the shallow lagoon beneath us. 'She must be freezing.'

'Shhh!'

Freezing or not, the ritual bathe seemed to go on for ever, but when Noo finished she left the lagoon in the expected direction. With my heart beating furiously and my hands trembling, I was light-headed with nervousness. Yito's mouth quivered slightly as we exchanged smiles, each of us squeezing as far into vegetation as we could to be hidden, silent and still. A timid meadow vole appeared and foraged in the grass.

Minutes passed. I hardly dared to breathe. Then, through the tall grass stems and tangled bramble branches, I glimpsed Noo's legs and striking black pubic hair as she headed towards us, jumping from stone to stone. I tensed myself; the first move was to be mine. But just a few metres short of our position, Noo stopped. And from the way her hips were swivelling, she was looking around, as if something had alerted her. Yito looked at me questioningly.

Without warning, Noo began bounding up the path again – so quickly and nimbly that she was level and nearly past before I reacted. I threw myself sideways and wrapping my arms round her thighs brought her cleanly to the ground in the grass by Yito's side.

Noo squirmed onto her back. I pressed a cloth over her mouth and Yito deftly handcuffed first her wrists then her ankles before sitting astride her thighs to pin them down. For a brief moment, Noo seemed paralysed by shock, then she began writhing, kicking, squirming and bucking, a diminutive but strong lithe woman, her skin still cold from the lake.

'Please stop struggling,' pleaded Yito. 'We don't want to hurt you. We just want to talk to you. Honestly. Stop, please.' But for an age, Noo continued to battle. It took all our combined strength to keep the cloth over her mouth and to keep her pinned supine on the ground. And in the end – one-against-two and shackled as she was – Noo gradually lost her strength until at last she seemed to give in. Her dark almond eyes flicked from one to other of us as occasional guttural sounds came from under the makeshift gag.

'Listen to me,' said Yito. 'We've met before. I tried to talk to you. You're the only person who can help me. Trust me, please. We won't hurt you.'

Noo stared at Yito while trying to say something to her.

'I'll lift the cloth,' I said. 'But if you try to scream I'll put it straight back on.' I eased the pressure.

'Are you who I think you are?' Noo asked Yito, her question muffled.

'I don't know. My father was John Doberfield. I think you knew him. My mother, too. His wife. Alice.'

Noo spat, either with contempt or to remove fibres from her mouth. 'Wife! Such a stupid word.' Narrowing her eyes, she studied Yito's face. 'So a spirit finally entered that bloated bloodless body of hers, did it?' Then she flicked her eyes sideways to look at me. 'So you must be Red.'

'How...?' but I already knew the answer. 'And you must be Ipomoea's grand-daughter. You are, aren't you?'

'Get this stinking cloth away from my face and I'll tell you.'

'Scream and it goes straight back on.'

'I won't scream unless you hurt me.'

I eased away the cloth. 'So... Are you her grand-daughter? Did she bring you here from the Amazon when you were a child? And what finally happened to her? Did she die here? Back in South America?'

Her expression had changed from angry to suspicious. 'She's here. In the forest. Listen and you'll hear her.'

'Not alive. It's impossible.'

'Spirits live forever... Oh, for God's sake, will you unlock these stupid bloody contraptions. Where the hell did you get furry pink handcuffs anyway? A sex shop?'

I laughed. So did Yito as she said: 'They're called "Love Cuffs". Sorry about the colour. I couldn't think who else would sell handcuffs.'

'"Love Cuffs?" My God. Come on! Take them off. This is stupid.'

Yito and I exchanged concerned glances. 'Soon,' I said. 'Just a few more questions.'

'No. Now. Otherwise no more answers.'

'OK, I'll free your hands,' said Yito. 'But not your feet. Not yet. We know you. You're too fast for us.' She did as she offered.

Still lying on her back with Yito sitting astride her thighs, Noo scrutinised her again. 'You can't be Alice's daughter. You're too dark. Too pretty.'

'My looks come from my father.'

Noo laughed with contempt. 'Father! Sperm! Seed! All crazy talk. Men trying to hijack motherhood, that's all.' She looked at me as if all male shortcomings were my fault. 'Men feed women and fight each other. That's all you do. All you're good for.'

Yito looked tense and irritated. 'OK! Forget "father". John Doberfield, then. I look like him, yes? My mother told me. Olive skin? Brown eyes? Black hair?'

Noo laughed again. 'Are we talking about the same man? John was fair, both hair and skin. And tall, with brilliant blue eyes. Very beautiful. Why would Alice lie to you?'

Yito seemed to reel, as if punched, so I asked the obvious next question for her: 'Who else fed Alice? Your brother? Your cousins?'

'Of course. All the men fed all the women. That was our way.'

I glanced at Yito, wondering if she was following this, but she still looked dazed. I turned back to Noo. 'Did others have children too? Did you?'

Noo furrowed her brow. 'One. A daughter. And my cousin Laguna was carrying a spirit when she left. Why?'

'And does your daughter live here, with you?'

'In this cesspit? Hell, no! She went back to South America with Laguna and the others. Back to the jungle, for a proper life. And one day I'll follow. Why?'

Yito shuffled off Noo's thighs and began unlocking the fluffy pink ankle cuffs: 'What was her name? Your daughter?' Yito looked up at me. 'We could be half-sisters. Have the same father.'

Noo sat up and began massaging her ankles. 'Her real name?' She shook her head. 'You wouldn't understand.'

'In Spanish, then. Did she have a Spanish name like you? Like all the others?'

'Yes, she did. How did you know that? From Alice?'

'It's a long story. So, what was her Spanish name?'

Noo gave a wicked smile. 'Caballito,' she said. 'The same as yours, so I'm told. Alice must have got the idea from me. She always said she liked it.'

Chapter 23

"Take the Stroud road out of Nailsworth, then the third dead-end road on the left. It's quite long and steep – upwards. Just after the second cattle-grid sign, turn left onto the dirt track until the road ends in a sort of muddy cul-de-sac outside some double white gates. Leave your car there and follow the gravel path round to the front of the house."

Noo had cut our conversation short the day we ambushed her – 'I'm expecting visitors, and I've still got a lot to do.' If we wanted to talk more, she said, we had to meet with her again, and for this, she gave us her telephone number, e-mail address, and directions to her house. 'But check with me first. Sometimes I have company.'

'Impressive place,' I said as Noo answered the door. Set in it's own clearing in the forest the house was a three story circular tower.

'Just walls, floors and ceilings.' She scrutinised us. 'Please – house rules – no footwear.'

Bare-footed herself and wearing a loose brown shift dress she led us into what seemed to double as a lounge and office. The room was semi-circular with large windows all along the wall making it feel like one huge bay-window. The midday autumn sun was streaming in. 'It's so light,' said Yito. 'And the view, it's just… Wow.'

Noo grunted. 'Hardly outside though, is it? This is such a stupid climate.'

But given the "stupid climate," the room was a very good substitute for the outside; with a southerly aspect, it would receive sun all day long. And the view was so panoramic a person could easily imagine being in the forest.

Even the leaf-motif brown and beige carpet contributed to the open air feel. Less 'mode al fresco' was a large circular wood-and-glass coffee table, and also a computer set in its own alcove. As for the seating… Instead of conventional settees and chairs there were a dozen large bean-bags scattered around the room, their rustic colours matching the curtains. But the lay-out seemed strange, the coffee table positioned uncomfortably near to the door, as if the priority was to have as large an uncluttered space at the far end of the lounge as possible.

'Big house,' I commented. 'Is this where the commune lived?'

Noo didn't answer, but instead offered us coffee. 'The percolator's on. I shan't be long. Make yourselves comfortable.'

Yito and I exchanged glances but not comments as we sank into our chosen bean-bags. 'No, please sit by the table,' Noo said when she came back into the room. 'At least while we drink the coffee.'

'So where shall we start?' I asked once we were all sitting around the table. 'I've got loads of questions for you.'

She shook her head. 'No. Seems to me that you two already know more about me than you should, so first I want to know how much and how.' She kept glancing at the door, her pretty oval face with its wide mouth and flashing almond eyes seemingly betraying every thought and feeling.

I began by showing her a photocopy of the bookmark; she gripped the paper so tautly I thought it was going to tear. 'But… Where did you get this?'

After telling her, I explained how the bookmark had led me to Inchfield Park and eventually to Ipomoea's manuscript.

'You found her manuscript? But how? It was destroyed.' She hesitated. 'At least, that's what we all thought.'

'In a way, it was. Any idea who ripped it up?'

'Ripped it up? Really? Is that what she did?'

'She? Who?'

'Ipomoea of course. She grew so frustrated with the thing. I mean... She knew she was never going to finish it. Each page took her so long – and if she made even a tiny mistake she'd start over.' She looked at the bookmark she was still holding. 'You can see here. Look at the big X.'

'What was that?' said Yito.

'What?'

'That noise?'

Noo just shrugged. 'It's a house full of noises. Forest spirits mainly. Sometimes Grandmother's.' She gave a muted smile. 'So, have you learned anything from her scribbles?'

'Not really. The manuscript is so torn it's virtually impossible to read. I learned more – at least about the commune here – from talking to Yito's mother, years ago. That's why I'm so keen to talk to you.'

'Really? So what did Alice tell you?'

'Well – all sorts. Like how you were the only one that enjoyed learning anything, for example.'

'There's that noise again,' said Yito.

Noo moved her head from side to side. 'Oh, that noise. Oh, I'm always hearing that. It's a rat, I think. In the ceiling.'

I struggled from the bean-bag and walked over to the window nearest to the door, to gaze out for a few moments at the forest. When I turned round Yito was looking at me quizzically, and Noo suspiciously. I raised my voice. 'Alice didn't tell us you'd become a Wiccan, though. A High

Priestess even. We only found that out the other week when we watched your Corn Moon Esbat.'

'You watched us? How dare you! Those ceremonies are private. Didn't we teach you anything at the Winter Solstice? That was you two, wasn't it? Where were you this time?'

'Across the valley, with binoculars – and a camera. You were easy to identify, but the person who really intrigued us was your High Priest. Doesn't do much, does he? He looked so familiar. Who is he? Someone else from the original commune?'

'I'm not telling you that?'

'No? Why not?'

'Well, for one thing, it's none of your business. And for another, I don't know who he is. We use Wiccan names, not real ones. And these days... Well – if you really watched us like you say, you will have seen: we wear masks, and he wears a cloak.'

'Not last Winter Solstice, he didn't. Not when there were only the two of you. You and he know each other.'

'I still don't know his real name.'

'Well we know who he is.' With two quick strides, I reached the door and threw it open. 'It's him,' I said, as Blakely nearly fell into the room. 'Here's your rat. I wondered why that table was so near to the door. What's up, Blakely? Worried we're going to sell the tabloids a few choice photos?'

Blakely turned on Noo. 'You stupid fucking heathen. Couldn't you do any better than that?' Then he sneered at me. 'Fuck the photos. It was driving me crazy trying to work out where you two were getting your leads. Now I know. I want that manuscript; I'll wager you have managed to read some of it. Where is it?'

'Why? What possible interest could Ipomoea's memoirs be to you?'

'Murder! Rape! Torture! A young girl. An old woman. A man. The clues could all be in there. Everybody said it had been destroyed.'

'Then get a warrant, because sure as hell unless you do I'm not handing it over. I found it. It's mine.'

'It fucking isn't. If it's anybody's it's Noo's. How much have you read?'

'You heard me. Nothing – yet. It's still in tiny pieces.'

'And I don't believe you, so I'll tell you again. Go home, get that manuscript and wait for me. This is the law you're dealing with.'

I strode up to him and stood face to face. 'Do you know what, Blakely? I don't believe you. This is you, not the law. You're shit-scared about something. And I'm going to make damn sure I find out what it is.'

He laughed. 'Do you really think you're a match for me?' Then he pushed me full in the chest, making me stagger backwards. 'Now get out, take the witch with you, and have that manuscript ready for me. It's police property now.'

I gestured to Yito that we should leave. We snatched up our footwear but didn't stop to put them on. With the sound of Blakely shouting angry obscenities at Noo fading behind us, we walked barefooted back to the car. I was still shaking with anger and nerves as we slammed the car doors and settled into the seats.

'It's not over,' said Yito, her face pale.

'What do you mean?'

'While you and Blakely were shouting at each other, Noo asked me when I was born.'

'I don't understand.'

'When I told her, she pushed this note into my pocket.'

> *Tomorrow.*
> *Wiccan glade. Midday.*
> *Meet me there. Both of you.*
> *I'll be alone.*

***

'I don't like this,' I said to Yito. 'Last time we climbed up here somebody used us for archery practise.'

The air was warm for October and eerily still. Rain threatened. The leaves on the trees were turning brown but few had fallen; mainly it was soil underfoot as we weaved our way upwards into the forest. Yito suddenly grabbed my arm. About thirty metres away and above us, standing at the edge of the Wiccan glade and looking down on our progress, was a hooded figure wearing a full-length brown cloak. Evidently seeing that we'd noticed, the person threw back the hood. It was Noo. As we drew nearer we could see that her cloak was open at the front and that underneath she was – as almost always – naked.

'I wasn't sure you'd come,' she said as we scrambled up the last few metres to stand breathlessly by her side. She had bruises, a large one on her ribs and another on her cheekbone.

'Did Blakely do that?'

She didn't answer, just scrutinised us then handed us each a cloak like the one she was wearing. 'Please – coven rules – no clothes in the glade except cloaks. Even then only if you're cold. Are you cold?'

I looked around. 'Are you really alone? Are you sure Blakely isn't up there somewhere with his bow?'

'Blakely? I call him Janus – that's the J in CJ – his mother's choice. He hates it.'

'Janus!' I laughed. 'A two-faced Roman God?'

'More an "eyes-in-the-back-of-his-head" God. But even he can't see us from Birmingham. That's where he is for a few days. There's a big child-abuse case brewing; another Catholic priest. Look, I'm sorry about yesterday but that's in the past. Today is for me – and maybe for you. Please...' she said, offering the cloaks again.

A single large raindrop fell on my head. Then another. 'Sorry, I'd rather keep my clothes on.'

'Humour me? Both of you. It's not just because of the coven code.'

'Why then?'

'I detest clothes. They're uncomfortable, unhygienic – and they make people look stupid.'

'Aren't cloaks clothes?'

She grunted. 'You have to stay warm somehow in this ridiculous climate. Please... I trust people more when they're naked.'

'And I trust people more when I'm clothed.'

The rain gathered pace. Noo's eyes were flicking from one to the other of us. 'OK. I'll tell you the main reason: I want to see Yito's body again.' She looked Yito in the eyes. 'I want to see your flesh. Sense your spirit.'

'But why?' Yito looked uncomfortable.

Suddenly we were in a downpour. With rain running over her forehead and dripping from her nose, Noo glanced at me then back to Yito. 'Why? Because I think you might be my daughter. Don't you?'

Chapter 24

According to Noo, in the spring of 1983 she gave birth in the forest at Inchfield. The previous autumn the baby-to-be had been given the Spanish name of "Caballito." But when born that 'baby' proved to be twins: two girls. Noo's small community – with Mariposa the most vehement – demanded that she follow tradition and bury the twins in the forest floor with just their heads above ground until at least one of the spirits departed.

Sprawled on bean-bags, hot coffee by our sides, we were in Noo's lounge, sheltering from the now driving rain. Our hostess had finally gained her wish: clothes as well as cloaks were drying elsewhere in the house.

'And the others let you?' I protested. 'John? Alice? The other Wiccans?'

'How could they stop us? It was our tradition, not theirs.'

'But you and your family had been living here, what? Ten years? More? You must have known you couldn't kill a baby just to satisfy some stupid superstition.'

Noo's eyes flashed. 'Spirits can't be killed. They move on.' She uncurled from her seat to kneel in front of me like a cobra. 'Your culture!' she almost spat. 'Your pompous certainty that your way is right… Let me tell you: our society works just fine and from everything I've read it has done so unchanged for probably tens of thousands of years. Only when – and if – your screwed-up culture with its absurd beliefs and obscene prejudices stands such a test of time will you have the right to call mine "stupid".'

Yito, who had been silent for a while, jumped to her feet. 'Stop it, you two. This isn't why we're here. Noo – carry on with your story. What were you going to say? That I'm the baby that survived that night?'

After a final glare at me, Noo turned to Yito. 'No. You can't be. She's in South America with my family. I was at the airport. I watched her go.'

'Then I don't understand. How can I be your daughter?'

'Because you might be the baby who died.'

'Oh, come on,' I snorted, but then Noo explained. The night the twins were buried alive, one disappeared, dug from the ground and carried away; a fox, they all thought. The forest spirits had spoken, taking one spirit back and showing Noo which baby to raise. But now, Noo was wondering if the 'fox' had in truth been Alice. 'She had been so jealous of my being pregnant; so desperate to have a child of her own.'

I actually laughed. 'You mean Alice disappeared the same night as your baby? And you still thought it was the forest spirits talking?'

Noo's look was pure contempt. 'Do you really think I'm that stupid? Alice was around for another fortnight or so – but kept coming and going. She hated our brutality, she said, and couldn't bear to live with us any longer. Then she disappeared. But maybe she was just being clever.'

'But she'd need help. Somebody to look after the baby while she was with you. Was it John?'

Noo shook her head. 'Maybe Ipomoea. That I could believe.'

'Red!' There was an anger in Yito's voice. 'I want to go.'

'Why?' said Noo.

I turned on her. 'Why do you think? Because she doesn't want anything to do with a mother who tried to kill her at birth. That's why.'

A look of panic spread over Noo's face, as if she had been fearing such a response. 'But Yito... It's our people's way. Imagine trying to raise twins in the jungle. Nobody ever tried. Both would eventually die, and probably the mother too, from the sheer effort. Think about it. Even just carrying twins is impossible. Much better to return one spirit to the forest quickly than to cause the drawn-out suffering of three.'

Yito's eyes flared. 'Not if you're the "spirit" who's returned quickly it isn't. Besides, you were here, not scraping along in the Amazon. Here it's called murder. Couldn't the others have helped? Your cousin?'

'That's not our way. And in any case, our plan was to go back to the jungle as soon after you were born as possible. As for Laguna, she would also soon have a baby to care for.'

'But she took the other Caballito back to South America for you.'

'That was different. It wasn't planned. It just happened.'

'That's stupid. How could it just happen?'

Noo laughed without humour, a strange distraught sound. 'Because when we all arrived at the airport, there was something wrong with my new passport. They wouldn't let me on the plane. All the others, but not me.'

'What? So the others went on ahead? With the baby? That's crazy.'

'Look, if you don't believe me, you don't believe me. Why should I care? But you weren't there. OK? It didn't seem such a big deal. I could be on the very next plane, I was told. Just go to the Passport Office in Liverpool and it would be sorted out while I waited. And it seemed much easier for my family to take the baby on ahead than for me to haul her around Liverpool. She had her own passport; John had arranged everything for us. But in the end it was months before I got mine. They needed some document from French Guiana. My whole life screwed by some stupid piece of paper, and a bad decision.'

'But you did get your passport eventually. So why not join them then?'

'Because I couldn't.'

'Why not?'

'Because I couldn't. OK?' Her face glared with a warning to desist, and an awkward silence fell.

'Do you still want to leave?' I asked Yito.

'Try and stop me. I'll go and get our clothes, dry or not.'

After Yito left the room, there was a brief silence, save for the sound of rain on glass. But after a few tense moments I looked straight at Noo. 'How did John Doberfield die?'

'The inquest said suicide.'

'And was it?'

'How should I know?'

I looked into her wide brown eyes. 'Ipomoea then? What finally happened to her?'

'Her spirit moved on, like all spirits do.'

'But when? 1983? And what did she die of? Where is she buried?'

'Why do you want to know?'

'I'm just interested.'

Noo stared at me for a moment. 'Look, I've taken a real risk today, telling you my story – and I didn't do it just to "interest" you. Yito and I, we need a maternity test. I thought that you, Red, might be able to arrange this.'

I laughed in astonishment. 'You believe in genes? DNA?'

Noo shook her head. 'I'll tell you what I believe. When a spirit enters a woman it gathers bits of her blood and flesh around it to build a body to live in. And from what I've read, a maternity test can tell us whether Yito's body is made from my flesh or another woman's. And that's all we need to know. So can you arrange such a test or not?'

Chapter 25

As I reached under Yito's pillow for the vibrator, she stayed my hand. 'Not tonight.' Her flushed face broke into a coy smile and she reached under the pillow herself. For a moment, her hand stayed hidden. 'About risks,' she muttered. 'Tonight, I will if you will.' She held up a silver packet and tore it open, releasing the smell of rubber and lubricant. 'But you must promise me. No thrusting, and definitely no coming. Just to be joined. Just for a while. OK? Promise?'

'Are you really sure?' I said after we both checked the condom was secure. She nodded, and as I gently began to penetrate, she bit her bottom lip and closed her eyes.

My loss of control was immediate, and so briefly was hers. But whereas my gasping groan was an apology for failure, her simultaneous squeal – or so she told me later – was an explosion of fear and panic.

'You promised!' she said, making me withdraw so she could look.

'I'm sorry.'

'Oh God, it's burst, look,' she said wiping the outside with her finger.

'No! It's alright, it hasn't, look,' I said, squeezing the teat.

The condom clearly hadn't burst, and once alarm subsided and emotions calmed, we saw a funny side to our panic. And at about six in the morning, when first light woke us, we dared to join again. This time, without thrusting, climax or panic, our union was so extended, calm and serene that we fell asleep while still engaged, until Yito woke with no feeling in one of her legs and made me pull out.

***

'Warrant!' I demanded after answering my cottage door.

'It's not that sort of visit. I've come to clear the air. Can I come in?'

'Can I say no?'

'No jokes. I'm naturally low on humour.'

I moved to one side and Blakely sidled in, then stood in the centre of my hallway, hands in his coat pockets, jingling his keys. His normally smooth-shaven head sported a couple of days' worth of bristle and his tie as usual seemed to be suffocating him. He looked tired. 'Aren't you going to offer me a drink?'

'I was hoping you weren't staying.'

He looked around. 'Where's the... Where's Yito? Is she here?'

'No. London. Press interviews. And somebody wants to make a documentary about her.'

He grunted, then began to speak, avoiding my gaze. 'Look, this is shit-difficult. I'm not usually wrong about people but... Maybe we three got off on the wrong foot.' At last he made eye-contact. 'Damn it, man! Give me a goddam drink!'

'Tea? Coffee?'

'Fuck that,' and he went into the kitchen and straight over to the whiskey in the corner. 'Do you want one?'

I shrugged and muttered, 'Why not,' and held out my hand for the tumbler he offered.

After downing his whiskey in a gulp he helped himself to another, taking it with him to sit at the kitchen table. 'I can't believe I didn't see it; when I was called in to question Alice and her daughter back in '96... Never crossed my fucking mind.'

'Surely the name: Caballito...'

'Well of course I knew that Noo had a daughter called Caballito too. But surprisingly enough, smart-ass, until your visit last week Noo had conveniently missed out the whole twins-and-burying-them-alive bit from her story. All Noo said was that Alice must have stolen the name. No hint that she might have stolen a bloody baby to go with it.' He took a swig, his hand showing a hint of a tremor.

'So what are you going to do about it? Shouldn't the Child Protection Unit take a dim view of mothers burying new-born twins up to their neck until one dies?'

He stared up at me, his close-set small blue eyes showing surprise and maybe even alarm. 'It was twenty years ago, for fuck's sake. All the witnesses are either dead or in some bloody jungle somewhere.' His eyes narrowed. 'And she's probably Yito's mother.'

'Just at this moment, I don't think Yito's too thrilled about that.' I sat opposite him. 'Is that why you're here? To see if we're planning to do something about Noo trying to murder her children? Protecting her, are you? Is that what High Priests and Priestesses do for each other?'

'Tread carefully, clever-dick. I told you: this isn't easy. Threaten or make fun of me, and we're right back to where we started. That's a promise, friend of Noo's daughter or not.'

'What happened to "Witch"?'

'Witch? You'll get no apologies for that. At the time, why fucking not? From Yito's looks I thought she was probably Mariposa's. Christ, could that animal fuck. And any bloody fruit from his and Alice's stinking loins just had to be evil.'

'But not from Noo's loins, eh? Yet the father could still be Mariposa. Brother and sister? Well, probably half-brother and sister. It's fine by them. The only incest taboo they have is mother and son.'

'Well let's just wait and see, shall we? Noo wanted everybody and everybody wanted Noo. It wasn't just the animals. All the bastards in Doberfield's coven fucked her. Especially him.' He helped himself to another whiskey, then sat down again. 'Any news on the maternity test yet?'

I shook my head – 'But any day now' – and we fell silent for a while. 'How come you know so much about the original commune? Just from Noo? Or were you part of the investigation into John Doberfield's death?'

He grunted. 'Only as a nobody. Just a plod.' Then he looked straight at me. 'I want to see the manuscript.'

I held out my hand. 'Warrant!'

'Don't fuck me about. I just want to see it, OK? I always thought it was a myth, this story of a crazy old crone scribbling away with her quill. I'm just interested.'

'OK. Stay there.'

After returning from my office, I shoved a piece of paper across the table to him.

'What's this?'

'A receipt. From the Stroud Museum of Local History. It's up and running again. Lottery grant. Whole new staff. I've given the manuscript to them. One day they're going to reconstruct Ipomoea's memoirs – maybe. I decided I couldn't be assed. All that effort it would take – and now that I've met Noo it seems a lot easier just to ask her everything I want to know.'

***

Heads turned, mainly men's, when the door to the public bar opened and Yito walked through the smoke-filled room to join me at the corner table. 'How was your drive?' I asked as she sat.

'London hell as usual, and a bit of a snarl-up on the M4, otherwise fine.' She unzipped her coat. 'I got your text. So it's true then. Noo is my mother. I knew she would be.' Her face was impassive.

'Mitochondrial DNA a perfect match. So... How do you feel about it all? Now you know for sure?'

'Numb. I can't get my head around any of it. She tried to kill me, Red – and Alice saved me. Which would you prefer as your mother?'

'Well not somebody who condoned, watched and photographed me having sex from the age of eight, that's for sure. HIV is one hell of a price for a young girl to pay for a roll of film.'

She shook her head. 'You're not being fair. You of all people should understand where Alice was coming from. She was just bringing the jungle ethos to Wales via the commune, that's all, with sex no big deal, not even for children. And she wasn't just watching and taking photos. She was standing guard. Making sure the men were gentle with me. I know it sounds weird, but I never once felt that any of it meant she didn't care for me. Quite the opposite – until I got her arrested. Then suddenly she hated me.'

'But lying that you caught HIV at birth when she knew it had to be from one of the men that she...'

'Red, stop! I don't want to talk about it. OK?' She was glaring at me. 'Look... I've got something to tell you, and I don't know how you're going to take it. I think it's brilliant, but you...'

'Oh. OK, sorry.' I took a sip of my drink. 'So go on. What?'

She reached across the table and helped herself to the tiniest of sips of my wine. Then with growing excitement she told me about her meeting with the TV company and a few details of the programme about her work and childhood they had in mind. 'But that's not all,' she continued. 'When I got your text I told the producer about Noo... Explained that I had a twin sister and a whole bunch of uncles and aunts, not to mention maybe a father, living a stone-age life in the Amazon. That they'd tasted English society, but hated it. Rejected it. Well, you can guess, can't you?'

I shook my head.

'Of course you can. If they can raise the funding, they want to send me into the jungle – with a camera crew – to search for my family roots. They'll do all the research, arrange everything, find the local help we'll need.' She placed her hot hands on mine. 'Can you believe it, Red? I might be going to the Amazon. Like Ipomoea. Like Isabel Godin. Just think of the adventure. Just think of all the pictures I can take.' Shining with excitement, her wide and beautiful eyes were searching mine. 'You don't mind, do you? Please say you don't.'

When I didn't respond immediately... While I sifted through all the different ways that I did mind... She seemed to panic a little. 'I did ask them, honestly. I mean... I knew how you'd feel when I told you. So I did ask, but...'

'Ask what?'

'Well... What else? If you could come too. Of course. Because I know it doesn't seem fair. This is what you always wanted to do when you were my age, but never got the chance. Yet it's just fallen into my lap.'

'So... What did they say? "No", I presume.'

'Oh, Red. They wouldn't even think about it. "No passengers" they said. Just like that. I am sorry. I really am. It would have been fantastic, wouldn't it? Going there together.'

'It would. Fantastic.' I took a breath. 'But it's OK. Really. I'm pleased for you. Honestly. It's a fantastic opportunity for you.'

The excitement returned to her eyes. 'It is, isn't it. I can hardly believe it. And not just an opportunity. Think of Ipomoea. All this time I've spent helping you piece together her life. Marvelling at the woman she was. Yet all the time she was my great-grandmother. Her story is my story too. And before I die, I want to know absolutely everything that happened to her. And my grandmother. Who was she, I wonder? And why did they all leave the jungle? How did Ipomoea die? Where's she buried? And I still want to know what happened to John Doberfield, because when all is said and done – he could still be my father. Never in a million years did I think my life would turn out so exciting.'

With a smile and a shrug I said, 'You could always make up with Noo – and ask her all these things. Maybe she'll answer, now that she knows you really are her daughter.'

Yito shook her head with an air of despair. 'If only… But she hardly ever answers anything, does she? Why is that? What are all these things that she doesn't want us to know?'

Chapter 26

26 October 2002
Dear Noo
We have the results. There's no doubt about it. I am the twin you tried to kill all those years ago. Sorry. I'll need time.
Yito

28 October 2002
So I did give birth to you. Well, well. But I see no other reason for your spirit to treat me as a mother. Take all the time you need. Maybe one day...
Noo

***

'I think I know how Ipomoea died,' I said, looking at scans of two different fragments of the manuscript on my computer.

Yito didn't answer, just continued to stare out of the office window, so I said it again.

'How?'

'Well, come here. Have a look at this.'

She didn't even turn round. 'Just tell me.'

'Yito... Are you OK?'

'Stupid question, don't you think? So how do you think she died? AIDS maybe?'

'Yito! Don't. I think it was a stroke, maybe several. Look...'

At last she turned round and gazed from a distance at the screen.

'Most of the manuscript – especially all of that describing life in the jungle – is written in these immaculate italics of hers. But then some of the later stuff about Inchfield… The writing is really shaky.'

'Let's see what your writing is like when you're ninety – not that I'll be here then.' She stared at me, her brow furrowed. 'You do realise you're never going to find out what happened to her – or John Doberfield – from the manuscript, don't you? You can't. You're wasting your time trying.'

I laughed, trying to lighten the atmosphere. 'You mean: because she can't write once she's dead? Believe it or not, that had occurred to me, yes.'

'Really?' She grunted, then turned to stare again out of the office window. 'Is this your way of asking me – again – to make up with Noo so that I can quiz her over everything you want to know? Because, if it is, the answer's still no. I'm never going to forgive that woman. Nor am I going to give her the pleasure of refusing to answer.'

Sighing, I tried to stay calm. Since Yito's initial euphoria over the prospect of a trip to the Amazon had faded, her moroseness had been unrelenting. 'Yes, you will eventually forgive her – because you'll accept that what she did to you was tradition, outside of her control. And you'll also forgive her because you know that she also had a rough childhood, not very different from your own. Look at everything she had to put up with from this new guy in the commune for a start.'

I had just completed a section of Ipomoea's memoirs that for once had been fairly easy to put together. It concerned a "Christian" and his time at Inchfield Park. Once Ipomoea begins writing about this person, she doesn't stop, quickly referring to him simply as "C".

Yito grunted again. 'Just somebody else who could be my father as far as I'm concerned.'

C is young, perhaps 14 when Ipomoea first mentions him. His father had been a vicar at a West Country diocese. But caught forcing the wrong sort of communion onto a young girl in his confirmation class, the father lost his parish, his liberty, and his wife. An old friend of Alice's, the wife retreated from the scandal by hiding away with her son in the commune, and much to her son's disgust had no hesitation immersing herself in the general pagan ethos.

'And even worse, he sounds totally repulsive. I just don't see how she could.'

Ipomoea describes C as a "plump and ugly youth with thin and straggling hair" and as possessing the "smallest man-nipple" she had ever seen on someone of his age. He is also "bombastic, pious and mean-minded, bent on causing trouble." But his initial adolescent tirades against John Doberfield and Alice for corrupting his mother, and against Mariposa for behaving "no better than an ape," all quieten when his own code of conduct slips beyond redemption. When a naked Laguna, then only about 10 years old, introduces him to Amazonian children's feeding rites, and Noo follows up by teasing that he can't manage to feed two girls in a night, his lust proves a lot stronger than his fear of his God.

'She was only playing with him. You know how little sex meant to them all. How was she to know he was going to start taking it seriously?'

Unfortunately for the commune, C's foray into fornication with under-age girls did nothing to stop his trouble-making, only caused it to be redirected. After professing undying love for Noo, he decided that if they were one day to marry they could be absolved their pre-marital weaknesses. He stoically became a one-girl boy, and did everything he could to make Noo a one-boy girl. Forever trying not to let her out of his sight, he threatened and sometimes fought any man or boy he found with her when he failed, which was often.

Yito turned to face me. 'Meant little? She made Alice look positively frigid. Look how many men could have been my father. Blakely was right. I don't stand a cat-in-hell's chance of ever finding out who he was.'

'Well at least he wasn't C. He left years before you were conceived...'

According to Ipomoea, the arguments caused by C's teenage obsession with Noo mixed with other tensions to "stir the group to boiling point." The stresses were only relieved – and "murder forestalled", Ipomoea says – when C's mother, having paired up with one of the Wiccan men, left the commune to live in a croft in The Hebrides, taking a lovelorn C with them.

'... as you well know. Now come on, Yito. Lighten up. What's got into you this last couple of weeks?'

***

'I told you,' Yito snapped at me one chill November morning on the patio. 'I don't want to talk about it.'

'But all I want to know is a bit more about that letter Alice sent you from jail.'

'I know you do. But I still don't want to tell you. It was horrible. Spiteful. As if I deserved to suffer like her. As if suddenly she hated me.'

'But surely it helps now, knowing that she wasn't actually your mother? Doesn't that make her spite easier to handle?'

'No! I've told you. It makes it worse.'

'But you haven't told me why? How can it possibly make things worse?'

'Because!'

'Because what? Tell me!'

'Because... It raises doubts. And I can't handle them. OK?'

And before I could ask her 'what doubts?' she stormed back into the cottage and with me in pursuit threw off her coat, launched herself on to the chair in front of her computer and pretended to start working. I swung her chair round to make her face me, dropped to my knees, took her hands in mine, and squeezed. 'I know you're hiding something from me, and I'm sure you have your reasons – but there's no need. Whatever it is, it can't be worse than I already know. We've been here before. Let me help. What doubts?' She looked at me with a mixture of panic, fear and uncertainty. Gently, I repeated, 'What doubts, Yito?'

'OK! OK!' She gave a big sigh. 'But be nice to me over it, right? Try to understand. In Alice's letter... Well, she said I was eleven years old when we were both tested for HIV.'

'I know that. You've told me before. So...?'

'So... The thing is... I don't remember. I don't recall having my blood taken. I don't remember anything. How can I possibly have forgotten something like that?'

'So what are you saying? You've blanked it out? That's understandable.' Yito didn't answer, just stared into my eyes as if she was expecting me to be angry with her. 'I'm sorry, Yito. I don't see... So you don't remember the first time, but since... I mean... You're being monitored. You told me. What does the first time matter?' Still she didn't speak, and still she stared into my eyes. My mind scrambled, then raced. 'Oh my God... You're not, are you? You don't remember being tested and you're not being monitored. This whole HIV thing. It's based on a single letter from a bitter woman who was dying of AIDS. And now that you've found out she lied to you about being your mother and about how you caught HIV, you're wondering if she also lied about your having it at all. To punish you. That's it, isn't it?' Yito didn't nod, just looked down at our hands on her lap and squeezed my fingers. 'Right. We've got to get you tested. Straight away.'

'No!' On the verge of tears, she was shaking her head. 'No! I know I should, but I just can't. What if Alice was telling the truth about our being tested and I just don't remember? What if I have HIV anyway? What if I really did catch it from one of the men? Sex with her, sex with me. They never used condoms. I don't think I could bear it. After all this time, to glimpse a normal life – a future – and then to have it snatched away from me again. You can see that, can't you? How could I possibly cope with that?'

Chapter 27

The walls were white, the posters were dire, and the virtues of condoms were being extolled all around us. The whole room looked ultra-clean, untouched. Even the abrasive receptionist looked un-kissed.

We were in a private clinic not too far from St Paul's Cathedral in London. The place was reputed to be discreet and friendly, and although we were there for Yito, I wasn't just an observer. It had needed more than a few days of empathy, reassurance and determined cajoling on my part to bring Yito to this place; it had also needed me to agree to be tested at the same time. To go through the ordeal with her. But when we arrived for our appointment, we were told we had to be seen separately. It was the clinic's policy, 'to aid openness.' It was also the clinic's policy that Yito should see a woman and I should see a man. After knocking on the consulting room door, I walked in and explained my situation.

'So how long have you been having sex with this woman?' asked the consultant.

'Since August. Just over four months.'

'But always safe, yes?'

'I think so.'

'You think so?'

'Well... Condoms... You know.' Yito and I had become the masters of ultra-gentle, ultra-safe sex – yet still we distrusted those evil-smelling sheaths of latex.

'Mmm! Any unexplained fevers? Sore throats? Swollen glands?'

'Not until today.'

He checked me over, asked all the details, then told me everything about HIV and AIDS that I already knew. 'OK. Roll up your sleeve, please.'

'What are the chances?' I asked him while the needle was in. 'Do we know?'

'Chances? You mean for a man? A single vaginal intercourse? Without a condom?' He pulled out the needle and gave me a wad of cotton-wool to press on my arm. 'Not bad. Around one in two thousand. Much worse for the woman.'

'And with a condom?'

'Maybe around one in thirteen thousand. But are you that one, eh? That's the question.' He gave a quiet chuckle. 'Don't worry. You'll know soon. You probably have influenza.'

***

We opted to be informed of the results by post, neither of us wanting to return to the clinic, nor to be told such news by a voice at the end of a telephone line. It became a race: which would arrive first, Christmas or the envelopes. The envelopes won by a day, dropping through the letter box with assorted Christmas cards – and on the mat they stayed while we picked at a breakfast for which we had no appetite, showered far longer than usual, and generally tried to pluck up the courage we needed. 'After Christmas?' said Yito. 'Let's not spoil the next few days, eh?'

We were standing in the hall, holding hands, and just staring at the two envelopes which looked unnervingly different from each other. 'No,' I said at last. 'Now,' and after picking them up I carried them into the lounge. 'But first I need a brandy.' I threw a log on the fire, then went to the drinks' cabinet.

'Get me one too.' There was a tremor in her voice. And when I glanced questioningly at her, she added, 'I promise I won't drink it unless...'

A few moments later, we stood nervously either side of the fire. 'You first?' I asked, but she refused. So with hands trembling and a sudden belief that even 'ultra' couldn't possibly have been gentle and safe enough, I opened my envelope and took out the letter. There were very few words, just a couple of sentences with some numbers underneath. I read aloud, "I am pleased to tell you that..." My head bowed with relief, and with the evidence in my hand, I wondered how I could ever have doubted the outcome.

Yito managed a smile but her lips were quivering. 'Congratulations.'

'Thanks. Now you.'

While taking tiny, rapid sips of my brandy, I watched her and waited nervously for the moment we had been dreading; her hands were shaking so much it seemed to take an age for her to tear the flap of the envelope. But even as she pulled out and unfolded the sheet, I could see that her letter, like her envelope, was very different from mine. The logo that formed the heading was more complex, and there was much more writing. A look of confusion and despair crept over her face as she scanned down the page.

'What is it? What does it say?'

She was almost imperceptibly shaking her head. 'I'm not sure. It's all about how they did the test.' She handed the letter across, her hands still shaking. 'I can't see the result. Can you?' Concentrating hard, trying to fathom the letter's contents, I took so long to voice an opinion that Yito became agitated. 'What are they saying?' she pleaded.

'I'm not sure. Just let me... But I think you're right, it's all explanations and provisos. There's no result. We'll have to phone them.' Exasperated, I turned the page over – and there, on the back, was what we were seeking. I lifted my head to look at her; her face was set, as if not daring to show emotion. 'It's negative,' I muttered, confused.

'Negative? What's that? Bad? Good?... Clear?' Then slowly: 'Like... I haven't got it. Are you sure? Really sure?'

My mind cleared, finding certainty at last; enough certainty for me to smile, even to grin – to laugh. 'Yes! Really!' And with a shriek and a bound Yito was in my arms, jumping up and down, swinging herself round my neck. Her display of joy went on and on as we jubilantly hugged, kissed, re-read the result, then hugged and kissed again.

'We have to celebrate?' I said after we separated at last and I downed her brandy as well as my own. 'Where shall we go? Which restaurant?'

'Later.' A huge grin was on her face as she took hold of my hand and led me out of the lounge. 'First, let's give less-gentle a try.'

Chapter 28

'You were up early,' said a just-awake Yito as I placed a breakfast tray of orange juice and croissant on her bedside cabinet.

'I couldn't sleep.' I threw open the curtains and let the early-morning April sun flood into the room. 'And now that I know which of Ipomoea's children was your grandmother, I'm dying to find out what happened to her.'

Yito plumped up her pillows and sat up. 'Estrella,' she murmured as if savouring the name. 'A spirit from the stars. I love it. And I hope you don't find anything. She'd only be about 70, wouldn't she? Maybe she's still alive?' She smiled. 'Don't laugh, but I met her last night – in my dream. I was on my Amazon trip; it actually happened. It was brilliant. I met my twin sister too. And Mariposa. Everybody.'

'I had a dream last night too. Well... More of a nightmare. Cochise reappeared.'

She chuckled, then watched for a few moments as I began sorting out some clothes for myself. Her long black hair was dishevelled, some caught up on the pillows, some tumbling over her shoulders and breasts. 'Aren't you coming back to bed?'

'I thought I'd carry on working while I can. Don't you want to photograph me in the copse later on?'

'Maybe. It depends how much those toadstools have grown overnight. Tomorrow might be better.'

'And one of us needs to go to the supermarket.'

'Let's both go. Have a pub lunch.'

'OK. In which case, I definitely need to work now.'

Her expression became mischievous. 'Well... It's up to you. But today is the last green-light for a while. It's back to condoms from tomorrow.'

I hung my head, then grinned at her, and ten breathless minutes later we were disentangling our spent and sweaty bodies then easing ourselves up the bed to sit side-by side. 'Ooh, what's the letter?' she said, noticing it on the tray as she reached for the glass of orange juice.

'From the only person we know who hasn't got Internet. It's from darkest Spain. Gemma. An invitation to spend Easter week at her villa. I think she's desperate for us to meet her new partner.'

'Oh! Bad timing, eh? Will you write and tell her or shall I?'

'I will.'

Yito and I were scheduled to spend Easter week in London. She had several radio interviews lined up, and I wanted to see my agent to talk over all the recent material from Ipomoea's memoirs. Yito put her hand on my thigh. 'Do you think you will ever do a Leo? Run off with a teenager when I'm all flabby and saggy after giving you your five children?'

'So it's five now is it?'

'Of course. I told you. Like Ipomoea.'

I smiled. 'But what about your career?'

'I can do both, can't I? I've got all the time in the world now – though maybe not start just yet, eh?' She finished her orange juice, then thought for a second. 'Actually, I'm surprised Ipomoea didn't have more than five – all that unprotected sex.'

'Probably something to do with breastfeeding each of them for four or five years.'

'So she's still not admitting to killing any?'

I shook my head. Most of the women Ipomoea wrote about openly killed and buried at least one of their babies at birth, "returning their spirits to the forest." Occasionally it was because the newborn was obviously ill or deformed and unlikely to survive, or because the woman had given birth to twins, but most often it was simply that the new mother felt unable to cope. But according to Ipomoea, she herself raised all of her babies – and the youngest was Yito's grandmother.

'But Ipomoea's five were probably all conceived with different fathers,' I said. 'Are you going to copy that bit as well?'

Yito rested her head back on her pillow and gazed at me. 'And lose all this? What could possibly be better than everything we have here?' And with lips still wet from orange juice, she put her hand behind my head, pulled my face to hers, and gave me a sweet and sticky long, long kiss.

***

The office phone rang and Yito picked it up, her squeals of delight telling me everything I needed to know. 'So when are you leaving?'

'September. And I'll be away three months they say.'

'Congratulations,' I said, doing my best to look pleased for her. She looked so happy.

'There's more. I've got a shock for you. They're planning on broadcasting the programme about eighteen months from now – and they think it would be absolutely brilliant if you could publish your book about Ipomoea around the same time and perhaps say something about her in the programme. Can you do that?'

I sucked in breath. 'It's tight, but possible – and they're right, it is a brilliant idea. Good job I'm not coming with you after all then.'

Her smile was weak. 'I still have another problem though.'

'What?'

'They want me to persuade Noo to come to the Amazon with me.'

'I thought they said "no passengers".'

'Red... Besides, she'd hardly be a passenger, would she? She could make all the difference. I guess I'm going to have to swallow my pride.' There was an embarrassed smile on her face. 'Is that too hypocritical of me?'

***

'No. Sorry.'

'But the program needs you. How else will I know how to find them?'

'You won't know, and you won't find them. But that's not my problem. And it won't be your problem either if you take my advice and don't go.'

'But you always said that you were going back one day. Come with me. It will never be easier.'

'"Easier" doesn't come into it. One day I shall go back. But not now. Not until I can.'

'When then?'

'I don't know. But not yet.'

On the grounds that she had a lot of Wiccan work to do that day, Noo had asked to meet us in the glade. This we had done, humouring her still further by wearing nothing but her cloaks while there. But when Yito finally dared to mention the TV company's proposal, Noo's response was immediate: she didn't want to appear on television; she certainly didn't want anybody to know what had happened at Yito's birth; and she didn't want to lead anybody to her family in South America. 'They went there to escape.' She felt equally negative about my writing a book about Ipomoea: 'Her spirit is free. And wherever it goes next, it matters little to anybody what it once did inside a woman called Ipomoea. Besides, there's nothing I can tell you.'

'Of course there is. How she died would be a start.' And when Noo looked as though she was going to refuse to answer yet again, I added: 'Was it a stroke perhaps? A series of strokes?'

Noo looked from me to Yito and back again. Then she shrugged her shoulders. 'Well if you know, why ask? It was a stroke, yes. Two of them. How did you know?'

'A lucky guess. And where was she buried? In the Park? Can we see where?' Again she hesitated. 'Come on, Noo. What does it matter? Here, near the glade? Near the Mansion?' She still wasn't responding. 'Where else? In one of the lakes?'

'There. You see. You don't need me. Just guess.'

Yito glanced at me and took over. 'But we do need you. You're the only person who really knows all the answers. You must do. Like... Take John Doberfield. I know what you told us last time we asked, but you didn't know us then. You probably didn't trust us. But I really, really don't believe he committed suicide. And... OK, so I never knew him, and I suppose I can't really trust anything Alice told me about him either, but... I still can't believe he did all those terrible things to that orphan girl that Blakely told us about.'

Not answering, Noo just stood facing us, looking uncomfortable, so Yito continued, 'Come on, Noo. I'm your daughter. You can trust me.'

Noo looked skywards, then sighed. 'Look... Yito... John did commit suicide – OK? I can't tell you anything different. But you are right about the other thing. Of course you're right. He didn't harm that orphan girl. He never even met her. That was just Janus being Janus. He hated John and wanted everybody else to hate him too. But John would never hurt anybody. He was a strong man, and he would stand his ground – but I never ever saw him use violence in any way. It just wasn't in him.'

'So why did he commit suicide?' I asked. 'And what did happen to the orphan-girl?'

Noo looked down at the ground and scuffed leaves with her feet. Then she looked up at us again. 'Why else? His spirit wanted to move on. Only it knows why. And as for the orphan girl, I've no idea what happened to her. Her body was never found. Maybe she's not even dead.' Suddenly, she waved her hands in the air. 'Don't sit there. I've just purified it for High Beltane tonight.'

I had without thinking perched myself on the edge of the stone altar. I quickly stood and apologised. 'High Beltane? Tonight?'

Yito answered for her. 'Of course! May Day! I'd forgotten. The celebration of fertility. High Priest and Priestess are supposed to have sex during the ritual.' She looked at Noo. 'But do you? Most covens chicken out, don't they?'

Noo chuckled. 'Not us. First all the others do their stuff, then High Priestess and Priest. It's almost like being back in the jungle.... You seem to know a lot about Wicca.'

'Are you surprised? All my parents, real and false, have been Wiccans: High Priests and Priestesses, no less.'

Noo looked from one to the other of us, her manner relaxing. 'Well, to be honest with you, the whole High Priestess thing was a bit of an accident. And a bit of a fraud. I only initiated because John was the High Priest.' Her expression became coy. 'He really was very beautiful. I was young, and beliefs seemed – I don't know – flexible. Then, when Alice ran off three years later, I was the only woman left in the coven. So John made me his High Priestess. Taught me everything.'

Yito was frowning. 'So... Tonight... You... And Blakely.'

'If he can manage it, yes.'

'In front of the rest of the coven?'

'Of course.' She glanced at both of us. 'None of the others know who he really is, you know. He always wears a mask, and even when it's warm he keeps his cloak on, mainly because he likes to see but not to be seen.'

I began looking around the glade. 'When you say "all the others do their stuff"... What do you mean? And where do you do it all? In the house? Not in this mud, surely.'

Noo came over to the stone altar and began stroking it. 'On here, when the weather lets us. One of our coven is a stonemason. He made it specially. See the shape?'

'Reminds me of an extracted tooth,' I said as Noo moved me out of the way.

'Tooth? Ceremonial sex, that's what it's for.'

'But you can't get the whole coven on here.'

She laughed. 'It's a ritual, not an orgy. Of our own invention. The fantasy was Janus's, but I choreographed it. Made it seem Wiccan. It's one of my best. It's ordered. Symbolic.' She grinned at me. 'Maybe you don't know, but Wiccans believe that sexual joining generates great positive energy that can then be harnessed.'

'But...'

'Isn't it obvious? One woman at a time, on her back, legs either side of the V. Oldest first, youngest last. And for each woman the men queue, again with the oldest first and youngest last. Twenty-nine thrusts, the days in the lunar cycle – we chant the numbers. That's all each man is allowed with each woman. Penetration is best but if a man can't, he just simulates.'

'Does Janus join in with this? Or you, with the other men?'

Noo shook her head. 'We just chant the numbers and watch. Janus enjoys that. It helps him with his bit, later on.'

Yito was frowning. 'But he's so... I can't believe that you and he...' Suddenly she looked panicked. 'Oh my God! When did this start? The first time, I mean. What year?'

Noo clapped her hands and laughed. 'Ooh, I know what you're thinking. You're thinking fathers and sperm again aren't you? You're worried that part of you might be Janus. Ha! And you don't like the idea – right? Well listen to me Yito. Men feed us, that's all. Their milk keeps us healthy, gives us energy, nothing more. No part of a baby is theirs.'

'I know that's what you believe...'

'Because it's true.'

'I'd still like to know...'

'OK. Let me tell you. After your and your sister's spirits entered me, I collected the milk of ten men before you were born. Ten! I'm proud of that. And you should thank me. Why else do you think you are so healthy and beautiful? What does it matter which men they were?'

I tried a different approach. 'So there were ten. OK. But which man gave you the most milk while Yito was inside you? John?'

'By a long way.'

'And Janus...?' Yito and I asked simultaneously.

'You really don't like the idea, do you? Either of you?' Noo smiled, as if playing with us. She looked from one to other of us again. 'OK. Relax. Janus didn't come into the valley until 1983, after you were born, soon after Alice had run off with you, Yito. He was a young policeman, sent to interview us. There had been all sorts of rumours in the village about the things we did – most of them probably true.'

'Did he arrest anybody? John, perhaps, for producing his own milk in front of the class? Blakely told us about that. I guess John was trying to convince you all that sperm existed.'

Noo smiled to herself. 'No chance. And of course nobody was arrested. Back then, Janus was easy to control. But his visits did scare all the Wiccans away. Except John. And me – waiting for my passport. Nothing was the same after that though. We couldn't keep Janus away from the valley. Then, when John died and I started recruiting, building up a new coven... Well, Janus knew nothing about Wicca – still doesn't – but he really liked the idea of being a High Priest. Especially at High Beltane...'

Yito suddenly looked angry. 'You mean... You chose to stay here, to build up a new coven with Janus, instead of going to South America to join your baby and your family?'

'Now don't you start judging me again Yito. I didn't choose, because I had no choice. And I didn't re-build the coven for Janus, I did it for John. His spirit is still here, you know. In the valley. In this glade. Every ritual. He watches me do all the things he taught me. Keeps me company during all the preparation. Makes sure I do everything right. I do it all for him, not for Janus.'

'But your baby. Your family.'

Noo stared at her daughter. 'Didn't you hear me? I had no choice.'

'Of course you had a choice.'

Now Noo shouted. 'No! I had no choice.'

An awkward silence fell, Yito probably regretting the past few moments but seeing no way back. In the end it was Noo who adopted the conciliatory role. 'Look... Go, both of you. I have loads to do before tonight – and John would say that I can't purify anything with non-Wiccans here. But come back soon, please. When I'm not so busy. When we're all calmer. I really would like to know both of you better.' Suddenly, a look of concern flooded her face. 'And please listen, Yito. The jungle is a dangerous place for those who don't belong there. I know that your flesh and blood is mine, but your spirit was last an English Caballito in this quiet valley. It might never have experienced jungle dangers, not in any of its previous lives. Remember that. Take my advice – don't go on this trip.'

Chapter 29

'Yes, it was good. Didn't enjoy the Yellow Fever vaccination much, but the rest… Especially last night. They took me to a fantastic little fish restaurant in Soho. We must go sometime. You'll love it.'

'How many of them?'

'Oh just the Producer and the Researcher. Plus the "camera crew" who are coming with me to the Amazon, of course. They're a husband and wife team, did I tell you?'

'And did you get on?'

'Oh, well enough, I suppose. Though there seemed a bit of tension in the air to me.'

Yito had been in London for three days, and for once I had not gone with her, wanting to press-on with finishing Ipomoea's memoirs; as the unused pieces grew fewer, I was speeding up. Yito came over to me, sat on my lap, and we kissed and said how much we had missed each other. 'So how did you get on?' she asked.

'OK, I guess. At least I've found out why they left the jungle. But it's not cheerful. Your grandmother's dead, Yito. She died quite young. Just before Ipomoea decided to leave. Everybody was dying. Some sort of plague. Here, look at this.' I displayed a partly-reconstructed paragraph on my computer screen.

> With dreadful speed, a raveno... army of the most vicious of spirits invaded our forest. Just like the grotesque v... seemed to be avengers, the spirits of enemies past that my people... killed. But unlike the vultures, t... spirits have no visible form a... healthy not the dying. Even the st... of our men ... women w... o resist. Suddenly, death was everywh...

'And you think these "avengers" are a disease?'

'What else? Measles, Pneumonia, Small Pox... Take your pick, or even several. And it's really virulent. Look... It killed your grandmother.'

> ...y children - Estrella - still ... her. She had been abandoned by ... River of the Caimans. Her face and ... appetite. Huddling in the sh...e, she complained that all brightness hurt her eyes. And every time she coughed, blood filled her mouth and dribbled down her chin.
>
> ...fever and ...y. 'Not the vultures,' she kept mumbling ... distant caiman's eyes glowed red in the moonlight, my... coughed, spattering me with ...r blood, until with her last breath her spirit left her to return to its home among the stars. From there it watched as Capuchin and I placed her cast-off body in a hollow tree, safe from vultures' reach.

Yito's eyes were moist when she finished. 'So what do you think? There's been first contact and the diseases have spread faster than the news?'

'Probably a new evangelical post somewhere. A few Christian missionaries to do the praying plus a load of already converted Indians to do the dirty work.'

'Dirty work?'

'You know... To go into the forest, make the contacts, risk getting shot, tell the hunters how wonderful life is at the mission – and in the process pass on just about every bloody disease known to the civilised world. It was genocide. They may as well have mown your grandmother and her people down with a machine gun.'

Yito read the sheet again, and this time real tears formed. 'How old do you think she was when she died?'

'Estrella? In her mid- to late-thirties, I would say.'

'So young.' Yito read the sheet again, then stood to go over to the office-window to gaze wistfully out at the huge Horse Chestnut tree, it's canopy laden with still-green conkers. She turned and faced me. 'Didn't they have any medicine? You know, bush medicine or something. Weren't there any… What are they called? You know, the medicine men, witch doctors… What's the posh name?'

'Shaman? Not according to Ipomoea. Their attitude to illness is what I would call "biological": you get ill, you put up with it, and you either get better or your spirit moves on. It's all just totally amazing. And I can't begin to tell you… Learning about them in such first-hand detail like this, it's just so…'

'"Wow?"' Yito gave me an indulgent smile. 'I can see it is. But shall I tell you what I really like about it all? Ipomoea and Capuchin. Don't you think their story is romantic? I mean, they have no ties, certainly nothing approaching marriage. They've had more sexual partners each than… Well, you know. Yet here they are, maybe both in their seventies, friends nearly all of their lives, and still supporting each other. Which reminds me – did you ever find out why Capuchin spared her? That day he killed her Aunt Matilda and the three bearers.'

'Ah! Yes. Not so romantic. Because he had only four arrows, that's what he told her. But then, when he came close, and looked into her eyes – then he couldn't kill her.'

'There! You see? Love at first sight. Well, second sight, anyway. A bit like us.'

I smiled at her. 'You like to think of Capuchin as your great grandfather, don't you?'

'Of course. So what happened? Did they stay together until the end?'

'They did. After Estrella's death...'

Yito held up her hand. 'Let me have a shower first. Make a coffee for me? Something tells me this might take a while.' As she reached the door, she paused. 'Are you sure we shouldn't let Noo in on our secret? That we kept a copy of the torn-up manuscript? It could really speed up your finishing off of Ipomoea's story.'

'And risk Blakely turning up with a warrant? I don't think so. Though I still can't see anything in the writing that need frighten him.'

***

We settled side-by side on chairs either side of the computer. 'OK. Tell me all,' and each holding a coffee, I told her the story I had pieced together.

After Estrella's death, Ipomoea rounded up her surviving children and grandchildren, and set off with Capuchin to "place a large distance" between themselves and the "awful avengers." Initially, the escaping group numbered about twenty, including several adults, but with terrible echoes from the story of Isabel Godin, one-by-one people died of illness. Eventually, only Ipomoea, Capuchin and seven grandchildren remained; the youngest, a girl called Ranito – meaning little frog – being only a toddler. She was Noo's younger sister...

'My Aunt,' said Yito.

... and at an awkward age for fast long-distance travelling. Often needing to be carried, she was too heavy to carry far.

They were two septuagenarians and a gaggle of children, all desperately wending their way through the forest trying to escape from an enemy that they couldn't see and didn't understand. In normal times, such a long journey across neighbours' territories could have been dangerous, requiring great stealth and cunning or, if those failed, diplomacy. At any moment they could have been shot – but these weren't normal times. Ipomoea describes how at some point along every track they would come across a corpse stripped of its flesh.

'Oh God! Not children?'

'Actually, not often. For some reason, children seemed to have more resistance.'

Almost all the corpses were adults, unburied because of a lack of healthy adults to bury them. Occasionally, the group disturbed vultures at their meal, and once...

'Look at this. This is terrible.'

…oman, old like myself, who w… …alive but who begged us to release her… …her pain. She was a pitiful and horr… …ing sight. Too weak to walk or defend… …she had been attacked by a single vul… …re which first pecked out her eyes. …ived and scared the bird awa… …ust as it bega… …earing flesh from her breas… …od covered her body, as… …d ants and flies.

Nubes and I begg…d Capuchin and Mariposa to do a… the poor woman… …ut afraid to releas… the avenger within her into our midst, bo…h refused a… …to hurry on be…ore she died.

The group's progress was slow, due more to Ranito than Ipomoea and Capuchin, and they all began to argue,

Mariposa wanting to abandon his little sister on the trail to allow the rest of them to travel faster. But Ipomoea and Noo wouldn't hear of it

'It's always Mariposa,' said Yito. 'He comes across as so heartless.'

'I know. But Ipomoea – and your mother… Look!'

Nubes stoically carried her little sister the most.

Then Capuchin began to show the first signs of illness: "twice my old friend stumbled and once he fell, laughing at his clumsiness, breathlessness and incessant coughing." At first they blamed it on his age, until his "skin began to glow red" and then "blood appeared in his mouth."

Mariposa insisted they had no choice: "'He carries inside him the very spirit we are trying to escape, Grandmother. He was there by your side when mother died. When the avenger left her it chose him. If he dies in our company, one of us will be next. Who do you care for more? Your grandchildren? Or an old man whose flesh will soon be vulture's meat anyway?'" And Capuchin agreed with him, telling Ipomoea:

'Go, protect your grandchildren. My spirit will find you. Then when your spirit is also free, the two of us will take root side-by-side on a river bank and grow into great trees, with our branches always intertwined.'

Yito held back tears and smiled limply, then reached out to take hold of my hand.

Mariposa hadn't finished. He took Ranito from Noo's arms and placed her on the ground by Capuchin's side, saying "Great man, my friend, take my little sister's spirit with you on your journey and one day let her grow alongside you and grandmother." Then he stood guard, keeping Ipomoea and Noo away from her. It was the last act:

Amidst all the horrible shouting and Ranito's crying, none of us noticed that Capuchin closed his eyes and slumped to his side. When we saw ... nicked and ran into the forest until, short of breath, I asked them,

...uchin die?' Nubes asked, her eyes wide in terror. 'Did the avenger ...ack one of us? Did anybody see? Did anybody feel anything?'
'Ranito was the nearest,' said Rio with his still high voice. '... her, wouldn't it? Not us?' He glanced like a frightened mouse ... and back again. 'Grandmamma? It would, wouldn't it? Attack her?'

... Dark shapes were circling beneath the dist... ...utes later, between the forest sounds of rustling leaves, raucous insects, screeching monkeys, we dimly heard a small child scream and shriek, then stop

Chapter 30

Noo laughed in disbelief when Yito and I spread the largest scale map of the Envira region we could find over the coffee table in her lounge. And it was a daunting sight: a vast sea of green with endless meandering rivers; tributaries joining tributaries *ad infinitum* until eventually they form a river that flows into the Amazon itself.

'It's not quite as bad as it looks,' I said, 'because we do have a starting point. Ipomoea and the rest of you arrived on the south bank of the Tarauacá River at a place just two days' walk west of where the Tarauacá joins the Envira.'

'We did? And how do you know that?'

'The TV company have been doing some research and found that the Consulate in Cayenne has notes filed away about you. Evidently Ipomoea told the Consul something of your journey out of the jungle. There was a small mission by the river, run by nuns, which Ipomoea said wasn't too far from Envira village itself. So everybody reckons that puts the place where you arrived at the river about here,' and I jabbed my finger at a position on the map.

'I remember arriving at the big river,' said Noo at my side, peering at my finger-tip. 'But how does that help?'

'Because we know that when you set off from your home area, you walked North for around three weeks.'

'Ipomoea told the Consulate details like that?'

'She did. So the next step is to work out how far you walked in total and work that far south from the Tarauacá river. How far would you say you walked in a day? Two kilometres? Five? Ten?'

Noo turned her head and laughed gently into my face, the stale smell of coffee on her breath mingling with a musky but just-pleasant odour from somewhere on her as-usual naked body. 'You don't measure jungle distances in kilometres. You measure them in days.'

'I know, but try.'

With a sigh, Noo turned back to the map. 'I remember we followed the River of the Caimans, always going downstream, always to our right.'

'So this tributary of the Tarauacá is the one you called River of the Caimans.' I traced it with my finger.

'But sometimes we had to trek through the forest itself – if the trees and bushes were too thick on the river bank, or we had to cross a wide stream. Travelling was difficult. We moved slowly. Mainly because my little sister...' Noo looked across into Yito's eyes, then into mine. Hers were watering – and suddenly she grew angry. 'This is stupid. A waste of time. You won't find them, Yito. You can't. You shouldn't even try.'

'I might find them.'

'No! You won't.'

'Why not?'

'Because...' Noo stalked away and disappeared into the kitchen, and when she came back she was carrying a single cup of steaming black coffee. 'If you want one, help yourselves.'

We declined. 'Why won't I find them?' repeated Yito.

'Why? The jungle is a huge place. A dangerous place. And they might not even be where you look. They might not have tried to return to where we used to live, or they might have tried but failed. Got lost. Died. Been shot.' Her hand was shaking so much she slopped some coffee on the map as she placed the cup on the table.

I glanced a warning at Yito which she understood, and for Noo's benefit she smiled and gave a carefree little laugh.

'Look, it doesn't matter that much whether we find them. Most of all, the camera crew want to film me returning to the jungle home of my family and ancestors – and that's what we're going to try to do. We just need somewhere to aim for. If we succeed then it's great, and if my twin sister, and Mariposa, and the others are there then the story's absolutely incredible. But if they're not...' She shrugged. 'It still makes a good story. Good television.'

Noo seemed distracted, focussing on the distant wall. Suddenly, she swung round to Yito. 'OK. If you just want somewhere to aim for, follow the River of the Caimans upstream. Use a motor boat. Make it easy. Check out every muddy bay on the right with a small river flowing in. There are loads, but look for one with five huge Brazil Nut trees in a perfect row and an orchard of Sweet Orange trees all around them.' She sighed. 'I never saw another place like it in all of the jungle. Those trees arranged like that. All those nuts and sweet fruit in one place. Fat Agouti and Capuchin Monkeys to shoot. Swarms of huge brightly coloured butterflies feeding from the mud. I so loved visiting that place as a child. And later my mother died there and we placed her body in a hollow tree. My spirit still flies there while I'm asleep, and one day I'll return there to stay. Then I'll die happy and my spirit can move on to its next life.'

'Now why didn't you just tell us that earlier?' I said, unable to keep a note of irritation from my voice.

Noo looked up at me with her dark eyes wide and her full lips parted. 'Because you and I, Red... Do we really want Yito to die there as well? And so young?'

Chapter 31

'It's no wonder Ipomoea had a stroke. It's just argument, argument, argument between her and the grandchildren.'

Yito, kneeling on the office floor, threw up her hands and gave a scream of exasperation. 'Not now, Red. I'm on the verge of a stroke here myself.' With her departure date just days away, almost everything was panicking her. 'I'll never learn how to use all this in time.' A parcel had arrived: a pocket-sized digital camera with 15x optical zoom; a mini solar-powered battery charger; neat little waterproof cases for them both that could hang from the belt; and innumerable memory cards.

With a grin, I went over to join her and help pore over the instruction manuals. An hour or so later she had calmed down, experimented, and found everything was easy. 'It is fantastic,' she said eventually. 'I could stay in the jungle for years and take a million photographs without ever going near a power socket if I wanted.' She looked at me and smiled. 'So... Now you can tell me. What were they arguing about? Still money and returning home?'

I nodded. I had dealt with all the fragments that were written in Ipomoea's immaculate italics. Now I was trying to make sense of the hundred or so written in her much less legible scrawl which, if my hunch and Noo's endorsement were to be believed, were produced after her first stroke and before the one that killed her.

'What I don't understand,' said Yito, 'is why Ipomoea had such control over the money.'

'I'm not sure I do either. I mean, I know none of the grandchildren were eligible for Trust money in their own right until they were 25 – but surely Mariposa at least was older than that by this time.

'Maybe Ipomoea deliberately didn't tell him his rights, and John Doberfield went along with it. She obviously didn't want them to go back to South America, not before she died, anyway. And once she had died, John made sure they had the money, passports and everything they needed. Have you fixed the year yet? It must be nearly 1983.'

'Not yet. But from the way Ipomoea is phrasing everything, she's writing in real-time now. This scrawl is much more a diary than memoirs.'

***

'Here it is,' I said, holding up the small fragment of paper. 'The last piece. Do you want to do it or shall I?'

With scissors and glue-stick, Yito did the honours and silently read the result. Then she shrugged and handed the sheet to me. 'I guess it makes sense enough. Can't be long before my birth.'

I read enough to get the gist:

'And it can't be that long to Ipomoea's death, either. Not if she doesn't write any more.' We loosely rested our arms round each other's waists and looked at the scrappy piece of paper as fondly as if it were a new-born child. 'Right, I'm going to open that bottle of champagne.'

'Pour me a quarter glass,' she said as I disappeared into the kitchen. But when I came back into the room she was waving a large envelope and looking mischievous. 'You'd forgotten, hadn't you? So had I. All those really tiny fragments. We haven't actually finished.'

She was right. I had forgotten, but pretended I hadn't. 'Ah! I decided ages ago not to bother with those. They'll just fill gaps and tell us nothing new. It's not worth the effort. I should just get on with writing my reports and the book now.'

***

'Go find your family,' I said as our farewell hug and kiss at the drop-off zone at Gatwick Airport came to a lingering end. 'Make a great TV program and take lots of fantastic photographs. I'll see you at Christmas.'

'And you go write a brilliant book about my great grandmother.' Then she hesitated. 'Are you sure you don't want to come in and meet Simon and Jessica at check-in?'

I wavered, but in the end decided it wasn't worth the time trying to park the car. 'And if I go now I might even beat the rush hour on the M25.'

'OK, you go then.' And after one last kiss and hug she added: 'Right. No last words.'

Those were always our last words when we parted.

Chapter 32

Yito and I had agreed to keep in touch by text until she moved out of cell-phone range in deepest Brazil, and in the week after we parted she sent me three SMS messages: one from Miami to say she'd arrived in the States; a second from Eduardo Gomes International Airport in Manaus to say she'd arrived in Brazil; and a third a few days later confirming that she and her companions had met with 'the woman from FUNAI.' They now had in their hands a permit to enter the rainforest to the south-west of Envira 'for the purpose of making a television programme' about the home of Yito's ancestors.

Contacting FUNAI – Fundação Nacional do Índio, the Brazilian government's Indian affairs department – had probably been over-cautious on their part. The area they were to visit was neither a Terra Indígena reservation nor thought to contain remnants of any isolated tribes; any Indians they met should be immune to the most common diseases of the developed world.

Each text that Yito sent me ended with 'c u in 3m, luv, Y' just in case it was her last, and after her message from Manaus, I was convinced that it would be.

***

The large envelope containing the smallest and unusable fragments of Ipomoea's manuscript had remained on my desk ever since Yito removed it from my filing cabinet. I had no real intention to study its contents because I still thought I would be wasting my time. But I was equally loathe to put it away because every time I looked at it I thought of Yito.

Coincidentally, I had just glanced at the envelope again when an e-mail arrived, bringing a huge but pleasant shock:

13 September 2003

Surprised? So will I be if you actually receive this. No cell-phone signal here, so Simon decided we should try out the satellite phone we brought for emergencies: one trial call (Simon), one text (Jessica) and one e-mail.

We're at last in Tarauacá in Acre State. Flew Rico Airlines from Manaus to Río Branca, about 1500 km, about 2 hours. At the airport we met up with this Australian guy who couldn't stop ogling Jessica – she is pretty, by the way, you'd like her. She reminds me of Gemma. Anyway, this Aussie drove us in his 4x4 along the BR-364. About 300 km. Sounds like a major highway, doesn't it? But think dirt track, very wide and in places bright red, sometimes dust sometimes mud – the wet(ter) season is just starting. Now we've got to buy a boat, hire a couple of Indian guides and set off down the Río Tarauacá towards Envira. After that, all we've got to do is find the River of the Caimans. Easy! I can already see Mariposa and my twin sister waiting for us by those Brazil Nut trees (must find out what Brazil Nut trees look like!) I know – but a girl can dream, can't she?

Did you ever open that envelope containing those tiny bits of manuscript? I really think you should, just in case. I hope you're missing me madly, working hard, and not drinking too much. Oh, and I hope you're well. I'm fine – apart from the heat, the humidity, the mosquitoes, the mosquitoes and the mosquitoes. Maybe it's thanks to my Indian blood, but I'm so glad I don't react to their bites like Simon. He's covered with big red itchy bumps already, which makes him even more irritable than before. He and Jessica never agree on anything.

Probably no point in your replying. Simon says we have to save the satellite phone for when we really need it, though we still don't know how easy it will be to get line of sight with a satellite, once we're on the River of the Caimans.

So, my lover...

'c u in 3m, luv, Y'

I read and re-read her words then picking up the large envelope, tipped it's contents onto my writing desk and idly turned over some of the pieces that had landed upside-down. They were, as I had always supposed, just gap fillers for the sections I had already interpreted. But then I turned over a piece that immediately seemed different. It was still written in neat but perhaps smaller black italics, but... I rummaged around in various draws and eventually found a kiddie's magnifying glass The difference was unmistakeable. This fragment had been written with a biro. The phrase was strange too: "I died just as the sun w".

As I turned over or uncovered more and more fragments I found that perhaps the majority in the envelope – there had to be well over a thousand – had been written in black biro. And many of them used the word "I" strangely, such as "I kissed me" and "I shouted at me." Then I found "M's club hit I on" – and suddenly realised what was in front of me. In a daze, I sat for a while staring through my window, looking south across the Vale of Pewsey up to the edge of

Salisbury Plain beyond, cursing myself for not looking in the envelope earlier.

The phone rang; a wrong number. I opened a bottle of Merlot and went back to the fragments. Bewilderment and disbelief kept me working on through the night. For every hundred or so undecipherable or meaningless words or phrases, I would find something that bit by bit made me realise how stupid I had been:

neck at such an angle
I's mind was
I thought she was a Muntjac
such pain
arrow straight through
lake, weighed down by
hollow tree, like mother, as she always

And once I was as sure as I could be, I showered, changed my clothes and as the sun rose climbed into my car. Somebody had a lot of explaining to do.

***

'House rules!'

'Sod the house rules, I'm not taking anything off. And you... Put some clothes on, Noo. I'm fed-up with seeing you naked.' I pushed past her and stalked into her lounge. The morning sun so lit the room I was momentarily dazzled.

'My house. My body. My rules.'

'Ipomoea didn't die of a stroke, did she? She went senile and you killed her. You and Mariposa. Him with a club and you with an arrow. What was the hurry? Couldn't you wait until she died to get your hands on the money to go home?'

Suddenly unsteady, Noo sank onto a bean-bag and reached to the table for her ever-present cup of coffee. After a few sips, she put the cup down again. 'Who told you that?'

'So it's true.'

Open-mouthed and wide-eyed she stared at me for an age. Then anger came. She sprang to her feet and strode towards me. 'Of course it's not true. Whoever told you that is a liar.'

'Then the liar is you. You wrote the last part of Ipomoea's memoirs, didn't you? Once she couldn't write any more, and more after she was dead. Come on, admit it.'

'OK, I admit it. But you can't possibly have put my sheets back together. Ipomoea's, maybe. But not mine. I tore them far too small.'

Only inches apart now, but very different in height, we were staring up or down into each other's eyes.

'You should have burnt it Noo, not torn it up. I've read everything I need: the birth of the Caballitos, your burying them alive. The fox. And then Ipomoea's murder. It's all there. All the evidence anybody would need.'

'Evidence? What do you mean, evidence?'

'I mean "evidence." In your own hand. No wonder you didn't want to tell me and Yito how Ipomoea died. My God, Noo. Did it really take two of you to kill her? A frail and demented old woman like her? She'd totally lost it, hadn't she? She thought that her spirit had already entered a Muntjac. And why bury her in the lake? She wanted to be buried in a hollow tree, like Estrella.'

Noo poised to shout back at me, but then the anger drained from her face, and when she spoke her voice was almost gentle. 'You're right. Of course, you're right. But it wasn't for the money, Red. It's our way. And please don't change your final image of Ipomoea. She was a strong, brave and wonderful woman right to the end. She asked us to help her move on. Didn't you read that? She was in so much pain, and had been for months. But she was so determined to keep going long enough to see her first great-grandchild. And just the once, just after the Caballitos were born, she held the twins in her arms.' She placed her hand on my chest. 'Ipomoea really didn't want us to bury them, you know. Which is why I think... Maybe that's where she found the strength to struggle on for another fortnight or so. To help Alice fool us over Yito. So that both of her great-grandchildren could live. That, and to enjoy holding my other Caballito just a few more times. But then...' Noo's eyes began to moisten, and she turned away from me.

'I understand, and I'm not going to judge you Noo. But I do want to know the facts – and I feel really pissed off that you've been keeping them from me all this time. Look... there's one thing I don't follow. It's obvious why you tore up your own sheets – though why you didn't burn them is beyond me. But why tear up Ipomoea's manuscript too? Because it was you, wasn't it? Not her.'

Noo turned back to face me. 'But her manuscript was dangerous too. Think about it. She named names. Described how people behaved in the commune. Even Alice didn't want you to find it, did she? And she told everything about how our people behave in the jungle. How many English would understand our ways, eh? They'd think terrible things of us, maybe even that we were criminals. But... How could I just destroy it all? All that work. That was her life in there, and her legacy. And at first I didn't destroy it. Just kept it hidden away. But once John was gone, and Janus began...'

She stepped towards me and took hold of my hands. 'I couldn't risk Janus finding it could I? Think of the power those manuscripts would have given him over me. And over

John, too, while he was still alive. But what could I do? Not burn them; not total destruction. So, in the end...' Her tone became wistful. 'That room in the old mansion... That desk, where I placed all the pieces... Ipomoea really loved writing in that room in the summer – and I knew Janus was afraid to go in there; with good reason it turned out. Only a few days after I'd torn up and hidden everything – locked the desk – the roof really did fall in and bury it all. To me that seemed perfect. A shrine to her and her life.' Tears welled up, then rolled down her cheeks to drip onto her bare breasts.

I walked away, over to the window, to look out at the forest. When I turned, Noo was sipping her coffee again, holding the mug with both hands, gazing at me over the rim, as if studying me. 'So what will you do now? Report me for killing Ipomoea? Write about how she died in your book?' Then she thought for a second. 'Are you going to write about Janus too? Does he feature in your book?'

'I wasn't going to. He never met Ipomoea, did he? Or... Was she still alive when he came here to interview you all?'

She stared at me for an age, then shook her head. 'She'd just died.'

'And does he know how she died?'

Noo hesitated. 'Look... Red. I don't think you should write about any of this. For your own sake, as well as mine. Janus can be a vicious bastard when he wants. And he will continue to protect me you know. He won't want any of this becoming public.'

'Really? Why? Is it a Wiccan thing? Some unconditional loyalty between High Priest and Priestess? Are you two really that close?'

Noo didn't comment, just began prowling round the room. Eventually she came to a halt just in front of me. 'It's been twenty years,' she said, looking up at me.

'What's been twenty years?'

'Since I milked anybody but Janus.'

'That's crazy. What are you saying? That you and Blakely... You're a real couple?'

'Absolutely! Though these days the sex is only at Beltane. And only then if he can manage it.' She gave me an incongruous smile. 'He gets more of a thrill from hitting me. He can always manage that.'

'So I've seen. Any children?'

'I don't think the spirits round here like me.'

'You mean he's infertile.'

She smiled. 'There you go, talking about sperm again.' She placed her hands on my chest and began to unbutton my shirt. 'He's not here, you know.'

As I grabbed hold of her wrists to stop her, I glanced around the room, looking for anything that could be a camera. 'Are you seriously telling me Janus is the only man you've had sex with in twenty years? Why? That doesn't sound like you.'

'Partly lack of opportunity' she said, leaning her naked body against me and craning her neck to look up at my face. 'He watches me like a hawk. And partly – I suppose – because he said he'd kill any man who even so much as touched me.' She gave a tiny laugh. 'That's marriage for you. That's Janus.'

'You and Blakely are married?' I glanced around the room again, then stared at the door, waiting for it to burst open.

She nodded. '1984. Bath Registry Office.' Then she wriggled herself against me. 'Twenty years. How about it?

Something for you to think about, while you're deciding what to write.' She wriggled again. 'He really isn't here, you know.'

Quickly releasing her wrists, I eased away from her and began walking briskly to the door. But she caught up with me as I was letting myself out. 'OK, relax,' she said. 'I get the message. Maybe some other time. But look… In your book. Why not leave me out of it. Just write that Mariposa killed Ipomoea? He's safe from it all. Janus won't mind that, as long as you don't say he knew.'

I glanced around again. 'Tell Blakely this… I've left copies of the reconstructed manuscripts – Ipomoea's and yours – with three different solicitors. If anything happens to me, one is going to the Crown Prosecution Service, one to my publishers, and one to the *News of the World*: "Corrupt Detective Inspector covers-up for pagan wife over evil ritual murder of grandmother." I can see it now.' Then I left as quickly as I could.

***

'"Can't be assed" you said. Lying bastard. You made a copy, didn't you? So where is it? I want to see those fucking manuscripts.'

'Well you can't. The only copies not with solicitors are inside my head.'

'The names of the fucking solicitors then.'

Having seen Blakely getting out of his car, I intercepted him before he could reach my front door. Blocking the path, I shook my head, 'Out of the question.'

As he stood there on the gravel, with fading pink roses either side of him, Blakely looked manic. His eyes were bulging, his temple pulsating and his neck turning purple.

'You write one fucking word about me and I'll have you in jail even before the ink's dry.'

'About you! Write what? What is this? You never even met Ipomoea. Why should I write about you? What exactly are you afraid of? That I'll say you accepted sex in exchange for not arresting Noo? Tempting, but not exactly relevant to Ipomoea's life, wouldn't you say? Or that I'll say you're a Wiccan? With a Wiccan wife? I take it nobody knows. But that was months after her death too, wasn't it? Not interesting. So relax. I'll leave you out of it – but not for you. For Noo.'

He looked confused. 'Hmm! Well that's alright then. Because I'm not, you know? I'm no more a Wiccan than you are. It's playacting, that's all. I do it for Noo. It's something we can share.'

'How touching. So it's not just for a cheap voyeuristic thrill then?' I shook my head. 'What is it with you and Noo? I keep thinking I understand, then along comes another surprise. How the hell did you persuade somebody like her to marry you? I mean… You, I know: beautiful woman; money from the family Trust; big house; big car. But her? It had to be blackmail, because sure as hell you'd never have got her any other way. And don't tell me she wanted to be the woman behind the man.' I gave a sarcastic laugh. 'I'd always wondered how an ugly Gloucestershire plod like you could rise so quickly through the ranks. Or even rise at all. I knew it wasn't ability, but I hadn't guessed until today it was bribery. But it was, wasn't it? Backhanders at every step, using Noo's money. You and her are *NB Holdings*, aren't you? N and CJ Blakely. "Administration Costs" my ass. And when you actually sell the whole Trust…'

He squared up to hit me, but after a few deep breaths and snorts, he settled for shouting and jabbing his finger instead. 'Jealous are you? Well you can sneer all you like, pauper. But it was ability. I am bloody good at my job and if you know what's fucking good for you, you won't forget it.' He sucked in a mouthful of air. 'But you are right about one thing. I did start at the bottom. But a Gloucestershire plod? Fuck me, you don't know the half of it.' He shoved his face toward mine, his halitosis making me recoil. 'How far would you have got, eh, if your fucking mother had taken you to a God-forsaken place like The Hebrides when you were a fucking teenager?'

Chapter 33

First I chuckled, then I laughed, and as the policeman grew more and more perplexed I eventually slapped him on the back, put my arm around his shoulders, and said, 'It's no good, Christian Janus Blakely. I can't wind you up any longer. Come into the house. Have a whiskey. Let's share a bottle. And while we drink I'll tell you everything Ipomoea wrote about you in her memoirs.'

A few minutes later, we were sitting either side of the kitchen table with a bottle of Jack Daniels between us. Bit by bit, I told Blakely nearly everything I knew about him – and amongst all the revelations, I couldn't resist including with a smile, 'She said you had the smallest man-nipple she'd ever seen on somebody your age. Is that why you always wear a cloak during the rituals? Or why you don't "fuck around"? Nothing to do with principles.'

He grunted. 'I warned you about my sense of humour. You're not buying anything with this whiskey. So is that it? Is that everything?'

'Almost. But like I've said, most of it was about how possessive you were over Noo.'

'Possessive? Besotted, more fucking like. The moment I saw that girl... My God, man, she was so beautiful. And always bloody naked, showing everything. I was fifteen, for Christ's sake. I thought I was in heaven.' He shook his head and had a drink. 'She drove me totally fucking crazy. I so wanted her to myself. Save her for when... Just her and me. You know? Yet day after fucking day, I had to watch her let those bastards fuck her as if it meant nothing to her.' He looked up from his glass and a rare expression of humanity crossed his face. 'I loved her, you see. I loved her then, and I love her now. And I always fucking will.'

'So how did it make you feel, coming back here a few years later, watching John and Noo still together?'

'How do you think it made me feel? I don't know how the hell he did it. He was like some bloody Svengali with the women. You should have seen those evil blue eyes of his.' His grip tightened; so much that I thought the whiskey glass was going to implode in his hand. 'Not content with just fucking Noo, was he? He had to drag her into his religion as well. Make her his High Priestess. They were closer than if they'd been fucking married. Bastard!'

I leaned across the table towards him. 'Made you jealous did it? Jealous enough to kill him?'

His lips curled in a contemptuous smile. 'And wouldn't you just like that, eh? Me a murderer. But no, I didn't kill him.' He caught the expression on my face. 'What? I've told you. It was suicide. There was no cover-up.' He hesitated. 'Now...' his voice quivered. 'Is that all? Is that everything Ipomoea wrote about me?'

I sat back and took my time, deliberately searching his face before slowly smiling at him. 'Not quite.'

'For fuck's sake man. What else?'

'Oh, I think you know. All your worst nightmares.' I chuckled. 'I wondered why, when you got the job of interviewing the valley commune, you didn't arrest John Doberfield. I genuinely thought it was just the free sex, but it wasn't was it? They blackmailed you as well.' I paused as fear spread over his face. 'Laguna. It's all there in Ipomoea's memoirs. How you once had sex with a ten year old. Necessary experience for joining the Child Protection Unit, was it? All that crap about breaking the generation cycle with

Yito. You were talking about yourself, weren't you? Like father, like son, eh?'

His face sagged, losing all colour. 'Shit!' He downed his whiskey then poured another before looking up, his bloodshot eyes fearful. 'What do you want, Red? Money? We've got plenty of that? Or Noo? You want to fuck Noo?'

'For God's sake man. I thought you loved her.' I gave a sigh of satisfaction. 'Look, I don't know what I want. I can't even decide what you deserve. You were fifteen and a naked ten year old girl who thinks nothing of having sex with grown men comes on to you. So does Noo, who nobody could resist. Hell, which of us really knows what he would do at that age in that situation? I'm not going to judge you.' I stood up from the table. 'Yito comes back in three months, just before Christmas. Then we'll talk, the four of us. Decide what I put in my book and what I leave out. But until then, let's leave each other in peace, eh?'

When he stood to leave, his shoulders were hunched. He looked smaller, older. 'Does anybody else know yet?'

I shook my head. 'But the solicitors have letters telling them the important bits to read in Ipomoea's memoirs if anything happens to me.'

'Then we'd better make sure nothing happens to you, hadn't we?'

Chapter 34

Photographer and Camera Crew Still Missing in Amazon

The decision to proceed with an exhibition of the work of the prize-winning British photographer, Yito Doberfield, 20, at the Malpas Gallery, Newcastle-upon-Tyne, on 21 January was not taken easily, said her agent, Beth Ramo of the Ramo Agency, London. The exhibition had been arranged months earlier as a showcase for photographs to be taken in the rainforests of Amazonas State, Brazil. However, Miss Doberfield and two members of Phuman Films TV company have so far failed to return from their film shoot, and their apparent disappearance is causing concern. According to Inspector Gilberto Sousa da Costa of the Brazilian Federal Police in the state capital, Manaus, a helicopter search of the area they were to visit found nothing. Inspector Sousa said, 'We are doing everything we can. But they could have disappeared anywhere between Tarauacá and Envira and beyond. So unless they are still alive and can give us a signal of some kind, the chances of finding them or evidence of what has happened to them are remote.'

***

Unable to speak Portuguese, I left the badgering of the Brazilian authorities to those who could, and waited endlessly for their next report. Long days of anguish alternated with even longer nights of horror as I lay in bed imagining everything that might have happened to Yito, or might still be happening. I retreated into my Wiltshire cottage and emerged only for necessities. Dirty dishes piled up in the sink, dust covered the furniture, soiled washing littered the floor, my beard grew long, and as winter turned into spring, the garden disappeared amongst weeds. The only thing that interested me was receiving news.

***

Missing Amazon Photographer and Camera Crew – Boat Found

Brazilian Police searching for the missing British photographer, Yito Doberfield, 21, and her two companions, Simon Grace, 39, and his wife Jessica, 34, have located the boat hired for their photo-shoot foray into the Brazilian rainforest. When found, the boat was being used by an Indian farmer who lives in the remote jungle village of Envira, Amazonas State. 'I use it to carry Manioc to Manaus (the State Capital)' the farmer told the Brazilian Federal police. According to Inspector Gilberto Sousa da Costa, the farmer claimed that he bought the boat from a trader who had found the vessel adrift on the Tarauacá River last October. The search for the missing Britons continues. The Brazilian police are particularly keen to locate two Indian guides that the group are reported to have hired in Tarauacá before setting off on their journey downriver.

***

From Spain, I received a card of sympathy and hope from Gemma including another invitation to spend Easter with her family and partner, but I declined. Instead, I walked where Yito and I had walked, ate where we had eaten, slept where we had slept. And in between I sat in my office, surrounded by Yito's pictures and pictures of Yito, drank whiskey, and waited.

The phone rang. It was Beth Ramo. 'Sorry, Red. I'm going to put a damper on your Easter. Listen. I've just heard from the Producer at Phuman Films. The Brazilian Police have made an arrest in connection with the disappearances.'

'Who? The two Indians?'

'No. An Australian guy. The charge is murder.'

Chapter 35

Noo swayed along the aisle and stood at my row of seats. 'Can I sit with you for a bit? Spend some time with someone who cares?' It was almost the first time I had seen her wearing clothes.

I moved my hand-luggage from the seat next to me to make room. 'What about that ugly jealous husband of yours ten rows ahead? I'm surprised he's even letting you talk to me.'

'He's drunk, asleep and snoring. He won't even notice until we land.'

I was probably no more than a whiskey away from drunken, snoring sleep myself, but I didn't care. Suddenly, the plane hit turbulence and a minute or so later the seat-belt signs lit up. Noo fastened herself in, then linked arms with me, and as the plane continued to vibrate, she gave my arm a squeeze. 'This is so scary.' she said. 'I mean... We're actually above the clouds, where my spirit came from. Imagine that. It's just so...'

After opening another tiny bottle of airline whiskey, I didn't even bother to pour it into a glass, just put it to my lips and swigged. 'Why did you marry him, Noo? And stay with him? Not go back to the jungle and your family. I mean... I know he blackmailed you into it, over you and Mariposa killing Ipomoea, but...'

'But what?'

I shrugged. 'That's the problem. I don't know. Somehow, I just can't get my head round who knew what and when. I keep getting the feeling that there's something I don't know, or don't understand.'

'Oh, I think you understand well enough.' She looked past me for a while. 'Would it help if I told you he has photographs? Me pulling the arrow from the body. Us burying the body in the lake. He'd been spying on us for days.'

'The sneaky bastard.'

'It was jail or marriage, he said. And at the time I thought there was a difference.'

'But what about the underage sex that he had with you and Laguna? Couldn't you threaten him with that?'

'Of course. Mutual fear and blackmail, that's the bedrock of our wonderful marriage.' She gave me a wistful smile. 'A far cry from "unconditional loyalty between High Priest and Priestess," eh?'

I didn't smile. 'Twenty years is a long time to live like that.'

'Tell me about it. But where in England could I run that would be better than Inchfield? I at least had money, space and privacy there. Now if I really could have escaped to the jungle... But how could I do that from there? Janus destroyed my passport when it arrived and wouldn't let me get a new one. And even if I had managed to get one without him knowing, he would have had me stopped and arrested before I even boarded the plane. At least, that's what he always told me. He thinks he can own me, you see. Possession, that's what marriage means to him.'

'He says he loves you.'

'I know he does. But you've seen the bruises. What do you think?'

'He let you come on this trip. You've got a passport now.'

'For the trial of my daughter's murderer? He's a policeman. What choice did he have?' She looked up at me, her face bright like a child's; so much Yito incarnate that it unnerved me. 'This is the first time my prison door's been opened in twenty years. It's the chance I've been waiting for Red. Now you just watch me take it.'

***

Not only had Noo, Blakely and I booked the same flights to Miami and on to Manaus, we also by chance had chosen to stay at the same hotel, the *Lord Manaus*. But at least our rooms were on different floors.

While grabbing a nightcap in the hotel bar after checking in, I began talking to a short stocky ginger-haired man on the bar-stool next to me. He turned out to be the correspondent who had been providing snippets on Yito's disappearance for the English media. Like me he was staying in the *Lord Manaus* to attend the trial the next day.

'Three months is shit-quick,' he said, slurring his words. 'He'll have done a deal to jump the queue. A bit of money, perhaps. Offered to plead guilty. Bit of diplomatic pressure from Australia. Who knows. He just wants to get convicted as soon as possible.'

'Convicted? Why?'

'So you've never been inside a Brazilian jail then?'

'You mean…'

'Christ, no! I've just written a report, that's all. My God! Talk about medieval dungeons. They're dark, damp, wet and dreary – and boy do they stink. It's that prison smell: rotting food, piss, shit, and sweat. And our guy isn't even in a proper jail, just a lock-up. He could have waited years to be tried.' He leaned towards me. 'Did you know? The prison population here nearly doubled between 1995 and 2003. There's been a crime wave tearing Brazilian cities apart. Governments trying to crush the gangs, get them behind bars.

But the system just can't cope. You see cells built for four people – just four sleeping racks – yet there can be twenty-five people in there. The poor sods, villains though they are, have to take it in turns to sleep. No wonder we keep having prison riots. They reach the point where they'd sooner die escaping than stay any longer.'

'Riots? Die? I didn't know any of this.'

'Well you wouldn't, would you? Not many people outside of Brazil do. The trouble is, just occasionally these riots succeed. A couple of years ago we had the biggest breakout ever. Nearly a hundred prisoners. They tunnelled their way out. But since then...' He shook his head. 'Last April, fourteen killed, some mutilated, during a riot in a Rondonian prison. Only last June, another uprising in Rio. Thirty-four died then. If you were this Aussie, wouldn't you want to get out as quickly as possible?'

'I guess so, but... Pleading guilty to murder?'

'Why not? Ex-prisoners have told me they were treated better after conviction than before. Crazy, eh? And there's no death penalty here. Not even a life sentence. Thirty years, absolute max. But our Australian friend will probably be out in six. Less if he can come up with a few backhanders. They need the beds, see.' He laughed at his own joke and finished his drink.

'Six!' I downed my own drink and slammed down my glass. 'Is he guilty? Do you know what happened?'

'Sure I know. But it's *sub judice*, mate. Top secret – until tomorrow. Though... Maybe if you buy me another nightcap, I might see my way to telling you a thing or two.'

'And if I buy you more?'

He laughed and leaning forward slapped me on the back. 'Then I'll tell you bloody everything. Why not! Line 'em up.'

***

Unable to face the breakfast buffet, I helped myself to a black coffee, chose a table where I could face the wall, and when my eyes weren't closed I stared into my cup. My plan was to wait for the pain-killers to work, force down some food, then take a taxi to the courthouse, all the while doing everything I could to avoid talking to anybody.

A hand landed heavily on my shoulder and simultaneously another hand placed a cheque on the table-cloth by the side of my serviette. The hand I could see was large, it's skin silky-brown. 'I probably owe you money,' a sonorous voice said in my ear. 'I gather you ended up paying for Yito's defence. Will that cover it?'

I didn't even look up. 'Go away, Cochise. I'm having a near-death experience here. The last thing I need is for you to crawl out from whatever hole you've been hiding in and start spouting platitudes.'

He sat opposite me, looking serious. 'Pain is all in the mind, Red. And I have no room for trivia. My heart is crying for Yito. How did this happen? You were supposed to look after her, nurture her, not send her to the Amazon to get herself killed.'

'I didn't send her. I couldn't stop her. And where were you when she needed you, eh? A cheque…' I picked up the scrap of paper, tore it up, and threw the pieces across the table at him, '… does not give you the right to blame me for what happened to her? You let her down Cochise, not me. Where the hell have you been, anyway?'

'Recently? Rio.'

'And before recently?'

'Here and there. I had to get away from England. I was being blackmailed. Students. They were threatening to report me for sexual harassment.'

'And why doesn't that surprise me? Something to do with baring souls, was it? Don't tell me. They had photographs.'

'Of course they had photographs. That was the whole point.' He raised his hands, as if in despair. 'Students, Red, are not what they were. A few years ago, education was a shared adventure. Now it's just a series of litigation opportunities.'

The next moment, Noo appeared by my table, with Blakely lagging behind. I groaned. 'Not you two as well. I can't cope. Please go to another table.'

But I wasn't Noo's target. 'And you are?' she asked.

'Cochise,' he said with a warm and lazy smile, his heart evidently no longer crying. 'I'm part Apache. And you?'

'Noo – I'm full-blooded Amazonian.'

Cochise's eyes were wide open. 'I'm sure you are.'

'No she's not,' I corrected them both.

'OK. I'm nearly a full-blooded Amazonian.'

'And she's Yito's mother,' I added. 'And that – it turns out – is Yito's father.'

Blakely grunted and stepped forward, offering out his hand. 'Well... Step-father at least.'

Cochise refused to reciprocate as his face soured. 'You're the bastard who arrested her. And she was your step-daughter?'

There wasn't chance for Blakely to explain. My ginger-haired correspondent from the night before shouted in my direction then came scurrying over, looking impossibly lively; from the number of tequila slammers I'd bought him he should be dead. 'The trial's off,' he said loudly as he approached.

'Off? Why?'

'A riot. Five of the inmates got their heads beaten to pulp – and the Australian is one of them. He's dead.'

***

Ten hours in bed and three pain-killers later, I was woken by a hammering on my hotel bedroom door. I looked at my bedside clock: 19:02. While pulling on my dressing gown, I staggered over to answer. 'Get dressed,' said Blakely. 'Noo's gone mental. I need your help to talk some fucking sense into her. She's determined to get herself killed.'

In the otherwise empty downstairs bar, Noo was drinking coffee and looking far from "mental". By her side, also looking composed, Cochise was drinking brandy. 'Tell Red what you told me,' Blakely instructed Noo.

'I'm going up the River of the Caimans to look for Yito.'

'You see? Totally fucking mental.'

'And I'm going with her,' said Cochise.

'Then you're fucking mental too. Yito's dead.'

Cochise gave Blakely a pitying smile. 'Listen to Noo, man. What she says makes sense. We should take it seriously.'

'Seriously! Which bloody asylum did you crawl out of? The only thing we should take seriously is what Red's correspondent told him last night. Or weren't you paying attention? Remember? The Australian guy talks them out of hiring Indian guides – "too unreliable" he says – and offers to do the job himself. A few weeks later he sells their boat to a farmer in Envira, their satellite phone to somebody in Manaus, and all their bloody camera equipment to somebody in Río Branca. And a couple of months after that he gets pissed out of his head in a bar in Feijó, and starts bragging about how he slit the TV guy's throat, then stripped, tied up and repeatedly raped the two women until he got bored and shot them instead. There's nothing else to say. Yito's dead, and there's fuck-all we can do about it now except go home and get on with our lives.'

'You, Janus,' said Noo, glowering at him, 'can do what the hell you like. Go back to England for all I care. But I am going into the jungle to look for my daughter. The police never found the bodies, they haven't found a murder weapon, and one thing I learned from your ginger-haired friend while you were in bed with your hangover, Red, is that amongst all the camera equipment they recovered, they didn't find Yito's. So whatever anybody else thinks, I still think there's a chance that she's alive.'

'And so do I,' said Cochise.

Noo looked up at me, her eyes pleading. 'Come with us Red. Please? Let's go find her.'

Chapter 36

'They were attacked by forest Indians, that was his defence. The other three were killed, but he escaped. They'd just reached the Brazil Nut trees. Maybe every bit is a lie, but that's all we've got to go on.'

The boat we bought in Tarauacá was ten metres long, three metres wide in the stern, and sported a canopy over the back half to protect us from sun and rain. But once we had loaded all the spare fuel, supplies and equipment, there was scarcely room left for us. Noo was scornful. 'These are all we need,' she said, holding up a large bow and a quiver of metre-long arrows that she had bought from an Indian trader. 'And even these I could have made. But this one is so beautiful. Exactly like the bow Capuchin taught me to use as a child.'

River traffic seemed heavy on our first day out from Tarauacá. As we travelled past plantations and logged areas of forest, we saw nearly twenty boats, most of them small – one-man or with families – carrying produce. But on the second day, with lush and flooded rainforest on both sides, seeing another boat as we chugged effortlessly down the river became an event.

I should have been excited, knowing that I was about to enter the realms of my boyhood dreams at last. But as I watched the tangled vegetation sliding past… As I glimpsed the occasional bird and monkey… I felt more as though I was at the gateway to a mausoleum: Yito's tomb.

'Try not to see her, Red,' said Cochise, moving to my side. 'It's too painful. Listen to the forest instead. Hear its symphony.'

'You too? But how, when she's here, every moment; taking photographs, posing for Simon and Jessica to shoot film, chatting and joking with *him*. On her way to – what sort of hell? How can we not see her?'

***

'It's a total waste of fucking time. We're all going to catch Malaria or dengue fever or whatever the hell it's called for absolutely fucking nothing,' was Blakely's oft-stated opinion as he lounged in the boat drinking the rum as if it were all his own. Being a minion was proving difficult for him, yet the only way that he or I could avoid being a liability or making fools of ourselves was to do exactly what Noo and Cochise told us, but even that didn't always spare us humiliation. 'How the hell do you come to be so good at fishing with a spear?' an exasperated Blakely asked Cochise one afternoon after the policeman had spent an hour missing everything that swam near him.

Cochise winked at me before answering. 'An Arizona childhood. The perfect training for life.'

Unable to excel at or take control of anything, Blakely spent most of his time either drunk, bad-tempered, or both. Until the rum ran out. Then he was just bad-tempered – and more than a little jealous. 'What are you two laughing about now,' he shouted often at Noo and Cochise. And the first time that Noo stripped-off for a swim in the river, Blakely took Cochise to one side and said in an aggressive whisper, 'Look away, Injun. If I see even a hint of a hard-on in those fucking pants of yours, I'll slice the fucker off. Understand?' Then, almost as an afterthought, Blakely turned to me and said, 'And that goes for you, too.'

'Why didn't you try the "all property is theft" line on him?' I quietly asked Cochise later.

'Red, he is a man without philosophy or humour. And he has an axe.'

***

Once the Río Tarauacá stops meandering south to north and starts meandering west to east instead, there is only one significant tributary that joins it from the south – and that tributary, unless we were totally wasting our time, is Noo's River of the Caimans. On the map, the junction is about 15 km west of where the rivers Tarauacá and Envira join, so we knew that if we reached that confluence we had missed our target. In the event, the tributary was fairly obvious.

Compared with the Tarauacá, the River of the Caimans was difficult to navigate, and not only because we were now travelling upstream. The river soon became full of submerged branches and sandbanks. Often, it was difficult to know what was river and what was just flooded forest. We began using the paddles and a pole to keep ourselves clear of trees and branches and to help whoever was at the rudder avoid obstacles. It was hot and sticky work, and before long Noo took off all her clothes and threw them in the river. And only moments later, Cochise followed her example. Everybody then looked at me. My decision became one of allegiance more than preference.

'Oh, for fuck's sake,' said Blakely. 'Well you needn't think you'll ever persuade me to let my bits be used as fucking fly food.'

An hour later, nudity seemed much more *de rigeur* when the first Indian we saw spearing fish by the river bank was also naked. Noo shouted to the man in her native tongue and he answered. 'Well at least it's the right language,' Noo said to us afterwards. 'Let's hope it's the right river as well.'

***

Noo was very impressive with her bow. As day followed day and we slowly made our way upriver, it was rare not to have meat as well as fish for the evening meal, thanks to her. Usually it was an Agouti, but once a Capybara, so large we couldn't eat it all. Also impressive was that after travelling upriver for a week, Noo had lost only two of her twenty arrows. 'Shouldn't you be dipping those arrow heads in toad venom or something,' I once said to her.

She pulled a scornful face. 'Poison is for amateurs who can't shoot straight.'

Progress upriver grew ever slower, mainly because the boat kept tangling with unseen obstacles beneath the muddy water and taking an age to free. And each day, Blakely grew more agitated and aggressive. 'Two months compassionate leave they allowed me, that's all. I've got to be back at my desk in just over a month. And we haven't even found the bloody Brazil Nut trees, yet. This was such a stupid fucking idea. Another week and we turn back. OK? No arguments.'

Eventually, a riverside Indian told Noo that our Brazil Nut trees were only a day's journey further upriver, and there was an excitement in the air that afternoon as we set about making camp. While Noo and Cochise went their separate ways to forage and fish, Blakely and I set about preparing our small overnight corral. We chopped down and stacked brushwood around the perimeter to keep out Jaguars; built and lit a fire; then constructed a shelter of inter-woven leaves and branches. All things we had been taught by Noo. Even Blakely seemed less morose than usual, despite the ulcer on the back of his neck and the sprained ankle which was making him limp. A hornet-sized wasp had flown inside his shirt-collar and stung him, and as Blakely flapped around in panic his muddy shoes had slipped on a damp log.

'Just going for a dump,' said Blakely as he limped away into the privacy of the forest after we had been working for a while. 'This forest stinks,' he said some time later on his return.

'Probably something you ate.'

'Idiot. I mean this whole God-forsaken forest. All the fucking time. It reeks like a downmarket curry house.'

'Reeks? It's fantastic. It's like – I don't know... Cinnamon? Camphor? Maybe a hint of pepper and cloves? And when it rains, that fresh earthy smell...'

'Like I said, it stinks. So where are they? Why aren't they back yet?'

'No idea. Give them chance. They've only been gone an hour.'

He began to chop branches with his axe, pausing every few seconds to peer around. Then within the forest chorus, I heard a distant stifled giggle, and evidently so did Blakely. After glancing at me as if I was part of a conspiracy, he turned to hobble in the sound's direction. I disentangled myself from what I was doing, then chased after him. The pair were facing away from us, with Noo on all fours and Cochise in full rhythm while kneeling behind her. Blakely didn't shout, just limped in their direction with his axe raised.

I sprinted to try to stop him, shouting warnings at the pair as I ran. Whether he would have used his axe on Cochise, we never discovered. His wet shoes once again slipped on damp soil, his injured ankle twisted and failed to support him, and as he fell backward, the bottom of his spine landed with a crunching thump on a wooden stump. He bellowed with pain and the axe fell from his hand.

First to arrive, I snatched up the weapon; Cochise arrived next and grabbing Blakely by the shirt-collar, pulled him to his feet. Then pushing the hopping and squealing policeman backwards against a tree, Cochise made to throw a punch, but held back. Blakely pushed him away, 'That's it. That's it! You're dead meat. Both of you. I warned you, you fucking Apache bastard. So help me, I'm going to kill the pair of you. You hear that, bitch?' Fists clenched, he made to move towards Noo, but as his injured foot touched the ground he shouted with pain. So slumping back against the tree then supporting himself on his one good leg he swore at her instead. 'Fucking whore! You fucking promised. We're married, remember? You vowed, remember?'

Noo was on her feet, her face contorted with rage. 'Screw marriage. To hell with vows. I kept my promise. For twenty years I kept it. Which is more than you did. You hit me. You abused me. You blackmailed me. And like some pathetic idiot I let you get away with it. But not any more. We're in my home now. We'll live by jungle rules. And if I want to milk somebody else, I shall.'

'Like hell you will.' Blakely tried to walk again, but with another squeal once more sank back against the tree. His neck seemed to be getting larger, as on a croaking toad. '"A blessed estate,"' Blakely screamed at Noo, pointing at her. 'Remember? Made in fucking heaven. Let no man cast asunder. I told you.'

'Your heaven. Not mine. All that life I wasted. All that money on your stupid career. I should have let you send me to prison. I'd have been free years ago.'

Blakely was wincing with pain, his face florid, almost purple. 'Money? "For richer, for poorer," that's what you promised. Whore! To love and to fucking cherish. Remember? And what's the next line bitch, eh? Sure as hell not "Till the first fucking Indian stud comes along".' He glared at her. 'Come on, what is it? The next line? Forgotten it, haven't you? You stupid fucking heathen whore.'

In one fluid movement, Noo bent down, snatched her bow from the ground, nocked an arrow, and fired. The missile went through Blakely's chest with such force, and so cleanly between ribs, that I heard it thud into the tree behind him, pinning him to the trunk. His head fell forward, his knees bent, and once his body stopped twitching, his arms fell limp, as if a puppeteer had just released strings. Within seconds, the left half of his shirt was bright red and the stain was spreading down his trouser-leg. Cochise and I looked open-mouthed at each other, and then at Noo.

Her face was grim. 'I should have done that years ago. The moment he killed John.' She looked at me. 'Time his spirit moved on, don't you think? Give it chance to choose a body that's more appealing next time. Like a snake's.' Then she looked from one to the other of us, as if only just registering our expressions. 'What? I don't care. It's my jungle! My body! My rules! I'm free at last. You two can think what you want.'

Chapter 37

Noo was a veteran at disposing of corpses. In contrast, I had never physically buried anything larger than a hamster, but I confess there were more tears shed that day than while we were burying Blakely. Noo seemed to feel nothing and Cochise – if he felt anything – remained stoic and practical. As for me, I felt more panic than remorse; a burning fear of discovery, of ending up in a Brazilian jail. But whatever we each felt, we all worked quickly. We had a spade and a shovel, the ground was soft, and in no time we were manhandling Blakely's bloody corpse into a shallow grave, then covering him with a shroud of large leaves, and finally shovelling back in the soil. Within an hour from start to finish, the ground was flat and the job was done.

'Don't think about it,' Noo said, perhaps reading my face. 'The forest is full of dead bodies. All we buried was flesh and bone. His spirit has gone.'

'Aren't you worried that his body will be found?'

'We were ambushed by forest Indians. It happens. But nobody will find him. Nobody will come, and the forest destroys evidence very quickly.'

Our overnight corral was only twenty metres from Blakely's shallow grave, and all night long the rain poured, thunder crashed, owls screeched, and frogs chorused. I couldn't sleep, and when the Howler Monkeys began their other-worldly dawn chorus, I couldn't wait to clamber on board the boat and continue on our way.

***

'Come on, Noo. How did Blakely kill John Doberfield? He always swore he didn't. And so did you.'

It was the third time I had asked her since she let the fact slip, but the night before she wouldn't tell me. Now armed with a paddle and a pole, we were standing forward, alert for submerged obstacles while Cochise controlled the engine and rudder at the stern. For once, we were making good progress along a more-open stretch of river.

Eventually, Noo sighed. 'I suppose he didn't kill him, not exactly. It was the villagers; a mob. But it was Janus who worked them up. Told them how John had boasted about the orphan girl and how nothing could ever be proved.'

'You mean he convinced them that John would never pay for what he'd done? Said that none of their children were safe? That sort of thing.'

She nodded.

'Did you see what happened? Was there no chance of John escaping?'

'Oh, I saw all right. We were just sitting there, under the Beech tree. Suddenly there were about twenty men, Janus amongst them. Other policemen too. When they grabbed John, Janus shouted: "Don't bruise him. This has got to look like suicide."' Her voice caught in her throat, but quickly her expression changed from anguish to anger. 'He didn't care about bruising me though, the bastard. He tried to force me to watch John kicking and struggling on the end of that rope. Then they all just sat around gloating and drinking, making jokes about him while his body just hung there. Eventually they lowered him down and 'rushed' him off to hospital. They pretended they'd been a search-party for the orphan-girl, and found John just hanging there.'

'But why didn't you inform on them? You could have gone to some other police station.'

'Because they threatened to frame me. To say I helped John rape, torture and kill the girl. What choice did I have? It all became part of our mutual blackmail.'

'So that's why you couldn't say what really happened to John – until now.' I thought for a moment. 'But what evidence would Janus have used, if John didn't do any of those things?'

'Evidence?' She laughed. 'Eye witnesses, of course. As many as he needed. As many as he could afford or could blackmail.'

'But… Are you saying that it was Janus who killed the orphan girl? Was it all part of a plan to get rid of John?'

Noo shook her head. 'He was capable of it but… No. He didn't kill her.'

'So who the hell did?'

'I told you before. I've no idea.' Suddenly she began waving her arms and shouting. 'Cochise! Left. Go left. There's a fallen tree.'

***

'That's it! That's it!' Noo gave a whoop of delight and excitement as we rounded the bend. The vista was just as she had described. Even I would have recognised it – and I'm sure so would Yito, if she really did reach that far. We moored the boat then waded onto land. Noo ran ahead, disappearing here, exploring there, simply overflowing with excitement. 'These orange trees. They're so much smaller than I remember.' Then: 'Come here!' She was under one of the Brazil Nut trees. 'It's gone,' she said once we reached her side. Looking around, she laughed. 'Of course it's gone. What did I expect. It's been thirty years.'

'What's gone?'

'The hollow tree. My mother's bones. Estrella. This is where she died.'

Tears began streaming down her cheeks, but she was smiling too. And after a minute of tearful cheerful reverie, she walked over to us, her arms wide, still smiling and crying, asking for the three of us to hug. 'I'm home,' she said, holding us tight while looking at her feet. 'Now we really start looking for Yito, yes? And the rest of my life starts right here.' And after a further spell of pressing her naked body against ours, she raised her tear-stained face and gave us a mischievous smile. 'Now, no excuses. After twenty years of just Janus, I need to build up my health and strength. This is how we do it. I want milk from you both. So who's first?'

***

Noo's plan for finding Yito – 'The only way,' she said – was for us to work our way up the narrow stream that threaded past the Brazil Nut trees, try to meet as many of the Indians living in the area as we could, and ask if any of them had seen or heard of a woman who could be Yito.

'Won't they ambush us?' I said. 'Shoot first and talk afterwards.'

'Maybe you. But they won't shoot me.'

The stream we were to follow was far too narrow, obstructed, overgrown and overhung for our boat. So we dragged the vessel into thick riverside vegetation, concealed it as best we could, and prepared to perform the next stage of our search for Yito on foot. 'Are you crazy?' said Noo as I retrieved my small blue rucksack which contained documents and medicines from the boat. 'A bag like that will get you shot. Put it back. Hide it. Leave it here.' So we took only what we could carry Indian-style: Noo, the bow and arrows; Cochise, the axe; and myself, the machete. In addition,

Cochise had a braided fibre 'bracelet' round his left wrist in which he lodged a hunting knife. And hanging down my backbone from a fibre cord round my neck was a foot-long hollow bamboo quiver containing spare arrowheads for Noo. Tied to the quiver was the fire-drill we used to make fire each night, plus a jaw, complete with teeth, of the Agouti that had been the previous night's meal.

***

As always, Noo was leading. 'Snake,' she said, pointing up to a Green Pit Viper hanging from a branch. 'Watch that it doesn't swing down and bite your face.' And half an hour later, 'Anaconda. Over there. But see that swelling in its middle? It's eaten recently, so it's not hungry.' Suddenly she stopped and held up her hand. 'We've joined a trail.' She pointed at a broken twig at knee height, then another a few metres ahead. 'This is how we mark them.'

'How come you remember all this?'

'We learned young and we learned well. We had to.'

A few minutes along the trail, heavy rain began to fall, so breaking off leafy branches we found the most sheltered position available and squatted under our primitive umbrellas. Noo asked me to dig a splinter from one of her heels using the point of one of her spare arrowheads. It was difficult because even by day the rainforest interior is gloomy, especially when it rains; the canopy is so high and thick that little light reaches the ground. Most of the plants that aren't trees are either climbers or epiphytes; huge clumps of orchids or bromeliads, including the occasional Pineapple, clinging precariously to the trunks. The bonus is that relatively few plants thrive low down, which makes walking naked and barefoot relatively easy. But it was still rare to get through a day without one of us picking up a thorn.

Cochise reached out and touched Noo's thigh. 'Visitors.' Two young men were standing just a few metres away with their bows trained on us.

'Don't move. Don't speak. Don't even look at them,' Noo said, as she rose slowly to her feet. 'Leave this to me.'

Chapter 38

'Are you really going to fuck every man you meet?' I asked Noo the next day, after we had helped the two men build an overnight corral, shared a fire and all eaten the Peccary they had killed.

'No. But freedom is still a novelty. And they didn't shoot you, did they? So stop complaining.' But after we had left them, she told us the real story. 'Actually, they did nearly shoot you. They said they'd been watching us for a while, and decided we couldn't be trusted.'

'Why?'

'Because women carry children, not bows, nobody in the jungle has long hair, and not many Indian men can grow either a beard or hair on their chest quite like Red. And there was something else they didn't like about you two as well.' And before she would let us go any further, she insisted that we all take steps to conform.

The easy change was to give each other a basin-cut hairstyle using a sharp sliver of bamboo. 'This is criminal,' I said as handful by handful Noo's glorious hair was thrown on the fire. But all she did was shrug.

'Sensible, though. My hair's been permanently wet since we left the boat. And how many times have you had to untangle me from a branch?' Then she chuckled. 'And soon we'll all catch head-lice anyway and be grateful for short hair.'

Cochise, being a better shot than me, was to carry Noo's bow and metal-headed arrows, but we needed to make a second bow so that I too could look like a hunting man. It took a couple of days to collect everything, then we had to shape and put it all together, using Agouti teeth as chisels, a

Peccary mandible as a plane, and fine bark fibre as universal cord. 'Now the arrowheads,' said Noo, laying out four types. 'Guess which one is for killing people.'

In the end, we decided against shaving off my beard and chest hair on the grounds that such weren't totally unknown on forest Indians and might even give me extra presence. 'And there's not a lot we can do about those things, either,' she said, scrutinising us. 'Just try not to make anybody else jealous, OK?'

'Jealous!' I snorted. 'I'd gladly trade mine for the smaller model on both those Indians if it meant it didn't get whipped and spiked by bloody branches quite so often.'

***

Day-by-day we worked our way upstream and increasingly we met forest Indians. Some groups were small, others numbered up to thirty-or-so. 'They're beginning to seek us out,' Noo said. 'Ipomoea is a legend in the forest. They've heard I'm her granddaughter and want to meet me.' Then she chuckled. 'They're intrigued to see you two as well. Guess why.'

Every group we met, Noo asked if they had seen or heard of 'a young Indian-looking woman, taller than most, who couldn't speak the language.' And for some groups she added that the woman spoke English or a little Spanish, and possibly had a camera.

The people we were meeting knew that there was another world and way of life beyond the jungle. Some could even speak a smattering of Portuguese or Spanish themselves, a legacy of having spent at least part of their lives in a reservation or riverside settlement. Places in which, as one old man told me in Spanish, *"People live where they shit"* and are so crazy that *"They stay in one place. Their enemies know exactly where to find them."* So they knew what a camera was. They also knew about motor boats, cars, and lorries. And they were also aware of the existence of other religions, mainly Shamanism (*"Too much ayahuasca"*) and Christianity (*"Too many commandments"*) and had rejected them all. They had returned to the jungle, we were told firmly, through choice. Because in their opinion naked and nomadic hunting and foraging is the only proper life for a human being. And it pleased them to think that we three, and the young woman we were seeking, had made the same choice. They all wished us well in finding her, but couldn't tell us anything to help.

***

Another group, another conversation – but this time when Noo turned away she was frowning. 'There are strangers in the forest. Men. Wearing clothes and carrying guns. They sound like soldiers – and they are shooting Indians.'

Cochise gave a sharp intake of breath. 'Mercenaries? Here?' He glanced from Noo to me. 'That is such bad news.'

I asked him to explain.

'I heard about such people while in Rio. They're no-hopers. Ex-cons, maybe even on the run. Gangland survivors from the cities' streets. The perfect raw material. Cheap, nasty and expendable.'

'But who pays them? And to do what?'

'Who pays? Take your pick: illegal loggers, cocaine makers, oil or gold prospectors. The mercenaries' job is to find uninhabited areas of forest for their paymasters to use or exploit. And guess what? By the time the mercenaries leave, the area always is uninhabited. *Carte blanche* to rape and kill as they wish. That's their real pay. They live and die for the thrill of it. But here…' He looked around, as if surveying the forest. 'Yes, I can see. River of the Caimans is the perfect artery into the forest from the Río Tarauacá. Once the tributary is cleared, the whole area of jungle along its length can be exploited. Their only hindrance is that Indians live here – and that is easily remedied.'

***

'Yes! At last!' Noo turned to us, her face animated with excitement after talking to a small group we had just met on the trail. 'Yito's alive. And she's in the forest.'

'Really? Are they sure?'

'"A young Indian-looking woman, taller and paler than most, speaks only English or Spanish, and has a camera..." Who else could it be?' Noo peered at me. 'What's wrong?'

'Ah, I really want to believe it, Noo, but... Are you sure they're not just trying to please us?'

'Our description of her coming full circle?' added Cochise. 'Do they know anything we haven't told other people?'

Noo spoke to them again for a while, and looked thoughtful when she turned back to us. 'You could be right. They haven't seen her themselves, and they don't actually know anybody who has. But the story in the forest is that she is travelling with a group of about twenty men, women and children, and...' She hesitated.

'And what?'

'One of the children is hers. That's new. And it's just about possible.'

***

'Stop scratching,' Noo scolded me, slapping at my hand.

It was difficult, and not just because of the head-lice. In the stifling humidity, everybody suffered endless sores, largely from jiggers, a flea that burrows under the skin; also from scratching the bites of a myriad different types of flies. The stings of bees, wasps and ants could cause ulcers too, though the prospect didn't stop the Indian men from climbing trees to smoke out a bee's nest and collect honey whenever they found one.

The three of us hadn't moved camp for a few days because Cochise had become the latest to fall ill with a fever, in his case probably from a spider bite. But although camp-bound we had rarely been alone. Each day a new group would arrive, bringing food, staying overnight then moving on. And today the visiting group brought news that just three days further along the river was a band that had met a band that had "probably" seen the woman we were looking for. It wasn't the first time we had received such information, but as always we would act on the news and set off at first light to try to find them, undeterred that one of the bands in question had recently been attacked by mercenaries – and that three of their members were dead.

***

Noo's name was called by a distant man running towards us along the trail. We knew him well. Darker than most and with a little beard and chest hair he was becoming one of Noo's favourite men to milk. As they spoke, Noo's body language became increasingly excited until, with face beaming, she turned to us. 'This man has fantastic news. Somebody has told him the names of the people with the camerawoman.'

'Does that help?'

'It more than helps. They are names we haven't told anybody: the Indian names of Mariposa and the rest. Yito's family have found her. She's alive. And after twenty years my twin babies are together again. Isn't it wonderful?'

Chapter 39

Across the fire, an argument flared between Cochise, a woman and a young girl; the girl was crying and the mother was beating Cochise around the head with twigs. Then the trio fell quiet, and my attention strayed elsewhere.

Coquettish and giggly, a young woman approached where I was sitting cross-legged on soft-leaves and asked if she could have my milk; I knew those words and gestures by now. I also knew the reply: place my hand palm-down over my groin for 'no,' or simply smile for 'yes.' For her I smiled, and after her tiny squeal of delight and a little skip and jump to stand astride me, I helped her to sit comfortably on my lap, facing me, her knees either side of my hips. Cochise and I had dubbed this the 'milking' position, feeling it was more apt for these Indians than 'cowgirl.' It was the women's favourite way of having sex.

I knew this woman – this wasn't the first time we had camped with her group, nor was it the first time she had approached me and I'd smiled – but previously she had been subdued, even on occasion coy. Tonight she was totally different. Her eyes were sparkling, her body was animated, her manner frisky, and her voice bubbly – and one-by-one she was working her way round all the men in the group who would smile at her: potentially ten, counting Cochise and myself. The Indians had a name for this conspicuous spike of libido that each woman showed occasionally. According to Noo, the name was untranslatable, but had elements of heat and hunger.

After milking me, the woman moved on – still coquettish and giggly – to her next man, leaving me to continue with my meal; I was gnawing Coypu flesh from a bone. Noo, who had been sitting by my side throughout, smiled at me. Then, manoeuvring, she also sat on me in milking position. 'It's too soon Noo,' I laughed – and she also laughed as she made herself comfortable.

'I don't want your milk. Not tonight. This is just to be close. I want to share my excitement with you. My family have found Yito, Red. She's alive, she's got to be. Come on. Be excited. We should be joyful together.'

'I'm trying, but somehow... I still can't believe it's true. If it is, then of course it's fantastic news. But...' I paused. 'Besides, even if it is true, how the hell do we set about finding them?'

'We don't. They will find us. Just be patient. Yito, Mariposa and the others will already have heard that we are looking for them, but not how to find us. So I have told my friend to spread the word that you, I and Cochise will go back to the Brazil Nut trees. Eventually, Mariposa will hear this. I've said that we will stay in that area for as long as we can, until the place runs out of food for us. And even then we shall return there as often as possible. This will work – and in just a few weeks or months, we shall all be together again. Complete. Me and my family. I even have a grandchild. Maybe several. After twenty years of hell, Red, my life will be worth living again. And you will be with Yito.'

Cochise came round the fire to us, glancing at our groins as he sat alongside. 'Are you two just starting or just finishing?'

'Just talking,' I replied before asking, 'Did you really just do what I think you did? I thought we'd agreed, you and I. No pubic hair, no milk.'

He peered across the fire to where he had been sitting, then looked back directly at me. 'It was too dark to see.'

'You didn't need to see. You know that girl. And so do I. She hasn't a strand.'

Still we eyeballed each other in the firelight. 'Red, my friend. A weeping girl? An angry mother? The social norm? They think our milk, yours and mine, is special. Powerful. One day, you also will give in and conform.'

I said nothing.

'If we're going to live with these people...,' he continued, but then his voice tailed away.

***

At the Brazil Nut trees, we chose as our base the place where Noo's mother, Estrella, had once been interred in a hollow log. And from then on, we didn't see another person. 'Everybody is leaving us alone,' Noo explained. 'They all know why we're here – and understand that the fewer people who visit the area, the longer we shall be able to find food. It is their way of helping. That and spreading the word. A woman's family are very important to my people.'

'Or maybe there is something they all know that we don't. We are right next to the river here. If any mercenaries come this way...'

Our base campsite was larger and more complex than our usual overnight corrals, though the basic plan was the same. But the triangular rain-shelter boasted thick poles and a sloping roof of large overlapping leaves, much bigger and stronger than the haphazard inter-weaving of branches and leaves that were our normal more-temporary constructions.

Time passed and nobody arrived. 'Patience, Red. Just think how our hearts will sing when we see her.'

I raised my bow and aimed. 'Cochise. Talk properly, or not at all.' My arrow hit the tree but missed the mark we had scratched on the trunk.

'And you talk civilly, or not at all,' he retorted, throwing his knife, which embedded itself right on the mark.

'Show off!'

'Stop niggling at each other, you two,' Noo said as we all walked to the tree to retrieve our missiles. 'We could be here for weeks more yet.'

'Wait! What was that?'

'Thunder?'

'A falling tree?'

Cochise shook his head. 'Gunfire. Automatic.'

'How close?'

'Too close. Quick, put out the fire.'

'Maybe we should move camp.'

'And go where exactly? Have you forgotten why we're here?'

***

A few uneventful days later, Noo looked uncomfortable as the three of us breakfasted on fruit and partridge eggs. 'Red... Why do you keep looking at me like that?'

'Like what?'

'I don't know. Like that.'

I hesitated. 'OK, it's this. It's been nagging at me for weeks. Why did you bury Ipomoea in the lake? She wanted to be placed in a hollow tree, just like Estrella. I didn't think anything of it before, but being here, really getting to know you...'

Noo smiled at me. 'Let's be honest with each other, eh? It's time, don't you think? You never reconstructed my sheets of writing, did you? If you did, you would know the answer. You'd know all the answers. I think that you read just a few phrases then made a few wild guesses. You didn't even know that I'd described what really happened to John, did you? Or to the orphan girl?'

I hung my head, then grinned at her. 'Did you really? Shit! When did you realise?'

'Almost straight away – because I never wrote that I helped Mariposa move-on Ipomoea's spirit. Why would I? He did it alone – just him and her. With a club. That's our way. And we didn't bury her in the lake, either. She got her hollow tree. Of course she did.'

'So why…?'

'Shhh!' said Cochise, raising his hand at us – then pointing at the perimeter brushwood.

Silent, we all listened, yet amidst the sounds of insects and birds I heard nothing unusual. But as Cochise had proved often, he possessed the keenest hearing of us all – and soon there was no doubt that we had a visitor, or visitors. Despite partial screening by bushes and tree trunks, we saw the perimeter scrub bow in and out, as if being pushed, then pulled. We all looked at each other. 'Is it them?'

'Surely they'd be calling for us.'

'A Jaguar then?'

'Tapir?'

'My God. You don't think…?'

Noo stood and as we watched she cautiously wove her way towards where the brush had moved, then tried to see beyond – until the scrub burst open and people ran through. It was a long time since I had seen a clothed man, and even longer since I had seen one wearing a combat outfit and toting an automatic rifle. Now I saw three, all bearing down on Noo who seemed rooted to the spot. Briefly I also froze until, seeing Cochise slowly prostrate himself and crawl on his belly away to his right, I did the same to my left. Through the branches of the bushes that now hid me, I saw all three guns pointing at Noo while the men looked nervously around them. Without hats and with unkempt shoulder-length hair they looked more like guerrillas than soldiers. My breathing became snatched and my mind raced. Nothing in my past had prepared me for a moment like this.

Chapter 40

From our positions several metres apart, Cochise and I exchanged glances; he gestured at me to stay where I was. Then he picked up a stick and lobbed it onto the roof of the triangular shelter just a few metres from our visitors. As if falling from the canopy, the stick bounced on the roof's overlapping leaves, rattled down the slope and fell to the ground. One of the men reflexively swung and fired a volley of shots in the direction of the sound.

The other two men seemed to make fun of the one who had panicked, the sound of their laughter somehow as ominous as the sound of gunfire. As far as I could tell, they were speaking Portuguese, but I needed no words to understand what they decided: one was going to stay with Noo while the other two searched our camp. In such a small area, it would be only moments before they found and undoubtedly shot us. I looked around, desperate for a plan.

Cochise took his knife from his wrist-band, held it up for me to see, then pointed beyond me. I knew what he meant. Just a few metres from where I was lying was the tree we used to practise knife-throwing and archery, and on the ground at its base lay our bows and two arrows. But I couldn't retrieve them without being seen. With gestures, Cochise told me what we should do. I nodded and with my stomach knotted, tensed for action.

After picking up another stick, Cochise again lobbed it onto the roof of the shelter. The men were distracted, but not long enough. Hardly had I begun to move before they were glancing around the clearing again. I sank back to the ground, shook my head at Cochise, then peered through the bushes. The two men were resuming their search. We had only moments left.

I saw Noo look at where the stick had fallen, then in our direction – and the man guarding her followed her gaze. His first shout might even have been to direct his companions toward us, but his shouts that followed were aimed at Noo. She was attacking him, flailing at him with her hands, kicking him in the groin, trying to push him over, wrestling with him, trying to wrest away his gun; one slight and naked woman against a hefty uniformed fighting man. The other two men turned towards the pair, shouting encouragement to their companion and laughing at his struggles. Finally, he managed to grab Noo's arms, to envelope her in a bear grip and wrestle her to the ground. Once there, once sitting astride her, he began slapping her about her face. Then he began fumbling with his belt and trousers. So did the other two as they moved back to join him.

Mouth dry, heart pounding, I stooped and ran to our target tree, snatched up both bows and arrows, and scuttled back all the way to Cochise. Two parrots flew screaming overhead, but for the moment the men were engrossed. 'Now? From here?' I whispered.

'No, closer. Much closer. Three guns? Two arrows? One knife? One miss and we're dead. Look, we must make sure we aim at different men. When we get there, you take whoever's fucking Noo, I'll take the other two. And for pity's sake, try not to miss him – or to hit Noo. Let's go.'

Keeping low, using what cover we could, we edged towards the noisy group. One of the standing men, trousers now round his knees, was facing in our direction; when we broke cover he would be certain to see us. But for now his eyes were riveted on Noo, his hand working his penis preparing himself for his turn, his gun cast on the ground. All three guns were on the ground. Noo was resisting as vigorously as possible: wriggling, twisting, bucking, shouting, screaming.

Suddenly I stopped moving, and alerted Cochise to do the same. More people had appeared at the gap in the perimeter. Naked people: an Indian man and two women – two Yitos, each with a babe-in-arms. Quickly they were joined by more children, then more women, and more men. All clustered there, looking toward the fracas as if trying to work out what was happening.

Their hesitation gave way to action. Several Indian men ran forward, each nocking an arrow then raising their bows. But they had been seen. Trousers still round their knees, the two standing men had dived to the ground and were reaching for their guns. After snatching them up, they began to shoot. An Indian fell, then another. All first arrows from the Indians missed.

After nocking our own arrows, Cochise and I ran from cover, attacking the gunmen from behind. The man who had been raping Noo was rearing up, trying to pull himself free from her, to reach his gun. But Noo's strong legs were wrapped round his buttocks and she wouldn't let him go. He was punching her, pushing at her, straining to break her grip. When he glimpsed me approaching, he half-twisted towards me, shouting a warning to his companions, his words lost in the cacophony of gunfire, shouts and screams. From just a few metres away, I aimed at what little I could see of his chest; he was almost side-on. Nerves made me miss my mark, the arrow instead going straight through his neck, ripping out his larynx, severing his jugulars. The gush of blood was instantaneous; so was his collapse onto Noo.

Cochise also hit his first target, his arrow just one of several from different directions to find their mark. Face contorted, the gunman slumped to twitch on the ground, his weapon silent, fallen from his grasp. But the third man, despite pin-cushioned by arrows, despite screaming and writhing on the ground, continued to shoot, his aim becoming uncontrolled, wild. An Indian man fell to a stray bullet, then a woman, then a child.

Instead of throwing his knife, Cochise ran a few steps, stood unexpected astride the man's back, jerked up his head by the hair, and with one quick slice cut his throat.

I threw down my bow. 'Yito!' I bellowed.

Chapter 41

Once out of the compound, beyond the gap in the brushwood, I glanced around, my body still quivering. 'Yito!' I shouted. 'It's over. It's safe. Where are you?'

Not only men had died. Inside the compound, a young boy was also dead. So was a woman, and a second woman had a bullet hole through her shoulder but still lived. Outside the compound, I had no idea where Yito, her sister, and the children had gone. All I knew was that brushwood is no barrier to bullets, and stray shots had already claimed lives. I scanned the ground, looking for bodies or blood, but saw nothing. Then I scanned the forest, looking for figures hiding amongst the trees and bushes. Again, nothing. 'Yito! It's Red. Where are you?'

Previously frightened squawking birds had by now calmed or flown away, but a myriad stridulating insects were as noisy as ever, some sounds harsh, others shrill; some grating, some piercing.

'Yito!'

Frogs began to sing too. From all sides came croaks and grunts, almost shouts.

'Yito!'

A new sound emerged from the rest, more shrill, more wailing. A bird? A monkey? A crying child? Turning my head from side to side, I tried to focus my ears through the din, to pick out the sound's direction. Then I ran into the forest, ignoring the tracks, taking the straightest route through the undergrowth towards the sound. Now I was sure. Somewhere a child was crying. Or a woman was wailing.

'Yito!'

One moment stumbling over uneven ground, another pushing away branches, oblivious to the scratches, I ran on until in the distance – in an open glade, between two distant bushes – I saw the source of the sound: several children with three women, all distressed. Two of the women were kneeling by the third who was laid out on the ground, her back against a tree. I sprinted towards them and as I burst through the bushes, all turned to face me in panic. All, that is, except the woman on the ground. Unconscious or dead, one side of her face was covered with blood.

Yito sprang to her feet from the supine woman's side, took two steps, and threw herself into my arms. Nothing was said as we hugged each other. Then she pulled back to look into my eyes. Her face was streaming with tears, but she had been crying when I arrived. A moment later we were kissing, so hard it hurt, so briefly I wanted longer, but again she pulled away, and this time taking hold of my hand she pulled me towards the woman on the ground. 'It's Laguna. We carried her as far from the guns as we could. Something hit her head. There's so much blood. I can't feel a pulse.'

I knelt by Laguna's side, but there was nothing I could do to help. Her hair was so matted with blood, I couldn't tell what had hit her or exactly where, but if it was a bullet I couldn't see a hole. I tried feeling for a pulse – in her wrist, in her neck – but my hands were so shaking, my mind so racing, my breathing so wild, I felt nothing beneath my fingers except her warmth. While resting my palm on her left breast, I searched with trembling finger-tips for a heart-beat. But still I felt no sign of life, not at this spot, not at that...

'Wait!' I said. 'There! I'm sure.' And as I spoke, Laguna stirred, turned her head sideways, and retched, then retched again. And when she turned her head back to face me, her eyes – though glazed and unfocussed – were open. But the sight of me and the sound of my voice seemed to panic her, so I stood and let Yito's twin take over, to hold Laguna's hand and try to calm her, then to try to restrain her as she made a determined effort to stand.

Yito, wiping her eyes, managed a watery smile, then went to help her sister support and walk Laguna as the dazed woman regained her senses, stability and mobility. Eventually, Yito returned to me, on the way collecting a baby that until then had been held by one of the older children. The baby rested her cheek against Yito's breast and looked at me with wide suspicious eyes.

I smiled at the sight. 'Your daughter is very beautiful. How old is she?'

'I don't know. What month is it?'

'I don't know. Noo made me leave my watch on the boat. September? October?'

'Then she's three-to-four months.' Yito offered the child to me, inviting me to hold her. 'Red, meet Caballito Rojo.'

I took the girl, perched her on my hip, and gazed into her panicked brown eyes. 'Caballito Rojo? The red damselfly?'

Yito nodded and murmured, 'What else? But I call her Rocky, for short.'

Rocky immediately dissolved into tears. Yito laughed. 'I told you condoms couldn't be trusted. She's yours, you know. I knew I was pregnant weeks before I… I…' and the sentence dissolved as she gave me an uncertain smile.

***

'They had no ID. Absolutely nothing to identify them. Probably part of the deal.'

By the time Yito and I returned with Laguna and the others to the compound, the mercenaries had been stripped, their clothes burned, and their bodies dumped in the river to be pulled apart by Caiman and cleaned to the bone by Piranha. Their boat had also been found and sunk, along with their guns. No trace remained.

'We hear of them more and more,' said Mariposa with his deep growling voice; he was taller and more muscular than most of the forest Indians. 'What choice do we have but to kill them.' Pausing from lashing a roof pole to an upright with lianas he eyed me and Cochise. 'You two, my friends, are lucky you arrived with my sister and had the good sense to travel naked. Otherwise my people would have killed you on sight long before now.'

Distant thunder rumbled through the forest. The three of us were building an extra shelter which we finished just as Yito, Noo and a few others arrived in the compound. Yito, carrying Rocky, walked over to face me. 'There's something I have to tell you,' she said, looking awkward. 'The two men we've just buried. They... I...' She was watching my face closely; she wasn't crying.

'I didn't realise. I'm sorry. Were you – I don't know – 'close' to them? Or is that a stupid question?'

'Close? Now there's a word. I suppose I was, in a way. Life would certainly have been more difficult without them.' She gave me a weak smile. 'But, you know... It all seemed so simple then. But now that you're here, I'm not so sure. Maybe it's not simple any more.'

Another peel of thunder sounded, nearer this time. I reached out for Rocky. 'Of course it is. Really simple. I'm her father.' But no sooner was the little girl in my hands than she began screaming and reaching out for her mother again, so I gave her back, but Yito immediately passed her on to Noo.

On her grandmother's hip Rocky stopped crying. Noo looked at me, the bruises on her face from the mercenary's fists already black. 'She's an Indian girl, Red. She doesn't understand "father".'

I reached for Yito's hand and led her away. 'I was so convinced you were dead. Right up to the moment I saw you. Even now I'm afraid this is just a dream.'

She squeezed my hand. 'No dream.'

'So what happened? Was it the Australian? Has Noo told you what happened to him? Or were you attacked by mercenaries? Or even Indians?'

Yito waited while a loud clap of thunder echoed then died away. 'Honestly, I don't really know. But I expect it was the Australian. He was such a mistake, all the time trying it on with me and Jessica, and arguing with Simon. Simon and Jessica had some terrible rows too.' She shrugged. 'Then, one morning, it all got totally out of hand. So I stormed out of the camp, telling them I was going to spend the day taking photographs and that if they hadn't sorted themselves out by the time I returned, the whole project was over.' She looked up at me. 'And that was the last I saw of them.'

'You mean they just left you? Or you found bodies?'

'Neither really. I found vultures. Loads and loads of vultures, all fighting around two skeletons and the last few bits of gore. That sight, Red. I still have nightmares.'

'And the boat had gone?'

She nodded. 'Even so... It should have been easy for me to find my way back to the Tarauacá. Just follow the River of the Caimans, I told myself. But everything was flooded, I couldn't tell river from swamp from land, and somehow I just ended up deeper in the forest, and totally lost. Then I found a deserted overnight site – and I remembered Ipomoea's story. The rest you can guess.'

We paused in a rare ray of sunlight that had penetrated the canopy. Clouds of insects flew around us. 'How long before somebody found you?'

'About a week.'

'Were they kind to you? How did you lose your clothes?'

'Totally kind. And I didn't lose my clothes, I took them off before anybody saw me. Ipomoea again, remember? The women who found me…' She chuckled. 'They actually thought I was Indian, that I'd run away from one of the reservations, and that's why I couldn't speak their language.'

'But once you could, or at least could make yourself understood, why didn't you ask their help to leave the forest? Did you try?'

'We were too busy keeping ourselves alive. Avoiding the mercenaries – and a few hostile Indians from neighbouring tribes, too. We had so many close encounters, especially near the rivers, so we stayed as deep in the forest as we could. Honestly, sometimes it was so scary. But it gave me chance to take loads of photographs. From the inside, you know? As one of them. Sharing their lives, their dangers…'

'Where are they? Your photographs?'

She took off the extra-large bamboo quiver that had been hanging down her back. 'Did you think it was arrowheads in here? It's all my memory cards.' And I had already noticed the camera and charger cases hanging from her plaited fibre belt.

The sunbeam disappeared and rain began to clatter on the high canopy; the chorus of frogs grew louder than ever. Then the first drips fell from the high branches and we sought a sheltered spot, under a giant hardwood tree. A zip of lightning and a deafening clap of thunder warned that the storm was now almost overhead. Yito leaned back against the trunk and gave a mischievous grin. 'So... Are you just being polite, or have you really not noticed my new hairstyle?'

I smiled. 'Because of the lice, yes? They're buggers, aren't they?'

'Tell me about it.' She laughed, teeth still white, face still beautiful.

'Well, never mind. It'll soon grow when we get home.'

She didn't answer, just gave an awkward smile and adjusted her position, putting her hands behind her as if to protect the skin of her buttocks from the rough bark of the tree. Her body looked just as I remembered, unscarred by the jungle and scarcely changed by motherhood; just her breasts, turgid with milk. She removed her belt and lay it on the ground.

Inured to the now continual thunder, I took a couple of steps towards her, my throat dry, my palms sweating. She seemed to be scrutinising me. 'Nobody's taken a sharp bamboo to your beard yet I see.'

'Only to keep it short.'

'I'm surprised you kept it. The lice must love it.'

'Head lice don't like beards. The hair's too coarse.' I chuckled. 'It gets the odd pubic louse though.'

She gave a wonderful smile. There were only inches between us. I could smell her, a fresh and earthy aroma. 'I really can't believe that we're together again. That we have a beautiful daughter. It all seems totally unreal.'

Her face turned up to mine. 'And a long way from Wiltshire, eh?' The kiss began gentle and slow, but soon became so frantic it had to stop. 'Milking style?'

Normally, a man examines a site before sitting for sex. A quick check overhead for orchids or bromeliads containing snakes that might fall, a glance for holes in the ground harbouring tarantulas, for wood or stone that could hide a scorpion, for large leaves covering scolopendra. But we were in a hurry, and I was familiar with this particular patch under this particular tree. I had used it before with Noo. So had Cochise.

The rain began to penetrate the canopy, to drip around us as I sat on a cool damp cushion of moss, my back against the tree. A bright green tree-frog hopped away then turned to face us as Yito knelt astride my lap and took control, as Indian women usually do.

***

On the moss, in each others' arms, Yito fell asleep. My eyes were closed too when a shadow settled over us. Noo was standing there, holding a leafy branch as an umbrella. She wasn't smiling. 'You haven't time for this. Word has arrived that there are more mercenaries on the river. Many more. To stay here would be suicide. We must go deeper into the forest. Scatter. Come on, Yito. Wake up. we shouldn't delay.'

Chapter 42

'We can't fight them,' Mariposa was saying. 'All we can do is move away from the river. And we must do it now, before nightfall. So let's go. We've already waited too long.' And after turning on his heels he left to talk to others.

Noo looked at me and Cochise, then without warning threw her arms round my neck and hugged me. 'What's that for?' I laughed as she did the same to Cochise.

'For saving my life. For giving me a life. Helping me to find Yito. Getting rid of Janus. For everything.'

'We should thank you too. For distracting that mercenary. Giving us chance to get our weapons. Your sacrifice saved all our lives.'

'Sacrifice? Oh, the sex you mean. Still not a jungle man are you Red?' She laughed, then winced from her bruises. 'Isn't this exciting, you two? Isn't it wonderful? All the people that matter to me together again. Mariposa's been telling me about this brilliant part of the forest he knows. No mercenary would go that deep. That's where he's taking us.'

'Whoa,' I said, my laugh fading. 'You don't think we're staying in the Amazon? After what just happened? I didn't get Yito back from the dead just so she could be slaughtered by mercenaries. Did you?'

Noo backed away from me with a look of shock, then strode towards Yito who was sitting playing with Rocky on a distant log. Cochise and I followed. There was disbelief, even panic, in Noo's voice. 'Yito... Red says that you're not staying. That you're going back to England.'

'Did he?' Yito looked at me, her face impassive.

Noo sat next to her daughter. 'But you can't leave. You and Rocky belong here, with me. With our family.'

Again Yito looked at me, but again said nothing, so I spoke instead. 'Noo... We should all go back. Life has become too dangerous here. You should return to Inchfield. Maybe you too Cochise. The pair of you. That could work.'

Noo almost exploded. 'Inchfield! I've only just escaped from Inchfield. Don't you know me at all Red? This is my home. The only place I can be free. In England... I was always a prisoner – and I don't just mean of Janus. All those stupid, stupid rules. All that fear, that prejudice. That horrible intolerance. Nobody, absolutely nobody, can be their true selves in your country. They daren't. No. Nothing would persuade me to go back.'

In the distance, Mariposa and the rest were ready to leave. He called to Noo. She shouted a reply then turned to us. 'Look, we can't delay any longer. We must talk as we walk.'

'Only if you are heading for the Río Tarauacá,' I said. 'I was going to use the boat. Take it all the way to Manaus. But if there are mercenaries on River of the Caimans... Well, we'll have to go through the forest, then flag down a boat on the Tarauacá. But that's OK. From here, we'll just head north, always north.'

'No,' said Noo. 'You – we – must all go west, always west. Away from the River of the Caimans. Deeper into the forest. To go north from here is suicide.' And I could see that she was right; so first west, then later north.

After collecting what we needed, we moved out of the compound to follow Mariposa along the trail. As we walked in single-file, I spoke to Cochise behind me. 'Surely you'll come with us, won't you Cochise? At least as far as the States. Back to everything you enjoyed so much? Fast cars?

Good food and drink? Photography? Your fight against censorship?'

'All false, Red. All meaningless. At last I have learned what is important to me. Here my spirit can have free rein. Elsewhere, what happens? I am accused of harassment because I teach the young the meaning of freedom. I suffer blackmail. I end up in debt because I have too many children with too many greedy lazy women. One day, I probably would end up in jail – and for what? For just being myself. As for a cause... If I want something to fight for, what better than the preservation of this way of life?'

Noo turned to Yito who was walking behind her, carrying Rocky. 'You see, Yito. Did you hear that? Please listen to Cochise. Stay here, with us. And you too, Red. I would like you to stay. But if you must go... Please Yito, don't go with him.'

Yito glanced back at me, a hint of anger in her eyes. 'I never said I would go with him.' Then she turned to speak forward to Noo again, 'But nor did I say I wouldn't. Red and I haven't talked about this yet. Look, this discussion is too important to have like this. I can't talk to people's backs, or listen to people I can't see. The forest is making too much noise. Just stop a minute, all of you. There, on ahead. Where the trail widens. Let's sort this out.'

When we arrived, Yito turned to me. 'What happened to your dream Red? When you were a student? I admired that dream. Isn't this exactly the life you wanted back then? What changed? Why do you want to go back to England?'

'I fell in love Yito. With you. With our life together. That's what changed.'

'Aah... With our life. Our life in England.' She didn't smile. 'Listen... I have a question for you. If I insist on staying here with my family, what will you do?'

'Well... Stay with you, I suppose. But I can't believe that you would insist.'

'Really? But suppose I did... You would stay with me. Is that what you're saying?'

'That's what I'm saying. But you won't choose to stay. I know you.'

'Do you? The old me, perhaps. But the forest has changed me – and you, I'm sure – and I need to know something. If we did both stay here... Would you be prepared to share me with other men? Like I would share you with other women? Would you let Rocky grow up an Indian girl? Because there would be no other way.'

'I know. We'd have to be Ipomoea and Capuchin, not Romeo and Juliet. But... Is that really what you want?'

Yito's face slowly relaxed into a smile. 'No, that's not what I want. But I needed to know what was important to you – and you've just told me.' She turned to speak to her mother. 'I'm sorry Noo, but I'm going back to England with Red. Because I fell in love too, you know. With him – and our life together. No, don't pull that face Noo. Look... I don't deny what you and Cochise are saying. There is a freedom here in the forest. And while I was here I enjoyed that freedom. I really did. But... It's not enough for me. I need more.' She glanced at me. 'I think we both do.'

Perched low on Yito's hip, Rocky gave a tiny grizzle. Yito raised her a little and helped her to latch on, then turned back to Noo and Cochise. 'Besides... How much longer can that freedom last? Seriously? These mercenaries and the people who pay them... They won't just go away. They're here to stay – and they won't rest until you, our people, are all dead and every last dollar has been bled from this forest. It would be suicide to stay here.'

Mariposa shouted to us from further up the trail. He was losing patience.

I carried on from where Yito had left off. 'The thing is Noo... Is freedom really the most important thing in life? OK, so maybe English society is like a jail compared to here. But it does have a lot of other things going for it.'

'He's right,' added Yito. 'Call me shallow if you want, but – do you know what? I actually like sleeping in a comfortable bed...'

'Having a house to go home to...' I added.

Yito and I glanced at each other and smiled. 'Getting food at a supermarket,' she said.

'Not being bitten by bloody mosquitoes all the time. Or stung by hornets...'

'Or having a hairstyle dictated by head lice.'

'You're right,' said Cochise, looking from one to the other of us. 'That is shallow.'

'OK! Well how about less shallow,' Yito said. 'I also happen to like books, films, music and art.'

'And I want my children to have a bigger education than the jungle can provide,' I added.

'Bigger!' scoffed Noo, turning up her nose. 'What bigger education can there be than here?'

Yito ignored her. 'And I also quite like the idea of going back to having sex with nobody watching, and maybe being faithful to just one man.'

'"Maybe"?' I laughed.

'Yes, "maybe". Don't knock it, Red. Compared with here, "maybe" is good.' She turned back to Noo and Cochise. 'And I want life to be more secure. If Rocky is ill, or me, or Red, I want to be able to go to a doctor and get help. And believe me, next time I give birth, I want it to be on a bed in a hospital, not on the ground in the rain with a whole tribe of people watching me scream in agony. And guess what Noo? I know this is heresy, but I would actually like to know who's the father of my next child.'

Noo's expression was pure despair. 'Then there really is no hope for you.'

'But most of all,' Yito continued, now addressing Cochise, 'I want a career. I want to take photographs. I can't imagine being happy doing anything else.'

'Is that so?' Cochise hesitated, then reached out and, despite Yito's protestations, removed her bamboo quiver full of memory cards. He held it up. 'You mean photographs like those in here?'

'Yes. Just like those. Give it back.'

'You mean... Let me guess. Rivers and forests. Naked men and women on the trail, hunting, foraging, building shelters, lighting fires. All with fantastically atmospheric lighting: some misty or smoky; some sharp; some with sunbeams through the canopy; maybe some by firelight. Using all the techniques I taught you.'

Frowning, she nodded.

Cochise began to scowl. 'And of course...' Now he shook the quiver in the air. 'Photographs of children. Lots of naked children. And not just naked. Openly having sex with each other. Having sex with adults too. Teenage boys fucking grown women. Young girls milking men. Did you catch some of that action, Yito? I'm sure you did. You wouldn't be my protégé if you didn't. But let me do you one huge favour...' He made to throw the quiver into the forest.

Whether he would have done so or not, he never had the chance. I blocked his arm and wrested the quiver from his grasp, then handed it back to Yito.

Undaunted, Cochise continued his tirade. 'Are you really that stupid, Yito? Have you forgotten about your suspended jail sentence? Take one step onto English soil with photographs like those, and you will go straight to prison. And I wonder what value you would put on freedom then?'

Yito hitched Rocky further up on her hip again. 'Well then I'll just have to go to prison, won't I? Because I don't care. I have a mission now: to show people that being human isn't just black and white, right and wrong; there's more than one kind of innocence. I'm proud of these pictures, and the people in them. They are my people, and no matter how differently they behave they are no less worthy than anybody in England.' She turned to me. 'Let's go home Red. Let's write books. Let's show these photos. Let's see if we can find anybody with the balls to understand.'

Mariposa came running towards us along the trail. 'What are you stupid sloths doing? Do you want your spirits to be moved on? We've had fresh word. The mercenaries are in the forest. They're combing the area. They know how to follow tracks. Now hurry or die. I'm not warning you again.'

Epilogue

One peaceful night in the jungle, Noo told me about a tree. It is an Oak, very large and very old, and located about 30 metres upslope from the Wiccan Glade in Inchfield Park. The trunk is huge, almost fifteen metres in perimeter at the base, and totally hollow, nothing more than a shell. Yet vital juices must still flow beneath the bark because the crown is green and vigorous. Three metres above the ground, the trunk has a hole large enough for an adult man to stick his head and shoulders through, and from there with a strong torch it is possible to see inside. Nestling in over twenty years' worth of wind-blown forest debris is a human skeleton in foetal position with a broken neck. It is Ipomoea – and I have seen her now. So has Yito.

Once we had travelled far enough from the River of the Caimans to be safe from mercenaries, we turned north for the Río Tarauacá, all the while accompanied by Mariposa, Noo, Yito's twin sister and Cochise. The farewell as we boarded a small boat we flagged down was emotional, with lots of hugging and tears. One day, or so we told each other, we would all meet again. Exactly where, we didn't say.

The boat belonged to a farmer who was carrying Manioc to Manaus. Convinced by his Mission upbringing that nakedness was sinful, he gave his shirt to Yito and the oily old shorts he used for cleaning his engine to me, asking nothing in return for his favours but our company. Which was just as well, because armed with only the memory cards from Yito's camera and a few precious locks of hair, we had nothing but our company to give. But thanks to the help and kindness of people like him and others, Yito, our daughter and I eventually managed to metamorphose from jungle refugees to international travellers.

Yito's agent, Beth, met us in Manaus within forty-eight hours of our phoning her. After collecting all of Yito's memory cards, Beth flew with them straight to her subagent in The Netherlands. So when Yito and I landed some time later on English soil, Yito could face the army of journalists and photographers that greeted her without fear of immediate arrest. And still she has not been arrested, though the question of whether her Amazonian photographs breach the terms of her suspended sentence continues to be very much debated. Are they legitimate anthropological reportage? Or are they 'pornographic filth' that merit her being sent to jail? Both views have been voiced, and there have even been calls for an expedition into the area to rescue the children from the depravity of their culture. In the meantime, Yito is in great international demand to exhibit her less controversial images of Amazonian life and to talk about her adventure. She has also received approaches from several well-known biographers – but the book rights to her story remain firmly mine. Film rights are being negotiated.

The Downing family trust is no longer for sale; *NB Holdings* has been dissolved. So, as Yito's birthright, Noo's amazing circular house is now our home and Inchfield Park our domain, giving us at least some freedom to live by our own newly-acquired standards. And when the weather and our inclinations coincide, that freedom includes being able to wander around the valley jungle-naked with our daughter. But as Noo once said, in the valley one never feels totally alone. There are of course no floating angels, headless horsemen or the like, and sadly the naked temptress is now half-a-world away, but for Yito and I ghosts are everywhere nonetheless. We cannot go near the big Beech tree or the

Wiccan Glade without John Doberfield springing into our minds; he could still be Yito's father, because none of the locks of hair from the Amazon produced a DNA match. Nor, to Yito's huge relief, did the sweaty shirt that we once kept as collateral.

We cannot either look at the middle lake, the deepest, without thinking of the little orphan girl it shrouds; the girl who Noo – so she finally admitted – once so tragically mistook for a Muntjac. The arrow that Noo removed while Blakely lurked with his camera was from the orphan-girl's body, not Ipomoea's. And it was the orphan-girl's body that Blakely photographed being buried in the lake, giving him both the idea for ridding himself of John and the means to imprison Noo in his life.

As for Ipomoea, her spirit seems everywhere, sometimes as a pretty young woman in Edwardian dress, at others as a naked matriarchal crone. My biography of her has been published, and one copy lies in a waterproof bag alongside her remains in the hollow Oak tree.

Occasionally Yito and I also share our valley with the living. Hood – who insists that he played no part in any lynching – still fishes there most Saturday afternoons. And the coven with its new High Priestess and Priest, continues to worship in the Wiccan Glade. But in the early days, we used that glade more than they did. Yito thought that it would be 'really cool' to conceive our second child on a Wiccan altar within a stone's throw of the skeleton of her amazing great-grandmother.

And that may even be where it happened.

Acknowledgements

In January 1999, my view changed on how the earliest human societies behaved sexually. I had been invited to lecture at the annual meeting of the AAAS (American Association for the Advancement of Science) at Anaheim, California. My role was to compare the sexual behaviour of women in twentieth-century Britain with that of their counterparts in certain Amazonian tribes. Until that symposium, I had always supported the standard view that the earliest humans were little different from the modern: outwardly monogamous but open to infidelities that they strove to keep secret. But as I listened to my fellow speakers describing the behaviour of tribe after tribe from lowland South America, I slowly accepted that there was a much more likely alternative. And that alternative is the behaviour I have given to the otherwise fictional tribe around which this novel revolves. So my first acknowledgements are to Paul Valentine (who in 1999 was a senior lecturer at the Department of Sociology, University of East London, England) and Stephen Beckerman (then an Associate Professor at the Department of Anthropology, Pennsylvania State University, USA). If they hadn't invited me to lecture at their Symposium – "Partible Paternity: when matings with multiple men lead to many fathers for a single child" – I would never have conceived the idea for this book.

No known Amazonian tribe, past or present, either in the area of Brazil I identify or elsewhere, is *exactly* like the one I describe in this novel; in that sense this is a truly fictional tribe. On the other hand, each of the various aspects of the beliefs and behaviour my tribe exhibits is or was shown by some tribe somewhere; they are all part of the early human condition. A reader familiar with anthropological literature will recognise elements from the field work and writings of: Kim Hill and Magdalena Hurtado on the Aché of Eastern Paraguay; Stephen Beckerman's summary of the sexual behaviour and reproductive beliefs of the many and widely scattered Amazonian tribes that ascribe to shared paternity; Napoleon Chagnon on the Yanomamö; and last but not least the old (1952) but excellent summary of patterns of human sexual behaviour by Clellan Ford and Frank Beach. The result is my best informed guess as to how the earliest humans behaved, and how some may have continued to behave until at least the mid-twentieth century.

All of the Edwardian, Victorian and pre-Victorian adventuresses mentioned in this novel, with the obvious exception of Rebecca Downing (= Ipomoea), are real people. The details of Isabel Godin's remarkable journey are from the 1827 publication mentioned in the text, though her story has been told in more than one book since (e.g. *The Lost Lady of the Amazon* by Anthony Smith.) Biographical snippets about others are from *The Blessings of a Good Thick Skirt* by Mary Russell. So too is the information on Marianne North, with additional material from the publications of Kew Gardens.

In 2008, Anne Thomson, Archivist at Newnham College, Cambridge, patiently answered my questions about the nature of the records the College has on students who attended Newnham in 1910. Thank you, Anne.

Finally, I should like to thank: Howard Baker and Gareth Thomas for information on Amazonian rivers; Nathanial Baker for airline and flight information in Brazil circa 2003; Kate Brooke for social services information circa 1990; my agent, Laura Susijn, for advice and encouragement and for subtly reminding me at opportune moments that I was writing a novel, not a treatise on anthropology, sex and religion; and my partner, Elizabeth Oram, for once again freeing me from a great deal of domestic responsibility so that I could finish writing this book sooner rather than much, much later.

Robin Baker
2012, Spain

Lightning Source UK Ltd.
Milton Keynes UK
UKOW05f0438310813

216303UK00003B/554/P